Sunset on the Square

Lilac Mills lives on a Welsh mountain with her very patient husband and incredibly sweet dog, where she grows veggies (if the slugs don't get them), bakes (badly) and loves making things out of glitter and glue (a mess, usually). She's been an avid reader ever since she got her hands on a copy of *Noddy Goes to Toytown* when she was five, and she once tried to read everything in her local library starting with A and working her way through the alphabet. She loves long, hot summer days and cold winter ones snuggled in front of the fire, but whatever the weather she's usually writing or thinking about writing, with heartwarming romance and happy-ever-afters always on her mind.

Also by Lilac Mills

A Very Lucky Christmas
Sunshine at Cherry Tree Farm
Summer on the Turquoise Coast
Love in the City by the Sea

Tanglewood Village series

The Tanglewood Tea Shop
The Tanglewood Flower Shop
The Tanglewood Wedding Shop

Island Romance

Sunrise on the Coast
Holiday in the Hills
Sunset on the Square

LILAC MILLS

Sunset
on the
Square

1❶ CANELO

First published in the United Kingdom in 2021 by

Canelo
31 Helen Road
Oxford OX2 0DF
United Kingdom

A CIP catalogue record for this book is available from the British Library.

Print ISBN 978 1 80032 227 1
Ebook ISBN 978 1 80032 202 8

Look for more great books at www.canelo.co

Printed and bound in Great Britain by Clays Ltd, Elcograf S.p.A.

To my dad who was taken far too soon, and to my mum who was left behind.

Chapter 1

Early morning was Elspeth Evans' favourite time. Sitting in her courtyard, a cup of tea in her hand and watching the sun come up over the distant volcano at the heart of Tenerife, was a darned good start to any day. April was her favourite month, too, when the infrequent showers of winter had more or less subsided, and the earth rejoiced in the longer days by sending forth an astonishing display of flowers. The little town of Santiago del Teide was around a thousand feet above sea level and had a little more rain than on the coast, making the surrounding countryside green all year round.

Early morning was also the best time to discuss her plans for the day with Ray. 'It's Friday, so I'm in the shop,' she told him. She worked four days a week; it was enough to structure her week, but not so much that she didn't have any time for herself.

Her tea was cooling, so she took a good sip. There was nothing she disliked more than tepid tea. Mind you, it served her right if it had gone cold; she'd been too busy staring at the familiar view – one she never failed to tire of – to remember her drink. But now that the sun had cleared the mountains, and was happily hanging solo in a cloudless sky, she turned her attention to her cup. It was bone china, as was the saucer. Just the way she had been served it as a child. Her mother hadn't been able to abide thick cups, and neither could Elspeth. The one she was holding now was part of a set she'd rescued from her mother's house before the rest of the family had descended on the poor woman's possessions like a murder of crows on roadkill. Not a nice analogy, especially in the context of her deceased parent, but it was an apt one all the same, and described her brother and his avaricious wife perfectly. Then there was her aunt – her mother's sister – who'd had her eye on her mum's engagement ring for years. No wonder Elspeth had lost contact with them all – these days they didn't even exchange a Christmas card.

A gusty breeze ruffled her hair, and Elspeth lifted her face to the sun, concentrating her thoughts on the day ahead.

'We had all that new stock in yesterday,' she continued, setting her cup back on its saucer. 'I can't wait to unpack it. I hope the boots fit.'

As an avid hiker, she'd worn out her current ones, and had made sure to have the pair she'd been eyeing up for a while put on this recent delivery. They were darned expensive, and although she wasn't too strapped for money, neither could she afford to throw it around. Still, decent hiking boots were a must with the amount of walking she did, and the good leather ones she'd ordered should last her ages.

Reflectively, she glanced down at her slipper-clad feet. No matter how many years she'd been in Tenerife, she still liked wearing slippers around the house. They were comfortable, and easy to slide her feet in and out of, besides they kept her toes warm – marble-tiled floors could be a bit cool.

Neither the villa nor the outside temperature was ever particularly chilly, but the older she got, the more she felt the cold. Anything less than about twenty degrees Celsius was decidedly nippy, as far as she was concerned. Which was why she'd asked Ray to install a log burner in the corner of the living room all those years ago when they'd first bought the place. Back then it had been purely for the ambience on the rare evening when it did become cold enough to light it, but maybe she'd had a premonition that she'd welcome the heat from the flames one day. Fifty-eight-year-old bones tended to need a bit of warmth.

She smiled softly to herself as she thought of Ray's old cardigan, the one that was still hanging in the cupboard in the hall. She borrowed it occasionally when she felt in particular need of comfort. It was quite an eyesore after all this time and she should get rid of it, but she couldn't bring herself to. He'd loved that cardi, had brought it with him from England and, if she remembered correctly, he'd purchased it not long before they moved to Tenerife, after he'd given all of his scruffy old work suits to charity. He'd been of the opinion that cardigans would be far more comfortable to wear in the evenings than a jacket. He'd still worn jackets, of course, but not half as often as he used to before he retired. Fifteen years ago, it had been. Every day Elspeth marvelled at how quickly the time had passed.

Sounds of the streets coming to life around her intruded on her thoughts. Elspeth's home, Villa Cruz (*cruz* meant cross, Ray had informed her the first time they saw the modest two-bedroomed property), was tucked away at the back of the town's one and only square, with a view of the mountains. Although, to be fair, the little town of Santiago del Teide was barely more than a decent-sized village actually and, as it was nestled in a small plateau with mountains on three sides, it was hard to live somewhere without a view of them. Her villa had the best of both worlds — the square with all its comings and goings to the front and an open landscape of meadows and mountains to the back. One side was people, shops and civilisation — the other was untamed Tenerife.

Just outside the garden, the hoop-hoop-hoop call of a hoopoe bird signified that spring had well and truly arrived, and the meadows beyond Santiago del Teide were a riot of yellow, orange and purple flowers, with swathes of bright red poppies catching the eye. A capirote (she thought the Spanish for the little bird was so much more evocative than the English name of 'blackcap') sang from a bush on the other side of the garden wall, and Elspeth listened to its melodious song in delight. A tiny yellow chiffchaff searched for insects in the hibiscus shrub only a few feet away from her, happily chirping to itself as it hopped amongst the branches, and she watched its energetic antics as she tried to stay still so as not to frighten it.

A lizard scuttled up the garden wall and came to rest on the top, its head lifted towards the sun, much as Elspeth herself was doing, and she nodded a greeting at it. She liked to think it was the same individual she saw most mornings, but she guessed it probably wasn't. The lizard, for its part, ignored her, but her slight movement had startled the chiffchaff and it flew off, chirping crossly.

Traffic droned faintly from the main road, and Elspeth knew she ought to make a move, but it was just so pleasant sitting out here that she was reluctant to leave. Even the smell of freshly baked bread from one of her neighbours' ovens didn't prompt her into action, despite her tummy rumbling in response.

She should have a go at making her own, and she kept promising herself she would, but she never seemed to get around to it. It didn't help that the little shop next door down from the one she worked in, had a fresh delivery every morning. It was so much easier to pop in there and buy a loaf than faff about with all that kneading and proving. Which reminded her – there was half a loaf in the cupboard – she could have a couple of slices of toast drizzled with honey for her breakfast. The honey was local and tasted divine, and she could hear some of its little bee manufacturers now, droning through the many flowers in the garden.

Elspeth lovingly tended to those plants every evening, giving them a much-needed drink from the water she collected after having her shower. Installing a water-collection system had been a bit of a pain at the time, and she recalled Ray arguing in pigeon Spanish with the builder they had hired to renovate the villa about the plan to connect the waste water from the shower to a water butt in the garden. The builder's objection had been something to do with the angle of flow, but she'd kept out of it and had left her husband to deal with the problem; it gave him something to do and he'd always enjoyed a challenge. Besides, at the time she hadn't been bothered about it one way or the other, although she was grateful now – anything to help preserve the island's precious water reserves.

Her gaze came to rest on the orchid tree that Ray had planted during their first year on the island, when she had been wrestling with decorating and furnishing the inside of the villa, leaving him to make a habitable space out of the seriously overgrown and neglected garden. At that point it had contained more rubble and weeds than anything else.

'Look at it now,' she murmured, her eyes travelling around what she referred to as 'the courtyard'. It was her favourite place in the whole villa, and she tended to spend more time out here than she did inside. A plate of tapas, a glass of wine and a good book was all that was needed, and she often didn't retreat indoors until it was too dark to read outside. She'd originally wanted Ray to put a pool in, but he'd argued that it would take up too much room, and he'd been right. Besides, the upkeep of it would be too much for her now, but she had a couple of sun loungers placed strategically in the sunniest spot, although she found she was using them less and less as the years marched on. She might love the sun, but it played havoc with mature skin, and she was out enough in it already with all the hiking she did.

No hiking today, though. Today was a workday, although she would sit out in her garden later, she promised herself – she had a brand-new romance novel just waiting to be delved into. First, she had a full day at the shop to enjoy.

'Right, Ray, you might be able to sit here all day, but I can't,' she told her husband. 'Some of us have a job to go to.'

Pulling herself up out of her chair, she got to her feet, picked up her cup and saucer and blew her husband a kiss. She did the same thing every morning, without fail. And without fail, there was no response.

How could there be when his ashes were buried at the base of the orchid tree?

Still, Elspeth took comfort in knowing he was exactly where he would have wanted to be. She also took comfort in the knowledge that although he might have passed on, he was still with her in spirit.

'Bye, darling,' she called, as she prepared to spend another day without the only man she had ever loved.

Chapter 2

'Morning!' Elspeth chirped, walking into Libertad and propping the door open behind her to air the shop and to let customers know it was open.

Stefan looked up at her, scowled and grunted.

'Hangover?' she guessed.

Another grunt.

'I'll take that as a yes,' she informed him. 'Coffee?'

Her boss winced. 'Please.'

'Painkillers?'

'Do you have some?' His German accent was always more pronounced after a night of excess, and as a joke she used it as a gauge to tell just how much he was suffering. It must have been some night, she decided.

She nodded and patted her rucksack as she slipped it off her shoulder. Need he ask? He knew she always had a packet or two on her, along with antiseptic wipes, bite and sting cream, plasters, steri-strips and a solitary bandage. She put her brevity of bandages down to figuring that if an injury needed more than one bandage, then she didn't have the expertise to deal with it.

'I'll put the kettle on,' she said, and trotted to the back of the store where a door led to the stockroom, and then to a little room off that, which doubled as an office and a staffroom.

Elspeth dumped her bag, retrieved a packet of painkillers and her phone, and flicked the switch on the kettle. After popping two of the pills into her palm and stuffing her phone into one of the pockets of her cargo trousers, she poured Stefan a glass of water from the bottle in the fridge and took it out to him.

He pulled a face as he swallowed them, and she noticed that he looked a little green around the gills.

'Good night, was it?' she asked, listening out for the sound of the kettle switching itself off.

'Yeah, the best.'

'Who was she?'

'Who says there was a girl?'

Elspeth cocked her head at him, put her hands on her hips, and sent him a knowing look.

'OK, there was a girl,' he admitted. 'Man, could she drink.'

'Will you be seeing her again?' she asked, answering her own question before he had the chance to. 'Silly me, of course you won't.'

'I might.' He looked defensive, and rather sheepish.

'One day someone will break your heart,' she warned him.

'No. Not me.' He shook his head, then grimaced. 'Ow.'

'Serves you right. Where did you go?'

'Beach party at El Médano.'

Elspeth wasn't surprised. The resort was a magnet for surfers and hippies, and had a bohemian feel: just the kind of place Stefan enjoyed. He might run his own business – and very successfully, too, she might add – but he also played hard, and she was pretty sure if he could afford not to then he wouldn't work at all, but would spend all his time at the beach.

The kettle had come to the boil and she went to make coffee for her boss and tea for herself. Stefan often teased her about her love for tea. She might have lived on Tenerife for a decade and a half, but there were some English things she clung to with fierce determination, and her tea-drinking habit was one of them. Despite embracing the language and the culture, there was no way Elspeth was giving up her beverage of choice, and she had been known to carry a stash of tea bags in her rucksack in case of emergency – like being somewhere that didn't have English tea. It was rare, admittedly, but she had known it to happen and she wasn't prepared to take the risk.

'I'm just going to check the delivery off,' she told him after she'd finished her hot drink. There should be enough time before the first wave of walkers arrived in the town.

Elspeth knew the bus timetable off by heart. She should do, because she relied heavily on it, having no car of her own. She and Ray had owned one for a few years when they'd first moved to the island, but she'd been car-less for a long time now. She could time the business of the shop by the bus schedule. Santiago del Teide was the place where people caught the bus to Masca, the famous village at the top of the equally famous gorge. It was a mecca for hikers and sightseers alike, and many of them came through Santiago del Teide on the way, swapping one bus for another. And because there was often a wait between the two, the visitors explored the shops and cafes along the town's one and only main street. Being situated directly opposite the bus stop to Masca, and with a cafe next door on the one side, and a shop stocking provisions on the other, Libertad was ideally situated. The town was also a convenient stopping place for cyclists, and the lure of coffee, cake and everything bike-related, not to mention the ardour of the journey from the coast on incredibly steep and winding roads, meant that the businesses in the little town did a roaring trade.

Taking the boots she'd ordered out of the box, Elspeth wiggled her feet into them, did up the laces and pranced up and down, making sure they didn't pinch or rub. They seemed comfortable enough, so she kept them on while she checked off the rest of the delivery and prepared the stock for the shop floor. When, after twenty minutes she'd forgotten she had the boots on her feet, she declared them perfect and went to pay for them.

'You pay cost price,' Stefan said, when she handed him the box. He looked considerably brighter than he had when she first came in, and she marvelled at how easily the young shrugged off things such as hangovers. If she'd drunk as much as she guessed he had, she'd have been suffering for days.

'No. Absolutely not,' she protested, shoving her bank-card at him. She could have conducted the transaction herself, but she wanted everything to be open and above board.

'Cost,' he repeated. 'We do this every time. Why?'

'Because you have to make a profit.'

'Not off you. You work here. I will win,' he added. 'I always do.'

The last time Elspeth had bought something from Libertad and had insisted on paying full price, Stefan had refunded her the difference via her wages.

'How's your dad?' she asked hoping that a change of subject would distract him, and he'd ring the full amount through the till. Stefan's father had been having some problems recently and she knew he was concerned.

His expression became more serious. 'Not too good. My mother is worried that it may be a brain tumour. He cannot say words clearly some of the time, and he has become very clumsy. He has had some tests, and he is going back to the hospital on Wednesday for the results.'

'I'm sure it's nothing to worry about,' she said, hoping it was true. Stefan's father, Dieter, was younger than she was, and, from what Stefan had told her, he was just as outdoorsy as his son. She thrust her card at him again, her mind now focused more on Stefan's father than on her boots.

'Cost, or I won't sell them to you,' her boss said, firmly.

She gave in, muttering, 'One of these days I'll take my business elsewhere.'

'No, you won't,' he laughed. 'You are a… what do you say…? A creature of habit.'

He was right, she was, and she'd been buying her clothes and boots here since before Stefan had taken over the shop. If he'd stocked slippers and nighties, she'd probably have bought those items here, too.

'I like being a creature of habit,' she retorted primly.

'One day you will do something reckless,' he told her, and she sent him an arch look in reply.

'Never.' And she was about to go into the reasons why not, when her phone rang.

'Elspeth, my darling, my bestest friend,' the voice on the other end began, the tone wheedling.

'What do you want?' She let out an exaggerated sigh, knowing that Amanda would take it in the spirit it was meant.

'A favour, a ruddy great big one.'

'You've double-booked again, haven't you?' She took a stab in the dark. It had happened once or twice before, and Elspeth had stepped in. Neither she nor her friend made a habit of it, though.

'Not on purpose.'

'It never is,' she chuckled. 'How many and for how long?'

'One person and he'll only need to spend three nights with you, as he can come to us for the other eleven nights. I hate to ask you, but the couple in the room he's supposed to be in thought they'd booked their flights for today, and only realised this morning as they were about to check out and looked at their travel arrangements that their flight is on Monday. They're quite elderly and they're upset enough already about the mistake without me forcing them to move hotels, plus they've been coming to me for years. What was I supposed to do?'

'Tell them there's no room at the inn,' Elspeth joked, not meaning it in the slightest. It wouldn't be the first time she'd helped Amanda and Toni out, and no doubt it wouldn't be the last. No matter that the extra income would come in handy – she owed them a big debt of gratitude; they'd stepped in and picked up the pieces after Ray had died, when she'd been floundering badly and hadn't seen a way out of her despair. 'Do you want me to feed him dinner, too?' she offered.

'Oh, can you? That would be marvellous. I'd hate for him to settle in at yours then have to up-sticks and trek over to the hotel for his meals. It's bad enough that he has to spend three out of his fourteen nights somewhere other than the hotel he is supposed to be booked into. I owe you big time.'

Amanda owed her nothing. Anything Elspeth could do for her, she would. 'When is this person arriving?' she asked. The villa had two bedrooms, and she always kept the spare one made up with clean bedding. She'd have to get some extra supplies in though. Amanda and Toni offered half-board, so Elspeth would have to ensure her guest had a three-course dinner, as well as a substantial breakfast. The upside was that it was home cooking; the downside was that the poor guest wouldn't have a choice. Her villa wasn't a restaurant.

'His name is Charles Brown and he'll be landing at five-fifteen this afternoon,' Amanda informed her.

He should be with her by seven or so, Elspeth calculated, allowing for Passport Control and baggage collection. It was about a forty-five-minute journey from the airport to Santiago del Teide, depending on traffic, so if she aimed for him to arrive at about six-thirty, then that should be OK.

'Are you collecting him from the airport?' she asked.

'Yes, Toni is, so he'll explain the necessary to your guest then drop him off at yours.'

'Righto. Look, I'm in work – we'll talk later, yes? Oh, one last thing – does he have any dietary requirements? He's not vegan or lactose intolerant or anything?'

There was silence for a second as Amanda checked the man's booking. 'None that he's declared.'

'Great, that makes life easier.'

'Thanks, Elspeth, I owe you.'

'Everything OK?' Stefan asked when she popped the phone back in her pocket.

'Amanda and Toni have a bit of a problem.' She explained the situation, and he nodded, understanding that at this time of year – Easter holidays – everywhere was fully booked. With there being only three hotels in Santiago del Teide, it could be hard to relocate a guest at short notice.

'I told you that you would do something reckless,' Stefan said, grinning.

'This is hardly reckless. And I have done it before.'

'Not since Ray died.'

That was true; the last time she'd agreed to put up one of Amanda's guests had been years ago, when Ray was still alive and they'd dealt with the situation together. It hadn't been particularly successful, as she recalled. The two elderly ladies had thought they'd booked a hotel in Puerto de Santiago, a bustling little resort on the coast. They hadn't been too pleased to discover that Santiago del Teide was a fair distance from the beach and there was no bingo or karaoke for miles around. They'd done nothing but complain and grizzle, even though it had been their own fault and there was no way Amanda could be held responsible for the beach being nearly fifteen kilometres away.

Oh, well, Elspeth thought, she'd said yes now, and she wasn't going back on her word and landing Amanda with even more of a mess. She could manage three nights, even if her guest turned out to be as curmudgeonly as those ladies had been. Three nights and he'd be gone, and she'd be a few more euros better off. Besides, it might be nice to have some company for a change. Talking to Ray was all well and good, but the poor man was hardly in a position to reply, even if she pretended he did.

Chapter 3

Soup was always good for a starter and she could prepare it in advance and warm it through just before dishing up, Elspeth thought later that day, as she popped some overripe tomatoes into her basket, and then added a red pepper and some onions. Next, she turned her attention to the main course, and decided on chicken breasts in a sauce, with potatoes and a side salad, before adding the necessary ingredients to her shopping. She bought another loaf of bread and a selection of fresh fruit, half a dozen eggs (she already had five at home, but she didn't want to risk running out), bacon, sausages, yoghurt and a few other bits and bobs.

By the time she'd walked the couple of hundred metres from the shop to her villa, her arms felt as though her elbows were being dislocated and the handles of her reusable hessian bags were cutting the circulation off in her fingers. All this just for dinner tonight and breakfast in the morning! And she still had to plan and purchase food for two more dinners.

As the tomatoes, onions and peppers were roasting in the oven ready for the soup, she prepared the chicken. Once that was done, she cleaned the villa's downstairs rooms, dusting and sweeping her already clean house. She then transferred the contents of the oven to a large saucepan, filled it with water and put it on to boil, before popping the chicken dish in the oven to roast.

After that, she hastened upstairs to give the spare room that Mr Brown was going to be housed in a quick check over, along with the bathroom. Both bedrooms had en suites and she was glad that Ray had suggested it. At the time, all Elspeth had considered was that she would have two toilets to clean instead of one; three, if she included the downstairs loo. But her husband's foresight continued to astound her, and now she mouthed 'Thank you,' at him, and blew a kiss in the vague direction of the orchid tree.

Satisfied that all was in order, Elspeth took a moment to gather her thoughts. It was a long time since she'd had anyone to stay the night, and she felt a little odd about it, especially since that someone was a man and unrelated to her. She'd even felt a little out of sorts when her own flesh and blood had come to stay, although she'd loved having Gideon under her roof once again, and had wept buckets when her son had to leave. It was curious how used to one's own company you became, she mused as she straightened the fresh towels she'd hung over the rail, and fussed with the exact placing of the soap on the wash-hand basin.

It would have to do, and she'd have to get on with it and stop being such a worry-wart. It was three nights, that was all. How much work or trouble could one tourist generate? He'd be gone before she knew it, and she'd be on her own again, with the addition of a few more euros in her bank account.

And if he caused her any trouble, then she'd simply ask Toni and Amanda to stick him someplace else – she didn't care where. Ah, that must be Toni now, she thought, as a loud knock sent her scurrying downstairs.

'Toni, how nice to see you,' she declared as she opened the door and leant towards her friend. They hugged and exchanged kisses on each cheek, and Toni held her slightly longer than necessary, to whisper in her ear, 'Sorry, but he seems nice.'

'And you must be Mr Brown,' Elspeth said, turning to the gentleman standing patiently by the car. She hadn't known what to expect, Amanda having told her nothing about him except for his name, and she was surprised to see that he was around her own age, slim and tall, with salt-and-pepper hair. There were laughter lines around his hazel eyes, and he was clean-shaven and wore a ready smile on his face.

'Welcome to my home,' she added, stepping forwards and holding out her hand.

He took it in a firm grip and shook it. Up close, she could smell his aftershave, and his hand was warm. 'Nice to meet you, Mrs Evans.'

'You too, but call me Elspeth, please.' She smiled encouragingly. 'I hope your stay here will be pleasant. Toni has explained the situation to you?' She raised her eyebrows.

'He has. I'm Charles by the way, and it's good of you to put me up at such short notice.'

She blushed and waved her hand in the air dismissively. 'It's no problem, honestly. Right, let me show you to your room while Toni fetches your luggage, then I'll leave you to settle in. Come down when you're ready and I'll make some tea or coffee. Or would you prefer something alcoholic?' She bit her lip — she should have bought another bottle or two of wine. Drat.

'Tea would be great,' he said, and she breathed a sigh of relief. While he was unpacking, she could nip to the shop and rectify the wine situation.

She left Toni to haul her guest's luggage from the boot of his car, and led Charles inside. 'The lounge is through there – it's open plan with the dining area at one end – and the kitchen is through there, so help yourself to anything you need.' Within reason, she thought, but didn't say it out loud. 'I've got a pretty garden-cum-courtyard that you can sit in, but no pool, I'm afraid. If you want a dip, you'll have to use the one at the hotel. And this is the downstairs loo.' She pointed to a door next to the stairs as she made her way up them.

Charles followed behind her and Elspeth hid a wince at having a stranger so close. Three nights, just three nights, she chanted silently, as she pushed open the door to the spare bedroom.

'Oh, this is nice,' he declared, gazing around with pleasure.

'There's a bathroom through here.' She walked across the room and opened another door. Charles moved towards her and poked his head around it.

'Lovely,' he said.

'If you need anything, just ask. I'm bound to have forgotten something.'

'I'm sure you haven't.'

'OK, then, I'll get out of your way,' she said as she heard Toni plodding heavily up the narrow staircase. She moved aside to let her friend lug the case in, and then she darted onto the landing and headed downstairs and into the sanctuary of her kitchen.

She was in the process of checking on the chicken when Toni appeared, carrying a cardboard box under one arm and a cool box in the other.

'From Amanda. She says you need things to cook and beer. There is wine, also.'

'You shouldn't have, although I am grateful because I forgot to pick any alcohol up. I was going to nip out and buy some.'

'No need. It is in here.' He placed the cool box on one of the counters.

Toni had been speaking in English, but he suddenly switched to Spanish as he said, 'He was OK with not staying at the hotel, but if you have any problems, any at all, you phone me, and I'll take him away.'

'I'm sure there won't be,' Elspeth said confidently, also speaking in Spanish. 'But thank you for the offer.'

'You will phone if you are worried?'

'I will, I promise.'

'Good. I'll go now, but don't forget.' He mimed holding a phone up to his ear.

'Shoo,' she said, reverting to English. 'I've got soup to make.' She retrieved the blender from its home in the cupboard next to the sink.

Toni departed, leaving her alone in the house with a man she'd only just met, and with no idea what to do with until dinner was ready.

And there he was, filling the doorway...

'Dinner will be about half an hour. Would you like a drink?' Elspeth asked as she rooted through the cool box. 'I know you said tea earlier, but I've also got beer, cola, lemonade, white wine, red wine, rosé—' Crikey, Amanda had thought of everything.

'White would be nice, please.'

'White it is. If you'd like to go into the garden, I'll bring it out to you. It's very pleasant out there and you get a great view of the sunset.' She watched him go and let out a slow breath. Although both Toni and Charles were probably close to six foot and Charles was not as portly as Toni, but he seemed to take up more space. Or was she simply more aware of him?

Hmm.

Three nights, only three nights…

Carrying the chilled bottle of wine, a glass and some cutlery, Elspeth ventured into the courtyard to find Charles standing at the far end, staring out over the meadow.

'How delightful. All those colours,' he said. 'I was expecting Tenerife to be more barren.'

'It is in the south. But the further north you go, and the higher you go, the greener it gets. It's still nowhere near as green as England, but it's pretty in its own way.' She busied herself with pouring a glass of wine and laying the table. 'What was the weather like when you left?'

'Horrid. Damp and drizzling, and it's set to stay that way all over Easter.'

'Typical. I can only remember a few bank holidays when the weather was decent.'

'Have you already eaten?' His attention was on the table and its solitary place setting.

'No, but I'll have mine in the kitchen.'

'Please join me – I'll feel awkward eating on my own.'

Elspeth bit her lip. She didn't feel comfortable sitting with him, but it would be unfriendly of her to refuse. 'If you're sure?' she replied, uncertainly.

'Of course I am sure. I'd hate to think of you eating in there all on your own, and me eating out here all on my own. I'd welcome the company, to be honest.'

She wouldn't, but she felt she didn't have much choice in the matter. Oh, well...

'And a view like this,' he added, gesturing at the sky with its terracotta, pink and purple hues from the setting sun, 'deserves to be shared.'

Elspeth left the chicken in the oven and turned the potatoes off while she warmed the soup and sliced a couple of thick chunks of squishy fresh bread. As she carried the starter outside, she braced herself for an evening of awkwardness.

'So, how long have you lived on Tenerife?' Charles asked, breaking off a piece of bread and dipping it in the soup. 'Mmm, this is good.'

'I made it myself. Roasted tomato and red pepper.'

'It's delicious.' He ate some more and waited for her to answer, his gaze expectant.

'About fifteen years.'

'Do you live here on your own?'

Elspeth picked up her spoon after pouring herself a glass of wine. In for a penny, in for a pound... 'Yes. Ray, my husband, died four years ago. It was his dream to retire out here. He was a lot older than me and I wasn't quite ready to retire yet, but I knew how much it meant to him and our son, Gideon, was all grown up, so...' Now, why had she told him all that? A simple 'yes' would have sufficed.

'I am so sorry about your husband. It must have been hard for you.' His eyes were kind. 'It probably still is.'

She nodded uncertainly. It wasn't like her to tell her life story to a complete stranger, and the sympathy on his face perturbed her.

'After you lost your husband, did you consider moving back to the UK?' he asked.

'Not really.' Not at all, in fact. 'My life is here. My friends are here. I had nothing to move back for. Gideon, my son, had settled in Japan by then – he's married with a gorgeous little boy – so there was nothing for me to go back to.'

Talking about Gideon made her long to see him again. It was about time her son came to visit or she visited him and his family, but the logistics were a nightmare, and there was the cost to consider. Flights to and from Japan weren't cheap. Travel might have been easier if she lived in the UK, but nevertheless she knew she'd made the right decision to remain on Tenerife. She was happy – as happy as she could be in the circumstances. It had taken her a long time to achieve contentment, and that horrible, bleak first year without Ray had been simply dreadful. If it hadn't been for Amanda and Toni she didn't know what she would have done. As it was, she'd consoled herself with too much alcohol, drinking on her own in the dark, sitting in the garden, close enough to touch the bark of the orchid tree, and sobbing.

Thankfully she'd emerged from those dark times, happy enough with her villa, her job, her hiking and her friends. Of course, she missed Ray terribly and she knew she always would, but she had a good life now and she couldn't see anything changing.

'What about you?' she asked. 'Is this a holiday or are you on business?'

'Holiday. I love the outdoors. Always have done. My ex-wife wasn't too keen, which is probably why she is an ex. The most outdoorsy thing she did was attend a BBQ, or lounge around on the beach. It's what split us up eventually – that old cliché of having nothing in common, apart from the kids, was true in our case.'

'How many children have you got?'

'Two, both girls. They're grown up, of course. That's one thing I can say – we stayed together while they were kids to try to give them the best childhood we could. Not sure if it worked, or was successful, but it's done now.'

'How old are they?'

'Gina is thirty-four; Hayley is thirty-one.'

'Any grandchildren?'

'Two. One of each, both of them Gina's. Hayley doesn't show any signs of wanting to settle down.'

'I bet you dote on them.'

'I would, but I don't see much of them. Both my daughters live in Edinburgh, near their mother, while I live in Bristol,' he told her.

Over the main course and the rest of the bottle of wine, Charles proceeded to tell her more about his children: Gina worked for the local council and Hayley was a fitness instructor.

'Hayley follows me more than her mother, much to her mother's disgust. She's a bit of a triathlon addict, and I've lost count of the number of marathons she's completed.' The pride he had for his daughter was evident in his face.

'Do you run, too?'

'Not now. I used to, but my knees aren't what they used to be. Pounding tarmac is heavy on your joints.'

'I take it you're here for the hiking, then?'

'Am I ever! I understand that the walking on Tenerife is phenomenal, as is the cycling.'

'They are,' Elspeth agreed. 'I don't cycle, but I do hike a lot.'

'Add the year-round sun, and as far as I'm concerned, it's a perfect holiday.'

'Santiago del Teide is a great base, and there are some fabulous trails right on the doorstep,' Elspeth agreed.

'Are there any guides or walking groups?'

'There are a few around. Not that many though.'

'Pity. I was hoping to find a guide. You wouldn't know of anyone local, would you?'

Elspeth pulled a face. 'There are several around, but they do tend to be booked up months in advance. I can drop one or two of them an email, if you like?' She'd have to look them up on the internet, but that wasn't the problem — what might be more of a challenge was the length of time they took to reply. His holiday could be half over and even then there'd be no guarantee any of them would have any availability.

'Hmm, that might take a while. Never mind, I can always look up a couple of trails to start me off,' he said.

'There's a nice one that starts at the other end of the town and climbs up the side of the ridge. It'll only take a couple of hours, but it's a gentle introduction to the area and the views are stunning. I can show you if you like?'

'Oh, would you? That would be fantastic! I'm looking forward to it already. It's much more fun hiking with someone rather than on your own.'

Elspeth froze. That wasn't what she'd meant at all. She'd been talking about showing him on a map, not showing him in person. And she was of the opposite opinion — she much preferred being on her own. If she couldn't have Ray by her side, then she didn't want anyone.

Charles must have noticed her expression. 'If that's OK with you, of course,' he added.

She forced a smile to her lips; how could she backtrack now? It would come across as rude and unfriendly; this was his holiday and she didn't want it to start off on a bad foot.

'Of course it is.' She smiled wider, but her tummy was in her boots. She hadn't hiked with anyone since she'd lost Ray. If she was honest, she hadn't done a lot else since he'd died either and she was perfectly fine with things just the way they were.

It was done now, and there was no going back. She'd have to bite the bullet and get on with it. Surely she could manage to spend a few hours in his company without having a total meltdown; if she thought of him as one of the customers in the shop, she'd get by.

She'd have to, wouldn't she?

Chapter 4

Elspeth stirred restlessly in her large empty bed and longed for morning. Technically, she supposed, four a.m. *was* morning, but it was far too early to get up. Sometimes the bed felt too big, and right now the vast emptiness on Ray's side made her feel wretchedly alone. Even after four years, grief could hit unexpectedly. She kept telling herself that she should have moved beyond it by now, but for some reason she didn't seem able to.

Maybe she *should* have returned to England after he'd died, where the memories wouldn't be as sharp. When they'd moved to Tenerife, they'd sold the family home, so her return to the UK would have involved living in a different house and, if she'd felt so inclined, in a totally different location, which would have meant far less risk of being ambushed by images of Ray sitting in the same chair he'd always sat in or standing at the window staring out over his handiwork in the garden.

Tenerife, especially her little corner of it, held so many memories of her husband and their life together. They'd been so busy, so active. Their days had been filled with love and laughter, good food and even better wine, which had been enjoyed with friends and on their own. They'd hiked and danced, explored their adopted island by car and on foot, swum in the sea and hauled themselves out on the rocks like seals. They'd made a life for themselves, had made a home. Then one day it had been snatched away from her, and she'd been left adrift and rudderless, and had been forced to build a new life out of the devastation of the old. And there had been no way she could have done that on her own in England, not without the people who knew her (who knew *Ray*) and loved her.

Elspeth understood what had sparked off her current blue mood – Charles. Not him, specifically, but having a man in her house who wasn't Ray or Gideon. She'd heard him pottering around in his bedroom, after she'd retired for the night. There had been the sound of water running, the occasional cough, the creak of a floorboard; it was muted, admittedly, but she was acutely aware of the noises he made. Even now, with the house blanketed in a four a.m. silence, she could sense his presence.

It was quite odd indeed.

Ordinarily she would have got up, resigned to the fact that she probably wouldn't be able to get back to sleep. She would have made a cup of tea and sat outside in the soft darkness, watching the world wake up, content with her thoughts and the odd comment to Ray.

But not today. She didn't want to wake her guest. He'd been remarkably good-natured yesterday about being shunted off to live in a private house with a woman he didn't know, instead of experiencing the anonymity and convenience that a hotel would bring. She didn't think she'd have been as calm about it, if the shoe was on the other foot.

Maybe Charles had already done his spear-waving and tantrum-throwing in the car on the way from the airport, but somehow she didn't think so. And Toni had said that he hadn't seemed too upset.

Charles had managed to find himself a guide, though, so something good had come of it, although she most definitely had not meant to offer her services.

Maybe that was the reason why she was wide-awake so early? Elspeth liked routine and she liked familiarity. Over the past for years she'd become very used to her way of doing things, very used to her own company; she'd had to be because, despite how dear her friends were, she was alone and she had to get on with it.

Charles had shaken her out of her comfort zone.

It wasn't his fault. And neither was it Amanda's. If she had to blame anyone, she should blame the unknown couple who had booked the wrong return flight. But she found she couldn't blame them either. Mistakes happened. Then there was also the fact that she needn't have agreed to put Charles up. Ergo, she had no one to blame but herself. With that cleared up, she lay there quietly, waiting until she heard sounds of life from the bedroom across the hall.

To her surprise, she must have fallen back off to sleep, because she awoke with a start sometime later to the sound of a toilet flushing.

Instinctively she reached across the bed and, encountering the emptiness she knew would be there, her first thought was that she had burglars. Her second was to wonder why they were using the loo in the spare room.

It took her a few moments to recall the events of yesterday.

It was Charles, so that was OK, then. Or it would be, if it didn't remind her that she was normally alone at this time of day.

What time was it, anyway? The sun was up, and Elspeth was dismayed to look at the clock on her bedside table and see that it was nearly half-past eight.

No wonder the man was up and about. He probably wanted his breakfast.

With no time to shower, she hurriedly washed her face and hands, ran a comb through her neat bob and declared herself ready to face the day.

Charles was coming out of his door just as she flew out of hers, and she nearly barged straight into him.

'Morning,' she said hurriedly, as she met him abruptly on the landing. 'Sleep well?' She indicated he should go down the stairs ahead of her, which meant that by the time he reached the hall, she had to dodge around him to go into the kitchen. Maybe she should have gone first?

Ooh, having someone in your house when you weren't used to it, and a total stranger at that, wasn't easy, was it?

'Would you like to have breakfast in the garden?' she asked, aware he had followed her into the room.

'That sounds good.'

'Tea or coffee?'

'Tea, please.'

'Right, I'll put the kettle on. What would you like for breakfast? I can offer you churros with chocolate sauce, croissants, fruit and yoghurt, toast or, if you like, I can do you a full English.' If he wasn't the full English type, the food wouldn't go to waste. It was ages since she'd had a BLT, or a sausage sandwich for that matter, so she'd have one later and her mouth watered at the thought.

'Chocolate sauce? For breakfast?' Charles looked aghast and Elspeth chuckled.

'It's quite usual for Canarians to have a light, sweet breakfast and a far heartier, more substantial lunch,' she told him. 'Churros are a kind of lightly fried doughnut, sprinkled with sugar with honey drizzled over them. The chocolate sauce is to dip them in.'

'Er, I think I'll stick with fruit and yoghurt, please, and some toast for after?'

'Of course.' Goody, she could have BLTs for her lunch, followed by the churros she'd bought.

When she brought out a tray of tea things, she was surprised to see Charles gazing not at the iconic shape of the volcano at the island's heart, but to the west where there was a gap in the surrounding mountains leading down to the sea several kilometres away. Little did he know she was taking him in that direction this morning, while it was still cool enough to climb up to the ridge with its fabulous views of the Atlantic.

'Is the town of Los Gigantes that way?' he asked, pointing.

'Yes. If you go to the outskirts of Santiago del Teide, the road drops off rather steeply right down to the coast. It's about fifteen kilometres to Los G, and the road can be a bit hairy if you're more used to city driving.'

'I don't have any plans to hire a car,' he told her.

'There's a path if you want to walk instead. It's especially beautiful this time of year because it goes through meadows of wild flowers and many of the cacti are in bloom, too. The scent is to die for.'

'Maybe I'll try that tomorrow.' Charles looked thoughtful.

'You don't have to go all the way to Los Gigantes. You can stop at the next town along, which is Tamaimo, have a drink and walk back. Mind you, you can't come all this way and not take a gander at the cliffs. So, if you were happy to walk down to Los G but didn't want to walk back up, you could always hop on a bus or grab a taxi. You could have a spot of lunch there, too. There are some nice restaurants down by the harbour with the most fantastic views of the cliffs.'

'Sounds great. I'll have to look into it.'

'I'll write a few things down, if you like. Bus times in particular, as they're not that frequent,' Elspeth offered.

It had been a while since she'd last been to Los Gigantes, the delightful harbour town with the towering cliffs of the same name. Maybe she should take a hike down there soon, although she would almost certainly catch a bus back up. She could take a towel and sit on the little beach of dark sand and have a picnic. The sight and sound of the waves always invigorated her – she might even go for a dip.

After she'd supplied Charles with fruit, yoghurt and toast, she left him to eat his breakfast in peace, preferring to have hers in the kitchen where she could be alone. She'd kept him company most of yesterday evening and she'd be with him all morning, so she needed some alone time to settle herself. Being in the shop with Stefan and all those customers was one thing, but having someone in her personal space for hours on end was a different matter entirely.

It is only for three days, she kept telling herself – it was fast becoming a bit of a mantra. And Charles was pleasant enough. She wasn't talking about his looks, either, although he was a rather distinguished and handsome-looking man. He was friendly and affable, and not at all intrusive as far as houseguests went. The fact that she wasn't too keen on guests in any shape or form was her problem, not his.

Besides, a little part of her was looking forward to showing him around. She adored her adopted island and was extremely proud of its natural beauty. Far too many visitors hardly left their hotels or resorts. The ones that did were often on organised tours, usually to theme parks, and they missed the truly magical things, like the view from—

'Sorry to intrude, but what time were you thinking of leaving?'

Elspeth was jerked out of her thoughts as Charles stuck his head around the kitchen door. He was holding his plate.

'I would have cleared that away,' she said, jumping to her feet to take it off him. 'You're a guest.'

He smiled. 'I'm also aware that you're doing me a favour.'

'Nonsense!' She began to empty the tray. 'Shall we leave in twenty minutes? How are you off for water bottles? Have you brought one with you?'

'Two, but I could do with some water to go in them.'

'If you fetch them down, I'll fill them for you. And I'll pack a couple of cakes to have as a snack, too. And maybe a flask of tea.'

He gave her a curious look. 'I thought you said the walk would only take about two hours?'

'That's right, possibly a bit longer depending on how often you'd like to stop.'

'I'm fairly fit, so hopefully not that often.'

'Oh, you *will* stop,' she promised him. 'You won't be able to resist. The views are spectacular. And the tea and cake are for when we reach the top. I guarantee you'll want to linger, and it's always nice to have a snack along the way.'

'It sounds wonderful.'

'It is.' Suddenly she found she was rather looking forward to the next few hours.

It was only when she was out of the door and heading down the main road, Charles striding easily by her side, that she realised she had forgotten to say good morning to Ray.

Chapter 5

As far as Elspeth was concerned, their walk didn't start in earnest until they had veered off the main road and started down a loosely cobbled path with low walls constructed out of dark volcanic rock rising on either side.

They'd only gone a little way along it and already the sounds of the road could no longer be heard, apart from the occasional motorbike and the deeper drone of a lorry making its laborious way up the steep, winding incline.

Gradually, though, even those noises faded, to be replaced with the steady drone of bees and the calls of birds. The path Elspeth was taking Charles along bisected fields which had been left to run wild, with only the occasional attempt at planting anything in them, and she breathed deeply as the scent of assorted flowers filled the air with their sweet fragrance.

Now and again, stubby trees grew alongside the route, throwing their shade across it. From past experience, she knew she'd be grateful for any hint of shade on the way back. For now though, the temperature was pleasant; there was a slight breeze blowing inland from the coast, and there wasn't a cloud in the sky. It was a gorgeous day.

'Wow, this is fantastic. Just a couple of minutes' walk from the centre of town and we're already out in the countryside.' Charles was gazing around him with a grin on his face. He looked relaxed and happy, and she was pleased he appeared to be having a good time. She didn't like the thought of him not enjoying himself, especially since she felt he was her responsibility for the duration of his stay with her.

'Santiago is hardly a metropolis,' she replied laughing. 'There are less than a few thousand residents, one main street and a square with a church in it!'

'And from where we're standing now, you'd hardly know it existed at all,'

He was right. Almost as soon as they'd left the main road, Santiago had disappeared.

'That's what I love about living here,' she told him. 'If you want to strike off by yourself, you can. We might see the occasional tourist, or maybe Yeremi, who has a smallholding nearby, with his goats, and perhaps a farmer or two, but that's it. And if you know what you're doing, you can leave the paths and cut across country, and you definitely won't see anyone then.'

'Is that what you do?'

'Sometimes.'

'Wow!' he exclaimed again, when the almost flat path with fields either side became a far more rugged track which clung to the side of a mountain, the ground having fallen away dramatically in front of them. What Charles was impressed with, was the crossroads they had arrived at. The right-hand path would take them around the side of the mountain. The left dropped down a couple of hundred feet in a series of zig zags, to a wide valley.

'The town you can see in the distance is Tamaimo, but that's a walk for another day.' Elspeth smiled as she watched the expressions flit across his face, the predominant one being wonder.

'What a view,' he said, shading his eyes.

She murmured her agreement – she never failed to appreciate it and it was one of the things that made living in Santiago del Teide so wonderful.

'We'll go that way,' she said when he was ready to move, pointing to their right and the narrow path etched into the side of the mountain, leading up to the ridge. 'Watch your footing, it can be a bit tricky in places.'

Keeping his attention on the rocky track beneath his feet, Charles followed her, a couple of metres behind. She kept glancing back at him to check he was OK, and each time she did so, he looked up at her and grinned. Every so often she would stop so he could take in the scenery. She didn't want him to get so distracted by it that he wasn't watching where he was going. The volcanic rock was sharp and unforgiving, and there was a distinct lack of grass to cushion a fall. The ground cover was relatively sparse compared to back in the UK, and it consisted mainly of spiky bushes and cacti, which didn't make for a comfortable landing. Besides, some of the slopes were rather steep, and were about to become quite treacherous in places.

The track might be rough, but it was well trodden and clear to see. Charles would have been fine on his own; the only guiding she was doing was choosing which way to go when there was a fork. Seeing that he was breathing fine and not struggling in the slightest, she picked the higher path the next time it diverged. It would take them past a small cave with a little shrine in it where water sometimes dripped down.

She let Charles climb to the cave, which was off the path a little way, while she caught her breath and admired the view. When she heard the click of stone on stone, she knew he was making his way back down and she turned to face him. She saw that he looked thoughtful.

'Flowers have been left, and they're fresh,' he said.

'Locals like to tend to the shrines. You'll see loads of them all over the Canaries, and they're never forgotten. Was there any water today? Sometimes there is, sometimes not.'

'It was damp, but nothing was dripping or running.'

'There's a spring around the next corner if you need to fill your water bottle. It might look a bit rough and ready, but the water is fresh and sweet-tasting, and perfectly safe to drink.'

When they arrived at it Charles took a sip, and then they carried on, the incline increasing sharply as the path led almost straight up to the ridgeline above. From there, the views were breathtaking. Panting slightly when they reached the top, Elspeth took her water bottle out of her rucksack and took a hefty swig. Along with the altitude, the temperature had been climbing steadily too, and the breeze was welcome.

Charles was mesmerised, his face full of amazement as he scanned the jagged ridges and deep valleys which lay to their right, and she simply knew he was dying to explore them.

'We'll carry on along this ridge,' she said. 'There's a viewpoint where we can sit and have our cake and tea.'

It took them a while to get there, mainly because every step revealed new things to look at, and Charles was constantly stopping to take a photo or simply to stare in wonder. Elspeth found she was enjoying seeing his reaction as much as she was enjoying the walk for its own sake. Although she never tired of it, seeing it afresh through his eyes brought a smile to her lips. Having Charles with her hadn't been as bad as she'd feared, and she chided herself for her reluctance.

'I can see why you love this place,' he said. 'It's got everything – the climate, the food…' He nodded at her and she smiled in acknowledgment. Last night's dinner had been tasty, even if she did say so herself. 'The people are friendly.' Another nod in her direction. 'And you have scenery like this. It's so unspoilt.'

She swivelled around and pointed back up the valley towards Santiago del Teide. 'If you turn right when you come out of the square and follow the road for a couple of miles, that's where the trees start in earnest. It's higher again, and gets more rainfall, and if you visit the volcano, Mount Teide, you'll pass through acres and acres of tall pines.'

He sent her a quizzical glance, his eyes crinkling at the corners as he squinted against the brightness of the midday sun. 'I've seen the photos – I didn't think much grew on Mount Teide, let alone trees.'

'It doesn't when you get high enough, but the lower slopes are blanketed with trees. Above the tree line, though, nothing much grows. The photos you've seen show a moonlike landscape, right?'

'Yes.'

'That's the beauty of Tenerife: it might be a sub-tropical island, but the various microclimates make for a huge variety of landscapes. Some hidden valleys in the north of the island, where they get more rain, are positively jungle-like. Volcanic soil is surprisingly fertile if there's enough water around. Speaking of water and hidden valleys, you must visit Masca Gorge. It's just over there.' She pointed to the right. 'It has a permanent stream running through it, which is quite unusual for Tenerife.'

'It is on my list of things to see and do while I'm here – it sounds incredible,' Charles said.

'"Just over there" isn't that accurate a description,' she admitted. 'The gorge is a couple of valleys over from the ridge we are on, as the crow flies. But to get to it from here, you would have to be an actual bird. The mountains are so steep-sided, that it would be reckless to attempt to traverse them. I'm not even sure if there is a route from here. The only way I know is to catch the bus to the very picturesque village of Masca, then follow the signposted path down the gorge.'

'I might try that tomorrow,' he said. 'After all, I came here for the walking, and to do a spot of cycling.'

'I'll hike down Masca Gorge with you,' she offered suddenly. 'I'm in work tomorrow, but I'm off the day after.'

'Are you sure?'

'Totally.' She wasn't. Then again, what harm could it do? Nothing awful had happened today and it had been a novelty to show someone who was new to the island its beauty. It was a while since she'd been down the gorge, and it would be nice to show Charles. Besides, tomorrow night was his last one under her roof. If the day trip to Masca was a disaster, she never had to see him again. She might never see him again anyway, once he'd moved into Hotel Aventuras, she reasoned.

Elspeth packed away the flask and the foil that had held the cake into her trusty old backpack, then got to her feet and brushed the dirt off her bottom.

'Hang on, you've got…' Charles said, and she almost jumped out of her skin when she felt his hand brush across her shoulder. 'It was some kind of an insect but it's gone now.'

'Thanks,' she muttered uncertainly, her heart pumping and her nerves jangling. If he'd given her some warning, she wouldn't have been so shocked. But for him to have laid his hand on her seriously rattled her. It had been a perfunctory swat using his fingers, to be fair, not a lingering, whole-hand caress, so she told herself to get over it and move on. No harm done.

There was a little part of her that wasn't so easily placated, though. The part of her that had enjoyed the brief feel of his hand and his nearness as he'd reached across to brush the creature from her T-shirt.

'It's steep going down,' she warned him, pushing the treacherous feeling to the back of her mind, where she hoped it would wither and die due to lack of light. What the hell would Ray say if he knew she'd got all unnecessary over another man? It didn't bear thinking about. 'Be careful where you put your feet and take your time. We've got all day.'

In truth, Elspeth didn't have all day. Certainly not now. She was eager to get back home and disappear into her room. She'd known Charles Brown for less than a day, and he was making her feel uncomfortable, although it wasn't his fault, it was hers. She knew her reaction was over-the-top but the fact that her villa would have him in it for the next forty-eight hours made her even more uneasy. Amanda and Toni owed her big time.

These were the thoughts going through her head as she scrambled down the rocky incline, Charles following closely behind. She eased herself down over a particularly large boulder, scooting onto her behind, her foot feeling for any loose rocks that might come free when she put her whole weight on them. This perilously steep section was mercifully short, and she often went down it on her bum rather than on her feet. It felt safer that way, and she didn't have so far to fall if she happened to—

'Argh!' Her foot slipped on a loose stone and, unbalanced, she threw herself backwards rather than risk falling forwards.

She went straight into Charles who was directly behind her.

'Oomph,' he grunted as he too was knocked back, and she felt him hit the ground.

Before she knew it, she was sitting in his lap and the pair of them were semi-prostrate on the steep dirt track.

Elspeth, cheeks blazing with unaccustomed heat, surged to her feet and scrambled away.

'Are you OK?' he asked.

She had no idea if she was or wasn't. Her brain was too topsy-turvy to check whether all her limbs were working correctly, but as she didn't feel any pain, she assumed she must be. Gingerly, she waggled her toes in her new boots, and rolled her shoulders.

Apart from her pride, nothing hurt.

'I'm fine,' she said. 'You?'

Charles hadn't made a move to get to his feet, and worry ate at her. Although neither of them was old, at their age falls could still be tricky, and even if he had technically only fallen a couple of feet due to the gradient of the slope, he might have cracked a rib on one of the rocks, or twisted a knee, or – God forbid – broken a hip.

'I'm fine,' he assured her. 'I'm more concerned about you. You look rather pink. Do you feel faint?'

'No, I'm fine,' she repeated. Elspeth felt silly and embarrassed, but definitely not faint. 'Shall we get on?'

The rest of their walk was conducted more or less in silence. She wasn't so discourteous that she didn't speak to him – she did, pointing out things he might be interested in – but she said as little as she could get away with without appearing to be rude.

She even managed to hide her relief when she finally slipped the key into the lock and pushed open her front door.

Then her manners got the better of her, and she had to say, 'I'm going to make myself some lunch. Would you like some? It's only a bacon sandwich, I'm afraid, not very Spanish.'

'No, but thank you, that's very kind of you. I'm only booked in for half-board, so please don't feel obliged to provide lunch for me as well. Not when you've already done so much.'

'It's no trouble,' she said, kicking herself even as the words came tripping out of her mouth.

'Well,' he looked doubtful. 'If you're sure it isn't too much bother.'

'It's not.' And it wasn't. The bother wasn't in the sharing of her meal, nor in cooking the bacon. It wasn't in the glass of wine that she would offer him to go with it. The bother was in the expectation that they'd eat together – because how odd would it look if she served him his meal in the courtyard, and she ate the exact same meal on her own in the kitchen? She'd got away with it at breakfast, but she didn't think she'd be able to pull it off when they'd spent the morning together and she'd practically invited him to have lunch with her.

But if she hadn't asked him then she'd have been forced to not eat at all, or to pop to the nearest cafe – where she may well have bumped into Charles himself because it was lunchtime after all and he'd have wanted to eat, too… And, now that she came to think about it, that would have been even more awkward. She realised she was getting herself into a bit of a pickle.

Her mouth must have worked all this out before her brain had had a chance to, which was why she'd blurted out the offer. Once lunch was over, she could make herself scarce by reading in her bedroom or popping across the square to the church. It was dim and cool, and incredibly peaceful. She wasn't religious, but she went there frequently for the serene atmosphere, although she never stayed long. However, she might make an exception this afternoon!

'I'll just pop to my room and freshen up,' he said. 'I'll be down in a tick.'

'Take your time,' she told him. 'Lunch will be about half an hour.'

'Do you need a hand?'

'Most certainly not! You're a guest. I wouldn't dream of asking you.'

'You didn't ask, I offered,' Charles pointed out, but she shook her head and, seeing she meant it, he disappeared up the stairs, Elspeth watching his every step.

When he was finally out of sight, she sagged against the wall and wiped her brow. She was concerned to see that her hand had a slight tremor. That little fall she'd had must have shaken her up more than she realised.

With a frown, she pulled herself together; she had bacon to grill, and she'd better freshen up too, because she had half the dust from the mountain on her. First though, there was something else she needed to do, and she went into the dappled shade of the courtyard.

'Sorry, Ray, I forgot to say good morning.'

Chapter 6

'That was delicious,' Charles declared a short while later, pushing his plate to the side and wiping his mouth on a cloth napkin.

No paper ones for her – Ray had been old-fashioned like that and had preferred linen ones. Not only were they nicer to use, but they were better for the environment he used to say. He'd been right, as he so often was. Not always, but frequently. And if he wasn't, he'd always acknowledge the fact and offer an apology. An old-school gentleman, that's what he'd been, and Elspeth didn't think they made them like that any more. They'd broken the mould when Ray had passed on. His manners were one of the things that had attracted her to him, despite him being nearly twenty years older than her. When it came to love, age didn't matter. That's what she'd told him and that's what she still believed, even now. Still, she couldn't help feeling a little bitter – if he'd been nearer her own age, he might still be alive.

She began collecting the dishes and when Charles half rose to his feet and tried to help, she waved him away. 'You're on holiday,' she reminded him for a second time that day.

'That's as may be, but I don't expect you to wait on me. Especially since you have been kind enough to take me on a walk this morning, and have provided me with lunch. And,' he added, 'you've offered to accompany me on a hike down Masca Gorge.'

Damn. She was hoping he'd forgotten.

'I can manage,' she said. 'It's only a bit of washing up. It'll only take five minutes.'

'I insist. You finish your wine, and I'll see to the dishes. Just point me in the direction of the washing-up liquid.'

'That's very kind of you. It's in the cupboard under the sink.'

'I'll be back in a jiffy,' he promised, stacking the dishes so he didn't have to make two trips.

Elspeth listened to the faint noises emanating from the kitchen and picked up her wine. She enjoyed a glass with lunch, and sometimes one with dinner. But that was all she allowed herself. In the awful days after Ray's catastrophic stroke, the temptation to drown her pain in the depths of a bottle had been overwhelming. Amanda and Toni had stepped in and looked after her. And they would have continued to do that for as long as it took, but she stopped drinking a bottle (or two) a day, because she didn't want them to feel obliged to take care of her. She still didn't. Which was why she never drank more than a single glass at any one time, and never more than two in a day. She didn't trust herself not to slip back into old habits and, not wanting to intrude on her friends too much, she refused most of the invites they issued to have her over for dinner, or to pop to the island's capital, and so on (spare wheel, and all that), which was why she was very careful not to reach for the wine bottle for consolation.

She knew they thought her rather grumpy sometimes and she didn't blame them, but it was so hard being with Amanda and Toni and seeing them together when it used to be the four of them – it made her feel Ray's loss even more keenly. Once or twice Amanda had tried to set her up on a blind date, making some flimsy excuse that a friend of Toni's was in the area and she was needed to even up the numbers so this stranger didn't feel awkward. Elspeth had refused those invitations, too. She neither wanted nor needed another man in her life. Ray was gone, and she had no intention of replacing him, not now or in the future.

'All done,' Charles declared, sticking his head through the sliding glass doors which she and Ray had installed when they'd renovated the villa. He was wiping his hands on a tea towel and had splashes of water on his shirt. Ray used to get soaked every time he washed up too, and the memory made her smile.

'Thank you, but I still think you shouldn't have,' she said.

'It's done now. Er… is it OK if I pop out for a bit? I'd like to have a look around the town.'

'Of course! Let me give you a key,' she said and bustled into the hall to fetch the spare from a drawer in the table. 'Here you are. But I warn you, Santiago del Teide closes down between one and four for lunch, so there might not be a great deal open apart from a couple of bars and cafes.'

'That's fine. I need to walk off that wonderful lunch.'

He was very kind considering the lunch had been rather basic and hadn't been wonderful at all.

'Dinner at eight?' she suggested.

'I'll be back well before then,' he told her.

Immediately after he'd gone, she picked up the phone and dialled Hotel Aventuras.

'Everything OK?' Amanda asked as soon as she answered.

'Why wouldn't it be?' Elspeth's reply was a little tart.

'No reason, just asking. You rang me, remember?'

'Yes, so I did. Sorry.'

'Well? Is it?'

'It's fine.'

'Is your Mr Brown behaving himself?'

'He's not *my* Mr Brown. If anything, he's *yours*; I'm just putting him up. And what do you mean when you say behaving himself?'

'He didn't stay out all night and come home in the wee small hours roaring drunk? Or drink your orange juice straight from the carton? Or make a pass at you?'

'No! Why would you say such a thing?' Elspeth narrowed her eyes. 'You don't think he'd do something like that, do you?'

'Which one?' Amanda was laughing.

'Any of those things? All of them!'

'I don't know the guy. I've never met him, remember?'

'Oh, of course you haven't.' She rubbed her eyes. Broken sleep last night and then an unaccustomed lie-in this morning hadn't done her any good whatsoever.

'Do you think he'll do those things?' Amanda asked. 'I mean, if you're concerned I can—'

'No, it's fine,' Elspeth hastened to reassure her, not wanting her friend to worry. After all, there wasn't anything to worry about, was there? Charles had behaved like a perfect gentleman. It wasn't his fault that she felt unbalanced by having a strange man staying in her house.

'What's wrong?' Amanda knew her too well. She should do, having seen her at her absolute worst. Seeing someone at their best was no way to judge a person – see them at rock bottom and you saw the true soul hidden deep within.

48

'I took him on a walk.'

'You did?' The amazement in her friend's voice spoke volumes.

'And I'm taking him on another the day after tomorrow.'

'You don't have to do that, you know. That wasn't part of the deal when I asked if you could put him up for a few nights.'

'I know. It just felt... right. At the time,' she added hastily.

'And now?'

'I don't know.'

'Look, let me sort something else out for him. You don't have to do this.'

'It wouldn't be fair on him and it's not his fault. It's mine.'

'It's not your fault. It's never yours. You can't help how you're feeling. I know how hard it's been for you.'

'But it's been so long.' Elspeth trailed off. As she kept telling herself, there was no time restriction on grief. 'You'd have thought I'd be able to handle having a house-guest by now.'

'You've done well to get this far – no need to beat yourself up over a little thing like this.' Amanda sounded concerned, and Elspeth felt dreadful to have worried her.

'Never mind, I'm being silly. I don't know what's got into me,' she said.

She did though. She'd been perfectly fine until Charles had touched her. It didn't matter that he'd not meant anything by it, or that it had been fleeting, he'd still touched her.

And she couldn't forget how it had made her feel. Neither could she dismiss her guilt.

After she ended the call, she made her way to the church and prayed her husband would forgive her.

Chapter 7

'I've changed my mind,' Elspeth told Charles as soon as he walked into the villa later that afternoon. 'I'm taking you out to dinner.'

'Have you got fed up with cooking for me already?' he joked.

'Not at all. I think you deserve something better than I can rustle up. Something typically Canarian.' Elspeth was happy enough to admit that she was a dab hand at cooking traditional English food, but if ever she and Ray had wanted authentic Canarian dishes, they used to go out.

'I honestly don't mind. I'll happily eat whatever you cook. Please don't put yourself out on my account,' he told her.

'I'm not.' She smiled at him to diffuse the shortness of her reply. In all honesty, she didn't give a stuff whether he ate local cuisine or roast beef and Yorkshire pudding for dinner. What she did give a fig about was being alone with him. At least a busy restaurant would diffuse the intimacy of the little courtyard dinner for two, because she didn't think she could cope with that right now.

'Let me pay then, please,' he said.

'Certainly not. This is my idea. Besides, you've already paid for your dinner.'

'I don't follow.'

'By rights, you should be staying at Hotel Aventuras tonight and dinner is included in the cost of your room. Therefore, if you pay for tonight's meal you'll be paying for your dinner twice. Three times, actually, because there's my meal, too.'

Charles gave her a quizzical look. 'You've thought about this, haven't you?'

'Yes.'

'What if I refuse to accompany you?'

'There are plenty of eggs in the fridge,' she retorted. 'Help yourself.'

'You would go out and leave me to cook my own supper?'

She nodded.

'In that case, I'd better go and put my best bib and tucker on.'

'Oh, I wouldn't bother if I were you,' she said.

'No?'

'No.'

He frowned and looked so perplexed, Elspeth let out a giggle. But she didn't explain any further and just grabbed her bag.

'Let's go,' she said.

'Now? OK.'

'It's not far,' she told him, as she led the way across the square and onto the main road. There was a restaurant directly opposite and Charles glanced hopefully at it, but she continued on past.

When she turned into a small park with a kiosk-type building at one end with a paved section and several barbeque pits to the side, she could sense his confusion. Directly in front of the building were tables and chairs, but their accompanying sun umbrellas were closed at this time of the evening. In front of the barbeque pits was grass, and on it sat several benches and tables. Most were occupied, and the aroma of roasting meat filled the air, as did the sound of chatter and laughter. Children darted around, and everyone seemed to be having fun.

Most of the tables outside the cafe were also occupied, but there were a couple free and Elspeth went over to the nearest one and sat down. Her gaze, when she looked at a rather bemused Charles, was direct and slightly challenging.

'This wasn't what I was expecting,' he admitted, glancing around as he took a seat.

'It might not be, but look how busy it is and take a gander at the sort of people here,' she advised.

Charles studied the people as best he could without appearing to stare, and Elspeth stifled another giggle. What was wrong with her? She wasn't a giggler, but she'd done so twice in the space of an hour.

'They're locals?' he said, at last.

'Bingo! The food here is amazing, and it's relatively cheap. Tourists tend to go for the rather more upmarket, stylish restaurants, but you can't beat this place. And the view isn't too bad, either.'

Trees lined the park, providing not only shade, but also screening from the road traffic, and the whole feel was one of rustic simplicity.

'Do you ever use those barbeques?' he asked, staring at them.

'We… I… have done in the past. Not anymore.' It used to be fun to bring a selection of stuff to throw on the coals, and wash it down with cold Efes beer surrounded by laughter. Barbecuing on one's own wasn't quite the same, although she guessed if she did, there would most likely be someone she knew who would invite her to join them. Nevertheless, without Ray she hadn't been tempted.

She felt a flutter of unfamiliar excitement – eating out was such a novelty, and she was glad she'd made the suggestion (or demand, rather). Apart from joining Amanda and Toni now and again for dinner at the hotel, she'd rarely eaten dinner out since Ray had died. This was a treat indeed, although she had to ignore the guilty niggle at the back of her mind, and she told herself not to be so absurd, Ray wouldn't mind her getting out a bit.

Mind you, she'd felt that way for ages after he'd passed on, no matter what she did, whether it was finding pleasure in a sunset, or enjoying a pastry with her cup of tea. Guilt had become her constant companion and had been hard to dismiss. She'd thought she'd managed to overcome it, but every now and again it surprised her, like now.

'Elspeth, *cómo estás?*'

'Maria!' Elspeth rose and gave the woman a kiss on each cheek. Elspeth saw the cafe and barbeque owner around the town on occasion and often stopped for a chat, but this was the first time she'd been on the premises since Ray had died, and Maria was delighted to see her.

After Elspeth had taken a few moments to catch up on some news, she remembered her manners and introduced her to Charles, speaking in a mixture of Spanish and English so both of them could understand her. And after the introductions had been made, Elspeth was extremely glad that her guest didn't speak Spanish.

Maria wiggled her eyebrows and turned to Elspeth. '*Guapo! Es su novio?*' The well-manicured eyebrows wiggled some more.

'*No, él no es mi novio!*' Elspeth exclaimed. Boyfriend, indeed! Huh. Although she did have to agree with the cafe owner's assessment that Charles was a handsome man. Hurriedly, she explained the booking situation at Hotel Aventuras, but even so Maria gave her a quizzical look.

'*Definitivamente no es mi novio,*' she repeated, in case Maria hadn't understood the first time that Charles wasn't her boyfriend, and added, '*Negocios,*' for good measure. That was what Charles was – business. And helping a friend out. See, she thought, this was why she didn't go out much. People always tried to set her up. She didn't want, or need, a man in her life. She was perfectly content as she was. No matter how well meaning people were, they simply didn't understand that she'd had her one great love. It was enough. It had to be.

Why was she thinking about love and Charles in the same breath anyway?

She waited until Maria had fetched them each a menu, before she looked at Charles, dreading reading his expression.

Thankfully, he appeared to be more concerned with the choice of food and Maria's insinuations had gone unnoticed.

'The grilled cheese is a good starter,' Elspeth said, trying to keep her voice neutral, despite her heart beating a little too fast. This dinner was turning out to be more stressful than she'd anticipated. Thanks, Maria… 'Then how about a plate of goat's meat, with a side of potatoes with *mojo*?'

'Sounds good. What's *mojo*?'

'It's a sauce, either red – chillies – or green – green peppers and coriander. It's eaten with almost every dish in the Canaries, and especially with potatoes.'

Elspeth gave Maria the order, along with requesting a large beer for each of them, then sat back to watch the antics of the children in the play area. That was her one regret about living on Tenerife: not having Gideon and her grandson near.

Gideon had flown to Tenerife for the funeral, of course, bringing the woman who was to become his wife with him. Elspeth had been too caught up in her grief to spare the girl much thought, but ever since then Gideon and Sakura had holidayed with her once a year, and she'd flown to Japan for the wedding. It had been a wonderful wedding, only marred, as far as Elspeth was concerned, by Ray not being there. Travelling without him had been simply awful and quite distressing. She'd also visited Japan again shortly after her gorgeous little grandson arrived into the world; they'd called him Raidon, which meant 'spirit'. And whenever she thought about little Rai, she knew her husband was still with them. The little boy's name encompassed the heritage of both of his parents, she felt. He would celebrate his first birthday in a couple of months, and she sorely missed him. She missed Gideon, too. But she didn't miss either of them as much as she missed Ray.

'What is the best way to get to Mount Teide?' Charles asked, breaking into her thoughts.

Glad for the distraction, because she was in danger of becoming quite morbid, she replied, 'Car or taxi. There isn't a direct bus service from this side of the island. Of course, you could always go on an organised excursion.'

He grimaced. 'No, thanks. I prefer to set my own itinerary, as much as possible. Besides, I was thinking of hiking up.'

Elspeth tilted her head to one side. 'All the way from the road?'

He nodded.

'Really?' It was ambitious, she thought. She'd done it once and it was one heck of a climb.

'Yep,' he said.

'That's brave. You do realise how long it will take, don't you?'

'Five to six hours?'

'That's right, plus at least another four to get back down. And you won't be allowed to go to the very top unless you have a permit.'

'Ah ha! I do have one. It's for next Sunday.'

'You'd better hire a car then,' she told him. 'As next Sunday is Easter Sunday lots of things close down or will have limited service, taxi firms included.'

He sighed. 'I'll have to do that then,' he said. 'Who do you recommend?'

Elspeth had absolutely no idea. She'd never hired a car, and neither had Ray. 'I'll ask Amanda at the hotel. She's bound to know, although you are leaving it rather late to hire something; this is one of Tenerife's busiest times of the year, and there won't be much availability.'

Charles looked disappointed, but there was nothing she could do. He'd have to take his chances along with all the other tourists. And even if she had a car, she wasn't sure she'd offer to drive him up there. Anyway, after Monday, he'd be Amanda and Toni's concern, not hers.

'By hook or by crook, I'll get there,' he vowed. 'I didn't come all this way not to climb one of the highest peaks in Western Europe – and one that you don't need crampons and ropes to get to the top of.'

'Do you do a lot of climbing?' she asked.

'No, too much of a scaredy-cat.'

'Yet you want to hike to over twelve thousand feet and perch on the edge of the crater rim?'

He smiled slowly. 'Now you put it like that...' Leaning back in his seat a little to allow Maria to place their drinks and cutlery on the table, he added, 'You don't hike *all* of those twelve thousand feet though, do you?'

'Not unless you're completely insane,' Elspeth laughed. 'The easiest starting point is from the road at Montaña Blanca, at about seven thousand feet, so you'll still have some significant climbing to do, and it's terribly steep in places.'

'You sound as though you've done it.'

'I have. My husband and I hiked it once. I was so exhausted by the time I made it to the top, I insisted we caught the cable car back down.'

'You miss him, don't you?'

Elspeth looked at Charles in surprise. What a thing to say! 'Of course, I do.'

'I heard you talking to him. In the garden.'

'So?' She narrowed her eyes, her defences up. It was none of his business who she spoke to, and if she wanted to hold a full-blown conversation with her husband, then it was up to her. Her house, her rules, her business, and if he didn't like it then he could—

'I used to talk to my dad like that. I still do sometimes...' he said, and with that, he took the wind right out of her sails.

'When did he pass on?' she asked.

'Nearly twenty years ago.'

'I am sorry.'

'It was a long time ago, and that's what happens to parents, isn't it? You don't expect it to happen to spouses though. Not at your age, at least.'

'Ray was older than me, nineteen years older to be exact. We always knew he would probably go before me.'

The sympathy in Charles's eyes made her own prickle with tears. She looked down at her knife and fork wrapped in a napkin and blinked rapidly.

'That must have been hard,' he said. He'd said the same thing last night, too.

'Not really. Not until it happened, at least. Up to that point we just got on with our lives, like any other couple.' She lifted her head. 'You can't help who you fall in love with, can you?'

'No, I don't suppose you can.'

After that, dinner was a far less spiky affair. Elspeth was less on edge and relaxed a little more. Maybe dinner in the villa's courtyard wouldn't have been so bad after all, she mused, feeling better about the prospect of tomorrow evening's dinner at the villa. Still, it was nice to eat out for a change, and she took her time over each course, savouring it, relishing the novelty of having a meal cooked for her.

She even had a second (small, this time) glass of beer and a cup of tea to finish off. The indulgence scared her a little, and she tried not to agonise over how much the evening was costing her. She wasn't on the breadline exactly, but she didn't have an awful lot of spare cash to throw around, and she always, always lived within her means. Her treat for this month had been her new hiking boots. She shouldn't have splashed out on dinner, too.

It had been her own silly fault, she reasoned. If she hadn't reacted in such a ridiculous way to Charles's touch, then she wouldn't have felt the need to surround herself with other people rather than be alone with him. Still, she had enjoyed the food immensely, and she could always cut back a little after Charles left; salad and potatoes were cheap and plentiful.

She wasn't sure if her anxiety showed, or whether Charles was simply being a gentleman, but she didn't think anything of it when he excused himself to use the restroom. He still had half of his coffee left and she hadn't finished her tea, and she found she wasn't quite prepared for the evening to end just yet.

Eventually, though, their cups were empty and it was time to go.

'*La cuenta, por favor, Maria.*' She called for the bill when she spotted the restaurant's owner clearing a nearby table.

Maria beamed at her. '*Ya está pagado.*'

'Excuse me?' Elspeth reverted to English in her surprise. Then she caught Charles's rather sheepish expression. 'Maria tells me the bill is already paid,' she said to him, accusingly. 'I'm fairly sure the meal isn't on the house, so is this your doing?'

'Um… yes.'

'I suppose I should say thank you, but I'm far too cross.'

'You're welcome.' His grin was quite boyish and rather wicked.

'Hmph.'

'I didn't want to put you out,' he said, getting to his feet and walking around the table. 'I still don't.'

She blinked as she felt her chair being pulled out for her to stand up. Then he gestured for her to go ahead of him.

Before she did, she turned and called out, '*Gracias, Maria, estaba delicioso,*' then she brought her fingers to her lips and kissed them, making a smacking noise to show her appreciation.

When she turned back, her eyes met his, and heat rose to her cheeks at the admiration she saw in them. Honestly! Anyone could learn to speak Spanish, especially when they lived in the country for as long as she had. There was nothing to admire about her ability to converse in another language.

She strode ahead of him, aware he was hurrying to catch up, but once he reached her side his stride matched hers. So much for her stalking off. It had been more of a rapid shuffle than a stalk, and she knew she was being silly and a little childish. So what if he had paid for dinner? It was no biggie, and it meant she had more in her bank account at the end of the month.

Wanting to make amends somewhat for her surliness, as soon as they got back to the villa she said, 'Can I make you a coffee? Or would you prefer wine?'

'A glass of wine would be nice. Will you be joining me, or will I be forced to drink it on my own?'

She tamped down a sigh and made an effort not to roll her eyes. He was pushing his luck, even if he didn't realise it. 'I'll have a cup of tea,' she said. She'd already had two beers, which was above her self-imposed limit.

But when she poured him his glass of wine, she poured herself one, too, because it wasn't as though she was sitting on her own nursing a bottle – she was having a drink with someone in order to be sociable. An entirely different situation from those dark weeks and months after Ray had passed on. She carried them out to the table and chairs in the garden, where Charles was already sitting.

'I talk to Ray because he's still here,' she blurted after her second sip.

'I don't think our loved ones ever truly leave us,' Charles said.

'No, I mean Ray is *here*, in the garden. Underneath that tree over there.' She jerked her head.

Charles's eyes widened.

'Not his body – his ashes,' she clarified.

'Are you allowed to do that?'

'Not really. You're supposed to get special dispensation, or something.'

'I won't tell anyone.'

She snorted. 'It wouldn't matter if you did. The authorities could hardly remove them. They're part of the tree now.' She gazed fondly at it.

'It would be hard for you to leave here, wouldn't it?'

'Oh, I'm never leaving,' she declared.

'I mean, if you had to; when you get older, maybe, and can't manage the stairs. At our age we have to think of these things.'

'I don't.'

He cocked his head, his expression quizzical. 'Don't you? I do. Now that I'm retired, getting old seems a very real possibility.'

'That's probably it – I haven't retired. I still work, remember?' To all intents and purposes she had retired when she and Ray moved to Tenerife. The pair of them had enjoyed more than ten years of doing what they wanted, when they wanted. They hadn't lived in each other's pockets, because that wasn't healthy, and they both had separate interests. But their lives were so full and they had wanted to spend as much time together as they could, that Elspeth had never had the time nor felt the need to find herself a job.

It had all changed when Ray died.

Lonely, lost, and with all those empty hours, days, and weeks stretching ahead of her, she knew that for her own sanity she needed something to occupy her. Stefan and Libertad had been it.

She knew she owed that young man a great deal. Not many employers would have taken on a middle-aged grieving widow, especially in a business as vibrant and as youthful as one catering to the outdoors adventure crowd. Although, there were increasing numbers of older people enjoying hiking and cycling, she'd noticed over the years. She was just as likely to see a sixty-year-old on one of her more challenging walks, as she was to see a twenty-year-old. And the older ones tended to have more disposable income to spend on the high-priced clothing and accessories that the shop specialised in. So maybe Stefan taking her on had been more of a business consideration than she'd thought.

Stefan's motivation didn't matter. He'd given her a job and a reason for her to get up in the morning four days a week, and she'd be forever grateful to him.

'That reminds me,' Elspeth said. 'I'm working tomorrow and won't be around between ten and six, although I do get an hour for lunch, so I could pop back to the villa and make you something?' He might technically be half-board, but she'd provided lunch for him today and she felt she ought to do so again tomorrow.

'No need. I'm going to see about hiring a bike and going for a ride. Many of the top cycling teams train on Tenerife, you know.'

Elspeth bit back a smile. 'I know.'

Charles shook his head. 'Of course you do. I'm sorry, I'm just so excited at being here. Can you recommend any routes?'

'I can, and I can also recommend hiring a bike from Libertad instead of the hotel. I assume that's where you were planning on getting one from?'

'I was.' His look was questioning.

'The hotel's bikes are great for a dabble around Santiago, but if you want to do more serious cycling, you will need a more serious bike. Amanda will tell you the same thing. Did you bring your own cycling gear?'

'I did, as a matter of fact.'

'Good. How about shoes? Because most of the decent bikes in the shop have clip-in peddles, although Stefan will change them for ordinary ones if he's given enough notice. Or I can.'

'You can?'

She nodded. 'I might not cycle myself, but over time a fair amount has rubbed off on me. I know my drop bars from my classic.'

'I find knowing about the different kinds of handlebars rather attractive in a woman,' Charles joked.

'Stop it.' Elspeth's tone carried a mock warning. 'Loads of women cycle these days, and they're just as good as the men.'

He held up his hands in surrender. 'OK, OK, I apologise.' His expression sobered. 'I was only teasing, you know.'

'I know.'

'I don't want you to think…' He trailed off.

'I don't,' she replied, although she wasn't sure what it was that she wasn't supposed to think. That he found her attractive?

To her consternation, she realised she'd be rather chuffed if he did; she quite liked the idea of him fancying her.

Oh dear, time for bed. She'd had a tad too much alcohol this evening and it was making her silly.

But as she brushed her teeth, Elspeth couldn't decide whether she was relieved she was working tomorrow and therefore wouldn't see him for most of the day, or whether she was disappointed. And the fact that she couldn't decide was unsettling to say the least.

Chapter 8

The following morning, Elspeth had showered and break-fasted before Charles put in an appearance. It wasn't that he was having a lie-in or that he was tardy. The truth of the matter was that Elspeth had deliberately got up early so she wouldn't have to make small talk with him – or eat with him. Or interact with him in any way at all, really.

Yesterday had been an aberration. A pleasant one, admittedly, but not one she intended to repeat today if she could help it. Distance from him, mentally and physically, was what she needed. He'd upset her routine (and her composure) enough. It didn't help that she felt she was being disloyal to the memory of her husband. Enjoying Charles's company and the way she was reacting to him was making her feel guilty, as though she was betraying Ray. She'd not looked at another man since he'd passed away. And she didn't intend to do so now. The mere idea filled her with apprehension.

She was finishing the last few drops of the tea in her cup when she heard Charles coming down the stairs, and she gathered up her breakfast things hastily and took them into the kitchen.

'What can I get you?' she asked. 'There's the usual fruit, cereal and toast or I can do you scrambled eggs, if you like? Or poached? How about some bacon?'

'Toast will be fine, thanks.'

'Are you sure? It's no trouble.'

'I know breakfast is supposed to be the most important meal of the day, but I simply can't stomach too much.'

'Toast it is, then. Do you prefer jam or honey? I tell you what, I'll fetch both and you don't have to decide right away.' She knew she was fussing, but she couldn't help it; it was better than showing him how bewildered she felt.

'Are you joining me?'

Elspeth was sheepish. 'Not this morning. I'm going into work early... er... Stefan, who owns the shop asked if I could.' Stefan had asked nothing of the sort, and the lie sat uneasily on her tongue. To cover her guilt, she hastened to make Charles his breakfast. And to ease her conscience while his toast was browning, she swiftly made him a packed lunch for his day out cycling.

'That's so kind of you. You didn't have to do that,' he exclaimed when she handed him a bag with wrapped sandwiches, fruit, a couple of cookies and a flask of tea in it. 'I could have picked something up on the way.'

'It's not the same as having something made just for you, is it?' she asked, then bit her lip and turned away to hide an unexpected stab of sorrow. She used to do the same thing for Ray when he was going sea fishing for the day.

Maybe she shouldn't have made Charles a packed lunch, but it had felt like the right thing to do. And, although she didn't want to admit it to herself, she had enjoyed making it. It was nice to have someone to look after, to fuss over. Not that Charles needed fussing over – she got the impression that he wasn't used to it and didn't know how to deal with it – but it reminded her of how she used to take pleasure in doing little things like that for Ray.

She missed that – having someone to take care of, having someone other than herself to consider. Maybe she should get a cat? It would be somebody else to talk to, besides Ray.

Oh. She'd not said good morning to her husband *again* this morning. That was two days in a row now, and although she dearly wanted to speak to him, she didn't feel comfortable doing so in front of Charles.

Instead, she satisfied herself by whispering some words to her husband out of her bedroom window when she went to fetch her shop boots. She called them her 'shop boots' (they were actually regular hiking boots) because she only wore them at work. Stefan thought she was mad, but she felt she should wear the products they sold – a walking advert, as it were – and she had no intention of letting her work clothes and boots look worn or scruffy, which was what would happen if she wore them out hiking. She took pride in looking as though she could have stepped from the pages of a walking magazine. She often thought a customer might look at her and believe this is what they could look like while walking up a mountain if they bought a T-shirt like the one she was wearing, or the fleece, the cargo pants, the socks... The magazine would most likely be *Saga* though, not *Elle*, she had to admit. Still, she believed her modelling method worked, because she was a good saleswoman, and more often than not she hit her (voluntary) target for the day.

She might be an advocate for the business, but that didn't mean she sold anything to anyone regardless of whether it was suitable for them or not – she liked to keep her sense of integrity intact – which was why it pained her to fib to Charles.

'You've got a key, haven't you?' she asked, hovering uncertainly near the garden table. For some reason, she was reluctant to leave. 'Don't bother with the washing up, I'll see to it lunchtime. On second thoughts, why don't I wait for you to finish your breakfast, then I can tidy up?'

'I'm not going to steal the silver, you know,' he said, mildly.

Heat rushed into her cheeks. 'I didn't mean to imply that I don't trust you.' Oh, dear, now she'd gone and upset him.

'You didn't, I was teasing. And I'm perfectly capable of washing my own breakfast things. I've been doing it for years. I also know how to use a washing machine, and which end of a vacuum cleaner is the business end.'

'You're teasing me again.'

'I am.'

To her annoyance, she found she quite liked it.

'Go, or else you're going to be late,' he urged when she continued to dither. 'I'll come to the shop later, to sort out the bike hire.'

Elspeth went. Reluctantly.

–

'Has your guest driven you out of your home already?' Stefan asked when she used her key to enter the shop. It wasn't opening time yet, so she was definitely early.

'Not at all,' she replied, although he had, initially. Now, though, she wished she'd stayed and had breakfast with him. 'I was up, so I thought I'd come in.'

She rarely did that. This might be the first time in four years that she'd done anything so spontaneous as arriving at work early. A thought struck her. 'I don't expect to be paid for the extra hour,' she said. 'It's my choice. You didn't ask me to. If you had, that would be different.'

Stefan was staring at her with an amused expression.

She sniffed, stuck her nose in the air and marched into the back room to make some tea, then spent the next hour trying to look busy in order to justify her early start.

A little while later, she'd just about got into her stride and had recovered from her silliness, when Charles walked into the shop. Flustered, she busied herself with straightening some already neat hangers, and called to Stefan, 'Customer for a bike hire.'

Stefan stepped out from the back at the same time as Charles held up a paper bag and said, 'Good morning again, Elspeth. I've been exploring the town and these pastries looked so good, I thought I'd bring you some. I bought four because I didn't know how many people worked here and I didn't want to leave anyone out. You were up and out so early, I thought you might like a little something to keep you going until lunch.' He looked at Stefan. 'I'm Charles Brown, by the way, Elspeth's lodger for the time being, and as she was nice enough to make me a packed lunch, I thought I should return the favour, considering she was asked to go into work early.'

Elspeth wished Charles would stop speaking. She also wished he'd get lost and hire his bike from somewhere else. She was very conscious of Stefan's raised eyebrows and questioning look, and she shook her head briefly, hoping he'd get the message and not say anything.

He must have, because he turned his attention to Charles. 'What sort of bike do you want to hire?'

'A road bike, please, with dropped handlebars, and would you have any pedals to fit these?' Charles held up his cycling shoes so Stefan could see the cleats on their soles.

Elspeth had no idea how it was even possible to pedal when the sole of your boot was fixed firmly to the pedal. She knew, because she'd seen it with her own eyes, that it was a matter of a swift flick of the foot to release it from the pedal, but it was still a surprise to her how most cyclists didn't simply keel over when they got to traffic lights or junctions because they couldn't put their feet to the ground in time. She predicted that she'd never be able to get her foot out of the pedal quickly enough and would end up toppling over sideways.

She had no idea why she was thinking about this, but it was better than thinking about the man standing in front of her with his shoes in one hand and a bag of pastries in the other. Rounding up her scattered wits, Elspeth relieved him of the paper bag.

'Thank you,' Stefan said, and she had the feeling that he was reprimanding her for her lack of manners.

'Yes, thank you,' she repeated, slightly robotically.

'We do have pedals to fit,' Stefan continued. 'Come through to the workshop and we'll measure you for a bike.'

Elspeth tried not to peep through the open door, but it was impossible not to. Eventually, in annoyance, she marched to the front of the shop and fiddled with the window display until a customer came in to distract her.

She knew Charles had left when she heard the back door slam shut (it always did that) and guessed Stefan must have found Charles a suitable bike. She also guessed that Charles would be wheeling it along the pavement outside at any moment as he made his way back to the villa to change into his cycling gear, so she hurried to the rear of the shop and dusted a spotless shelf, studiously keeping her back to the window.

'Has he said or done something to upset you?' Stefan demanded, coming to stand next to her. 'Because if he has...'

Horrified that her boss should think that, she hastily said, 'No, of course not!'

'Then why are you acting so strangely?'

'It's not him, it's me. It feels a bit odd having a man in my house.'

'He's not just a man, he's a guest.'

Oh, Charles was a man, all right, and a very nice one. He was a very attractive one, too. 'I know, but it is odd all the same,' she replied, knowing what Stefan meant. But to her, Charles was becoming less guest and more man by the hour, and it wasn't doing her hard-won equilibrium any good.

The sooner he moved out of her house and into the hotel where he belonged, the better.

Chapter 9

Elspeth had to admit that Charles looked good in Lycra. Not many men could pull it off, especially middle-aged ones – they tended to be skinny in all the wrong places (bums, thighs) and fat in the wrong ones (paunch, moobs).

Charles was slim everywhere, apart from his shoulders (which were broad), his chest (which was deep) and his arms (which were muscular). Her eyes drifted down to his flat stomach and his muscly thighs, then moved to his—

What the hell was she doing? Heat swept up her neck and into her face and she dropped her gaze to his dusty cycling shoes. She'd expected him to have been home before her, but he pulled up alongside her as she arrived home from work, and got off the bike.

'I'll open the gate,' she told him without looking up. 'Will you cycle around the back, or do you want me to fetch you a pair of trainers?' She knew it was difficult to walk with cleats on the bottom of one's soles, and not only that, it would damage them, too.

'I'll ride it around, thanks.' He swung his leg over the saddle and clipped a shoe in. He was still wearing his helmet, and his face was covered in a fine film of sweat and dust. Abruptly she was reminded of Ray when he used to go off on his bike for the day.

Elspeth shut the door before Charles pushed off, and she darted through the villa to unlock the gate set into the courtyard wall. Then she shot back into the safety of her kitchen. She didn't need to see any more of him while he was wearing such figure-hugging clothes.

As she distracted herself by preparing dinner, she heard him prop the bike up, then clatter onto a garden chair in order to take his shoes off. Then she heard the patio door open and his soft tread on the hall stairs, before the door to his bedroom opened and closed directly over her head. Thankfully, that was where any similarity to Ray dissolved, and she breathed out slowly, letting her tense shoulders unfurl themselves from where they had been positioned somewhere up around her ears.

Charles was not Ray. They didn't look alike or sound alike. However, simply having this stranger in the villa made it feel as though Ray was still here. She told herself that having any man in her home would make her feel this way. The reality of having a male presence around was bringing memories of her deceased husband to the front of her mind (more than usual, that is), and nothing to do with the fact that the male in question was Charles. It was made worse because he liked similar things to Ray – hiking, cycling – was polite and gentlemanly, and generally seemed to be a genuinely nice man. If Charles had been into beer-swilling and sunbathing, then it would be easier to keep her distance. Similarly, if Charles had been a Charlotte…

But he *was* Charles, and Elspeth was forced to admit that he reminded her of Ray in all the ways that mattered.

But, as she thought about it some more, what was starting to worry her was how she was reacting to Charles. And the way he reminded her of how pleasant it was to share her home. Not to mention that he'd made her realise just how lonely she had been since Ray had gone.

She should consider getting a cat… or a dog. Now that was an idea. A dog could accompany her on her walks; it could probably go to work with her, as long as it was well behaved. It would be pleased to see her, it would be loyal and loving, and having another creature in the villa might go some way to dispelling the crushing loneliness that she'd been living under without even realising it until now.

Elspeth savaged an onion with her favourite vegetable knife, hacking away at it with more force than was necessary and considered that she had been perfectly satisfied with her life two days ago, until Charles had been foisted upon her. She'd thought she was content (not *happy* exactly – how could she be happy ever again now that the only man she'd ever loved was gone?), but then along had come this perfectly nice man to destroy all her carefully constructed illusions, leaving her feeling restless and discontented. Her peace had been shattered, and she didn't know what to do about it.

Oh, if only her son lived nearer, so she could try to fill the gaping hole in her heart with Gideon and her marvellous, sweet little grandson. But she knew that nothing and no one would ever replace Ray, and it was that knowledge which cut the deepest. No matter how full her life might be with the love of her family, she'd lost the love of her life and her heart would never be whole again.

'Mmm, smells nice,' Charles said from behind, making her jump, as she dashed an onion-induced tear from her eye with the back of her hand. 'What are we having?'

We. He'd said we, like they were a couple. The word carried connotations of togetherness and cosiness. So yes, she'd been right to insist on eating out last night, because this evening's meal for two would be every bit as awkward as last night's might have been. All she'd done was to postpone the ordeal. And there was still tomorrow's breakfast to get through.

Tomorrow? Oh hell, she'd promised she'd take him down Masca Gorge.

'Excuse me, I need to make a phone call.' She slammed down the knife, turned on her heel and pushed past him, knowing she was behaving badly but unable to stop herself.

After she had finished her phone call to book the water taxi for tomorrow to take them from the end of their walk where the gorge met the sea, around to the harbour at Los Gigantes, Elspeth paused for a minute and fought to regain her usual poise, before she returned to the kitchen.

To her surprise, Charles wasn't there. Neither was he in the courtyard. He must be in the living room she guessed, and she found him standing next to the sideboard with a photo in his hands. He was studying it intently.

Slowly, she walked across the room and gently took it from him.

'Is that you and Ray?' He continued to stare at it.

'Yes. We'd just moved to Tenerife and that was taken on our first night in this villa.'

'You look happy.'

'We were. We had no proper toilet, the electrics were as dodgy as hell, there was a hole in the roof, and most of the windows were broken, but we were happy.'

She returned it to its customary place on the sideboard. 'Sorry about dashing off, but I'd forgotten to book a water taxi for tomorrow.' She didn't want him to feel uncomfortable and she was telling the truth – it had slipped her mind. 'We're having beef casserole for dinner, with wild rice and roasted vegetables.'

'I've always wondered why it's called wild rice. Did it have to be rounded up and captured? Or did someone happen to come across it when they were out for a stroll and decided to bag it up and sell it?'

She shook her head, bemused. 'I think it's a type of grass,' she replied, going back into the kitchen. Charles followed her.

'Is it the seed of the grass that we eat?' he asked.

Elspeth blinked. 'Presumably.'

'That's cleared that up, then.'

'You're funny.'

'Funny ha-ha, or funny strange?'

'Both?'

'Thanks.' His tone was dry.

'You remind me of Ray,' she blurted. Then her eyes widened and she couldn't think what had possessed her to say such a thing.

'Thank you.'

She scrutinised his face, searching for any evidence of sarcasm. There was none. 'It's a compliment,' she said, in case he hadn't realised.

'I know.' His gaze was warm and intense.

As she stared into his eyes, something deep inside her did a slow roll.

Quickly she broke the contact, bringing her attention back to preparing their meal. With jerky movements, she scooped the chopped onion into an ovenproof dish, and then realised she needed some peppers which were in the fridge. Elspeth bit her lip.

Charles was leaning against the appliance in question, looking relaxed and at ease, despite the fact he almost filled the small space. Funnily enough, she'd always thought of her kitchen as fairly generous. But not with Charles in it.

It was too small, stifling and cramped, and she was having trouble catching her breath.

Whether he sensed her discomfort, or whether he was bored with the conversation (such as it was), he straightened up. 'Shall I leave you to it? Too many cooks, and all that?'

Her sigh of relief was far too loud. 'Yes, please. I've nearly finished, although it will be an hour before dinner is ready.'

'That's fine. Um, do you have Wi-Fi?'

'Oh, yes, of course! Sorry, let me get you the password. I should have given it to you the day you arrived.'

'No worries.'

She was flustered again, and she didn't like it. It seemed to be her default setting when it came to Charles, and she wasn't used to it. She was normally the most collected person she knew, but since he'd come into her life she continually felt she was on the back foot.

As soon as she gave the password to him, being careful not to touch his hand as she handed him the piece of paper she'd written it on, he went upstairs.

He was back down again within a minute, clutching his phone, and she watched out of the kitchen window as he settled down at the table outside and began scrolling.

Unable to hang around in the kitchen for much longer without appearing surly, she opened a bottle of wine and took a glass out of the cupboard. He was a guest in her house, he hadn't asked to be lodged with her, and she'd do well to remember it. It wasn't his fault she was having some kind of emotional crisis, and it was down to her to keep her feelings under lock and key when she was around him. He was here for a nice holiday and she shouldn't do anything to jeopardise that, she told herself.

'Here you go,' she said, setting the wine and the glass down on the table, then made to go back inside.

'Aren't you joining me?' he asked, eyeing the solitary glass.

'You're busy... and I'm sure you saw enough of me yesterday.'

'I'm not busy at all, and I most certainly haven't seen enough of you.' His voice was warm and his eyes held hers in a steady gaze.

Elspeth was unsure how to take the comment. 'I, um, the kitchen...' She gestured towards it.

'You can pop back and forth. I won't mind, and I thought you said it would be an hour or so before dinner was ready.'

'But what about...?' Another gesture, this time in the direction of his phone.

'I'm not doing anything important. Anyway, I've finished now.' To prove a point, he turned it off and put it on the table.

She wondered whether he'd been cruising the internet, or texting his family, and she realised that holidaying on his own might make him feel quite lonely, when the world seemed to be full to the brim with couples, families and groups of friends.

All of a sudden, she felt sorry for him and she sat down, before realising she didn't have a glass.

Charles did, though. 'Stay there, I'll fetch you a glass.' He got to his feet and headed towards the sliding doors.

She watched him go, then blushed as she realised she was staring at his bottom, and quickly turned away, only for her eyes to come to rest on the orchid tree and Ray.

I'm not doing anything wrong, she thought. *I'm not being unfaithful.* She was doing Amanda and Toni a favour, that was all – how could anyone construe that as being unfaithful? Especially her gentle, polite, considerate Ray. He always thought the best of everyone, and that included her. She knew if he had been the one who had been left on his own and Toni had asked him to put a lady up for a few nights, he wouldn't have hesitated. She also knew that he wouldn't be feeling awkward about it. He certainly wouldn't be feeling all hot and bothered as though he was doing something he shouldn't.

But she was sure Ray also wouldn't be feeling attracted to the guest in question.

There, she'd admitted it – she found Charles Brown attractive. And nice. Don't forget nice, she told herself. Nice was better than sexy.

Shying away from *that* thought, she had another. A far more unsettling one.

What if Ray did find his lady guest attractive? How would she feel about it? Betrayed? Jealous? Possessive?

None of those things quite fitted… what she'd be feeling for Ray, was happy. Happy that he wasn't wasting his life grieving over her.

And deep down, she knew he'd feel the same about her.

So why did she feel as though she was betraying him? Especially since no matter how she felt about Charles, she had absolutely no intention of acting on it.

She sent her guest a smile as he came into view, holding her glass.

'I've checked on the casserole and given it a stir,' he informed her. 'It's looking and smelling great. My mouth is watering already.'

'You shouldn't have, but thank you.'

It was many, many years since Elspeth had been on a date. So long ago she could barely remember what it felt like. What she did recall was the awkwardness, the tentative exploration of the other person's likes and dislikes, and trying to find common ground and topics they were both comfortable discussing.

There was none of that with Charles, which was a good thing, considering they weren't on a date. It didn't half seem like they were, though. To Elspeth, she felt as though they had moved away from the formal host-and-guest scenario but if this wasn't a date and it wasn't business or friendship, then what was it?

She had no idea, and that made her uncomfortable all over again. She liked to know where she stood with people. Stefan, for instance was in the employer category in her mind, but he also occupied a friend slot and maybe even an adopted son slot – but she put that down to the age difference between them and the fact that her real son was many thousands of miles away. Anyway, whatever category Stefan was in, she knew why she'd put him there; she knew the boundaries of their relationship, and when it was appropriate to treat him as her boss, and when she could mother him a bit.

She had yet to find an appropriate slot for Charles in her mind. All she knew was that he'd managed to wedge himself into it without even trying.

What would happen to her if he did try?

Thank God she'd never have to find out.

Chapter 10

Buses to Masca were rather infrequent, roughly every four hours, but with an extra one in the morning to take hikers and other tourists to the gorge. Elspeth thought that if she and Charles missed both of those or couldn't get on a bus because it was full, then they could always get a taxi, but she preferred not to do that because of the additional cost. And there wasn't the option to try again another day because she'd already paid over the phone for the water taxi to take them from the end of the gorge to the little harbour town of Los Gigantes.

'Charles, are you awake?' She tapped tentatively on his bedroom door.

There was no answer, so she tried again, making both her knock and her voice a little louder.

Still no answer.

A trickle of fear slid down her back, and she hoped he was OK in there. An image of when she'd found her husband collapsed on the bedroom floor leapt into her mind and she forced it away.

Aware she couldn't go downstairs until she knew he was all right, she put her hand on the handle and—

'Elspeth?'

She let out a shriek and jumped. Charles was standing at the foot of the stairs, peering up at her.

'You nearly gave me a heart attack,' she said, putting her hand to her chest and sagging against the wall. 'I didn't realise you were up; I was just about to wake you.'

'I've been up for ages. Come down, I've made you some tea and toast. I hope you don't mind.'

'Of course not. Thank you, that's very kind of you.' She hauled herself upright, her heart still beating wildly, although it was beginning to slow down, and made her way to the kitchen.

'I'm outside,' he called as her critical eye scanned the room. Everything was neat and tidy. If he hadn't told her he'd been pottering in there, she never would have guessed. There wasn't even a single crumb on the worktop.

Elspeth appreciated tidiness. She couldn't abide mess or dirt in any form. When she stepped outside, she was tempted to say something along the lines of 'you'll make someone a good husband, one day', but she didn't want to sound patronising or make a thing out of it. So she sat down, saw that he'd already poured her a cup of tea just the way she liked it, and she began to butter her toast.

'We need to leave in an hour,' she told him. 'I'll do us a packed lunch again. The walk is only about three hours tops, but to enjoy the experience I want to give you the opportunity to explore Masca village and then take our time going down the *barranca*.'

'*Barranca?*'

'It's what they call a ravine. Masca has a permanent stream running through it, but not many ravines do, and in drier years even Masca's stream is reduced to a trickle. We had some rain earlier in the spring, though, so be prepared to get your feet wet. And if you're feeling hot when we reach the bottom, you can have a swim off the jetty.'

'I think that's why I woke so early – I was excited for today. Although…' He paused. 'I can't believe it's Monday already and I'll be moving into the hotel this evening.'

Elspeth felt the blood drain from her face. So soon? She counted in her head – three nights, which had been Friday, Saturday and last night. She had been so keen for him to leave on Friday, so how could she have forgotten? The only excuse she could think of was that she'd been too busy showing Charles one of her favourite walks on Saturday, then working yesterday, that the days had flown by.

Her heart did a funny little squeeze as she imagined making dinner for one rather than two this evening – and eating it on her own. Then there was waking up tomorrow to an empty house…

Somehow, in little over fifty hours she'd grown used to Charles being there. The villa would feel very empty once he had gone.

Get over it, she told herself. It would never feel as empty as those first few months after Ray had died. She'd never felt so alone and hoped she'd never feel that way again.

Since then she had become used to living on her own. She didn't feel the need to have company all the time, so she might just as well get used to being by herself again, and quickly. By this time tomorrow she'd have forgotten what it was like to have someone else in her house, although she'd do well to remember the awkwardness and inconvenience, just in case she was tempted to repeat the experience.

'You'll love it at Hotel Aventuras,' she enthused. 'You'll have a choice of food for a start, and there'll be loads of other guests you can chat to.'

He made a face, but didn't say anything, and she guessed he might not be that much of a people person. Just like her. She wasn't the type to chat to random strangers, apart from when she was in work, and it was expected, encouraged even. She didn't used to like it much when someone would sit next to her and Ray on the plane and attempt to strike up a conversation, or if another couple asked if they could join them at their table during dinner, although Ray revelled in it.

'I'll go and make our lunch,' she said, finishing off the last bite of toast and trying not to think how nice it had been to have breakfast made for her.

Charles Brown was an awfully nice man, and in some ways she'd be sorry to see him leave.

Chapter 11

Santiago del Teide was quickly left behind as the bus trundled heavily up the road leading out of the town. The gradient was steep and Charles twisted around in his seat to catch a glimpse of the view behind, of the buildings nestling in a bowl of mountains with the ultimate peak, Mount Teide, beyond.

'Gosh, Teide looks clear today – not a cloud in sight,' he said. Elspeth turned her head.

'She is clear,' she agreed. 'Doesn't she look splendid!'

'Teide is female?'

'No idea,' she replied cheerily. 'But the mountain is capricious, unpredictable and can be very dangerous, so I tend to think of her as some kind of female secret agent or assassin.'

Charles narrowed his eyes at her and leaned away slightly. 'That's a bit of a weird imagination you've got.'

'I know.' She smiled at him. 'Ray used to say the same thing, so it must be true.'

'He was right. I wish I could have met him. He sounds like a top bloke.'

'He was. I think you and him would have got along like a house on fire.'

'I'm sure we would.'

Elspeth left the conversation there, parking it until she was on her own and could give it the consideration it deserved, because at that very moment the labouring bus had reached the crest of the ridge, and without warning, the road dropped away and a magnificent vista opened up before them.

There was a collective gasp of appreciation from the people in the bus, and even Elspeth, who had seen this view so many times before, felt her heart lift in response.

A series of rugged, jagged mountains marched away into the distance, the odd cloud or two floating along their tops. Deep, steep-sided valleys harboured deeper secrets in their convoluted shadows, and every so often it was possible to catch a glimpse of the azure sea.

The road snaked and coiled along the flanks of the mountains. It was chiselled out of the unforgiving bedrock and was as narrow as it could possibly be whilst still allowing two vehicles to pass. This road wasn't for the faint-hearted or for the nervous driver.

'Crikey! I don't think I'd like to attempt to bring a car down here, let alone a bus,' Charles said nervously. 'It's a bit full-on, isn't it?'

'I've never driven it,' Elspeth admitted, 'although Ray did once. It *was* only the once, mind you. I think he had his eyes shut every time we came up against one of those awful hairpin bends. I know I did. I kept expecting to go sailing over the edge any second.'

'Can you imagine cycling down here?'

'Don't you dare,' she warned. 'I don't want to have to visit you in hospital. And Stefan would be very annoyed if you trashed his bike.'

'You'd visit me?' He glanced at her out of the corner of his eye.

'Of course I would. I would hate to think of you in a foreign hospital all on your own, and not being able to speak the language.'

'You're a very nice lady, Elspeth.'

'And you're a flatterer. Now, keep your eyes peeled because you'll see the village of Masca any moment now— Ooh!' She grabbed his arm to steady herself as the bus swung around a ninety-degree corner, which almost threw her into the aisle.

'If I realised it was going to be a rollercoaster ride, I'd have suggested you sit on the inside by the window,' Charles said, catching hold of her around the top of her opposite arm and hugging her to him.

Elspeth was already holding her body as rigid as she could to prevent herself from being flung about like a towel in a washing machine, but she tensed even more at the unexpected contact. Her heart hammered and her pulse thrummed in her ears. She held her breath and tried not to lean into Charles any more than she had to. She stole a glance at his face.

But he wasn't looking at her, and she wasn't sure he was even aware she existed. His focus was on the view through the window. She stared at him in fascination, watching the emotions on his face – awe, incredulity, wonder. When he glanced down at her, his already wide smile widened even further, and he hugged her closer to him even though the bus had travelled out of the ridiculous bend and was now on a more even keel.

'We're here,' she said, extricating herself from his hold and getting ready to stand up as the vehicle pulled up at a small bus stop. She waited for it to chunter to a halt, then rose and made her way down the aisle, not looking to see whether Charles was behind her. She didn't have to look;

she could sense him, and she knew that if she put out a hand she'd be able to touch him.

Dear God, she needed to stop being so ridiculous. Of course she couldn't 'sense' him. The only sense to be had was the common sense that he was following her – he'd hardly still be sitting on the bus, would he?

'It's impressive,' he said as he climbed down the steps of the bus and gazed around.

'You ain't seen nothing yet,' she told him, and led the way down a narrow, cobbled path, which quickly became rather steep.

There were a few buildings on either side, one of them a cafe, a shop or two and a couple of houses, and they passed several people selling nuts, trinkets and fruit from makeshift tables. It was already hot, with little to no breeze, and when Elspeth put a hand on a rock to steady herself she felt the trapped warmth within the stone. She could already feel a trickle of sweat run down her back and she shifted her rucksack, debating whether she should buy another bottle of water from one of the stalls in case her supplies ran low.

Charles beat her to it. While she was hesitating, he'd handed a couple of notes over and had swapped them for four bottles of water, which he was now slipping into his rucksack.

'Better to be safe than sorry,' he explained when he saw her looking. 'If we don't drink them today, they won't go to waste. I can use them for my hike up Teide.'

Elspeth agreed. He'd certainly need plenty of fluid for that little jaunt.

This little jaunt, however, was not quite as arduous – there was no danger of altitude sickness for one, and for another, they would be trekking downhill – but it was still slippery underfoot.

As they made their way down into the gorge proper, the winding track became much narrower and steeper. Scuffed-up dust from their feet coated their hiking boots and Elspeth could already feel the strain in her knee and ankle joints, while the muscles in her thighs were making their presence felt. It was a good ache though, and she knew from experience that the gradient would taper off somewhat after the initial descent.

Watching where she put her feet – a sprained ankle or worse wouldn't be good in this difficult to access location – she made her way carefully down to the floor of the gorge, Charles following closely behind.

There, that was better. They were still descending and would continue to do so until the gorge ended where the sea began, but the path was far less steep now and Elspeth could risk raising her head from her feet to look around her.

The first thing she looked at was Charles.

'OK?' she asked.

'I'm good. This is great, isn't it? Is that the sound of running water?'

'It is. If you look down there, you can just spot the river. It's never much of one – not like those back in England, because we don't get enough rainfall – but it usually flows for most of the year and can be quite impressive if there's been a storm. We'll end up walking through it when we get nearer to the end.'

They paused for a moment on a wooden bridge which spanned the small river, and Charles took some photos on his phone. The water itself was at least twenty feet below them, mostly hidden in surprisingly thick undergrowth, and was in reality little more than a gurgling stream.

'It makes you think what Tenerife could look like if there was enough rain,' she said. 'It would be positively jungle-like and lush.'

Photos taken, Elspeth led Charles to the other side of the bridge and up a small rocky incline. They were now on the opposite side of the gorge, and they could just about see the village of Masca high above them, perched on its rocky crag.

'Crikey, we've walked a fair way already,' Charles said, squinting up at the mountainside above and shielding his sunglass-clad eyes for a better look.

Elspeth studied the muscles in his arm and how the fine hairs were lit up by the sun. She glanced away hastily, concentrating on the towering gorge sides instead. Far from feeling enclosed, the gorge had always made her feel cocooned and sheltered, although that was a risky feeling to have about this ravine. It might be stunningly beautiful, but it was definitely not a safe place to be.

So why did she feel the gorge was safer for her well-being than the man by her side?

It was because he was quite good-looking, she decided, clambering over a particularly large boulder that lay directly in the middle of the path. It was certainly not because she liked him, not romantically anyway. There was nothing wrong with appreciating a handsome man – she certainly appreciated Aidan Turner, although it might be his *Poldark* character who turned her head, and she also thought George Clooney was a fine-looking specimen and more her own age. She tried to imagine how she'd react if it was either one of those delectable men who was accompanying her on this hike, and decided she'd probably feel just the same. To be honest, she simply wasn't used to anyone joining her on her walks, and hadn't been since Ray had passed away.

Therefore, she reasoned, not only was Charles attractive, which she found slightly disconcerting, but she was far too used to being on her own, so her vague nervousness was undoubtedly down to a combination of those two things and not anything to be concerned about at all.

Roughly halfway into their trek, Elspeth called a halt for some refreshments. Both of them had been steadily drinking from their water bottles, but she was beginning to feel the need for something more substantial and a cup of tea would go down a treat.

Spying a flat rock just off the trail, she gestured towards it. 'Fancy a spot of early lunch?'

'You bet!' Charles followed her and sat down on the rock next to her, slipping his rucksack off his shoulders.

Elspeth did the same and pulled out her flask. Charles had his own drink, and he poured himself a cup of tea before he tackled a sandwich.

The pair of them sipped and nibbled in contented silence, listening to the wind in the bushes and the birds calling. There was also the sound of voices now and again, followed by the sight of people walking past on their way to the beach, with a few hardy souls hiking in the opposite direction up the gorge rather than down it.

'This is so peaceful,' Charles said, after the sounds of another group of hikers had faded away. 'I could stay here all day.'

'It is gorgeous, isn't it,' Elspeth agreed, letting the beauty of the gorge soak into her. There was nothing like a good long walk in nature's garden for soothing the soul, and she gradually felt calmer. It was very pleasant having Charles with her, she decided. Sharing an experience like this with another person was a delight in itself. Although, she conceded, it did depend on who that person was. Charles was a good companion: he didn't talk too much, he wasn't needy or whiney, or overly enthusiastic and loud. He'd just walked calmly alongside her, or just behind depending on the width of the track, quietly taking in the sights and sounds, and making the odd comment now and again. Not only was he easy on the eye, he was easy on the ear, too.

'What are those?' He pointed to a stand of tall-stemmed plants further along the track. 'They look like bamboo.'

'Yes, they are. Are you ready to go on, because you're going to get a good look at them in a moment.'

They packed away the remains of their lunch, hoisted their rucksacks on their shoulders and rejoined the trail.

They'd only gone a few hundred paces, when they were met with a wall of waving bamboo about twenty feet or more high, their leaves fluttering in the breeze. A tunnel went straight through the middle of the plants, their stems arching overhead, and, as Elspeth picked her way through the leafy passageway, she felt like a kid again, creeping through the ferns on the moorland above the Yorkshire cottage her parents used to take her to on holiday.

Charles couldn't stop grinning as he turned around, craning his neck to study the thick arching stems, and she was smiling with him.

'This is like being in the jungle,' he exclaimed. 'All I need is a machete in my hand and a bandana on my head.'

'You'll have to make do with your water bottle and a baseball cap,' Elspeth laughed. 'The great thing about Tenerife is that there are no snakes or nasty creepy-crawlies. Imagine if this was full of scorpions and poisonous centipedes?'

Charles shuddered. 'No, thanks. I'm a bit of a wimp when it comes to that kind of thing.'

'I couldn't rely on you to rescue me from a man-eating spider then?'

'It depends on the size of the spider,' he replied seriously.

She shook her head, a smile playing about her lips. 'Some knight in shining armour you are.'

'Is that what you want me to be? Because I can be… However, I must warn you, armour doesn't look the least bit comfortable and I suspect it chafes something awful – and I haven't been on the back of a horse since I was ten.'

She rolled her eyes and playfully tapped his arm. 'You're daft.'

'It's been mentioned once or twice.'

Elspeth's smile remained in place as she carried on walking, but it was only with some degree of effort. Had she been flirting with him? Had he been flirting with her? Because it had certainly felt like it. And what on earth had possessed her to tap him on the arm? She wasn't a tapper, or a toucher or a hugger for that matter. She kept herself to herself, and only tolerated the double-cheeked kiss and accompanying hug when greeting someone like Toni, because that was the custom here. If left to her own devices she'd be happy to make do with a nod and a smile.

She was still musing on this when they approached the most dangerous and difficult part of the hike – a wall of rock on which a narrow ledge had been carved out of. The ledge had to be traversed if one wanted to continue down the gorge; there was simply no other way forward. The drop was a substantial one and the height was dizzying.

'You're kidding me!' Charles stopped and eyed the ledge with trepidation. 'You can't honestly expect me to walk across that.'

'Thousands of people have,' Elspeth pointed out, much more calmly than she felt. She disliked this part of the hike, too. The only way she'd been persuaded to go across it the first time she and Ray had hiked down the gorge, was the fact that she couldn't face going all that way back up. That, and the rope bolted into the rock that ran along the whole length of the ledge, which she'd clung onto with a hand–cramping grip for the duration.

'It's not as bad as it looks,' she said encouragingly, thinking to herself that it was *exactly* as bad as it looked. She tried to gather her courage. 'It's only for about thirty feet, and then the path gets easier. There's a bit more scrambling involved after that, but only the kind of stuff we've already done.'

'Yeah, I really enjoyed slipping into that gap beneath that giant boulder,' Charles stated dryly.

Elspeth giggled. 'Your face was a picture.' The boulder he was referring to was larger than a house and had fallen from the mountainside above in the past. Too big to climb over and with no room to go around it, there was sufficient space underneath for people to squeeze through. She'd done it several times now, but it still didn't prevent her from speculating about what would happen if the enormous lump of rock decided the best time to shift and close the space between it and the ground was when she was directly underneath it.

'I bet my face is even more of a picture now,' he said. He certainly did look worried. 'I don't like heights.'

'I like the drops even less,' Elspeth said, her tone wry.

'Are you sure there's no way around?' He glanced over the edge; the fall below them was almost vertical and Charles stepped back quickly.

A babble of voices alerted them to other people coming along the path behind and Charles moved to the side to let a group of three young women pass.

'I'll see how they do it first, before I give it a go,' he said, looking rather pale beneath his light tan.

Elspeth and Charles watched the women confidently work their way along the ledge, their hands holding the rope, the front of their bodies brushing against the rock face as they slipped by, faces close to the stone.

Soon they were out of sight, having disappeared around the wall of rock and Elspeth supposed they had emerged safely on the other side.

'It's OK for them,' Charles muttered, 'they're still young enough to think they're immortal. Besides, if they were to fall, they'd probably bounce at that age. Me? I'd break a hip.' He inched forwards to peer over the edge again. 'Or worse,' he added ominously.

'We can always turn around and go back up,' Elspeth suggested, half of her hoping he would agree. Each time she arrived at this spot, she always regretted her decision to walk down the gorge in the first place.

'You *have* done this before, haven't you?' he asked.

She nodded. 'At least five times, probably more.'

'Right, that does it! I'm not going to be outdone by a girl.'

'To be fair, those three were possibly a third of our age,' Elspeth pointed out.

'I wasn't talking about them,' Charles muttered, and she felt ridiculously pleased that he'd referred to her as a girl.

Giddy, and feeling slightly reckless, she offered to go first, so he wouldn't feel embarrassed if he freaked out a little getting across.

Taking a deep breath, she stepped onto the ledge, grabbed the rope firmly with both hands and began to inch her way sideways, her face so near to the rock wall that the dust from its stony surface tickled her nose. Her back was to the drop, and to an observer she probably looked cool and composed, but internally she was screaming and praying for it to be over.

She deliberately didn't look at Charles, but she could hear his shuffling feet dragging on the ledge and his ragged breathing. He was clearly as unsure about the situation as she was, and when the ledge eventually widened into a proper path and the rope petered out, he breathed a huge sigh.

Feeling a bit shaky, Elspeth turned to face him, only to find him inches away from her, and as he stepped onto the wider path, he bumped into her, almost knocking her over. Instinctively her hand shot out to grab him and save herself from falling. His hands reached out, caught hold of the tops of her arms and pulled her into him.

For a second, she froze, her face in the space between his neck and shoulder, breathing in the masculine scent of him.

Lord, but he smelt good.

He felt good too. She'd forgotten what it was like to be held by a man.

With a start, she pulled back, and he immediately released her.

'Are you OK?' he asked. 'I didn't mean to walk into you.'

'I'm fine.' Her tone was brisker than she'd meant it to be, but she couldn't help it. The way she'd reacted to him when he was only trying to help, had scared her. And after that horrid shuffle along that perilous ledge, she had been scared enough to begin with!

Inhaling deeply and closing her eyes for a second, she reasoned that he'd simply taken her by surprise, and it was no wonder she'd been short with him. It was a natural reaction to being terrified out of her wits, that was all.

'I'm fine,' she repeated in a softer voice, opening her eyes and seeing the concern in his.

'Good.' He smiled uncertainly, and she beamed back at him, anxious that he didn't think she was being off or in a mood.

The remainder of the trek to the beach went without incident, although neither of them spoke a great deal. Until, that is, they were forced to stop and take their boots and socks off, or risk getting very wet feet indeed, as the stream had spread out diagonally in front of them and there was no alternative other than to wade across it.

Laughing at the chill of the water on his hot feet, Charles went first. 'Would you like me to carry you across?' he asked.

'No, but thank you anyway.' Elspeth tugged her boots off and peeled her socks over her toes. Wriggling them, she dipped one foot in the water, then the other. It was deliciously refreshing and she made her way carefully across to the other side, wishing she didn't have to put them back on again to negotiate the rest of the rocky path to the pebbly beach which could be seen beyond it.

'The boat should be here in about twenty minutes,' she said, leading Charles to a wooden walkway which ended in a circular stone jetty with a set of wide steps facing out to sea.

'Can you swim here?' he asked.

'Yes, you can.'

'I'm going in.'

Elspeth sat on one of the stone steps and watched him disrobe whilst trying not to stare. He didn't take everything off, thank goodness, just his boots, and socks (again), and his T-shirt. He was wearing good-quality below-the-knee hiking shorts on his bottom half, ones that she knew would dry extremely quickly – and, to her relief, he left those on.

Her eyes were drawn to his torso, and she noticed the muscles on his chest, which were defined, but not too much, and his flattish stomach. He didn't have a six-pack (not many sixty-year-olds could boast they did), but he clearly took care of himself, and her gaze focused on the smattering of grey hairs on his chest, which travelled over his stomach and disappeared into the waistband of his cut-offs.

Clearing her throat, she looked away as he descended the steps, heat flushing from her stomach, up her chest, and into her face.

Damned menopause.

Reluctantly, and without her express permission, her attention returned to Charles, and this time she was treated to a view of broad shoulders, a tanned back and a relatively narrow waist.

He was certainly in good shape for his age, she mused. He was fit and toned, and for a fleeting moment she wondered how it would feel to run her fingers down his spine—

'Gosh, that's fresh,' he cried, yanking her from her thoughts.

Thank God he had, otherwise she didn't know where they would have led. 'It is the Atlantic,' she replied mildly, pleased that no hint of what had been going through her mind had shown in her voice. She did feel rather hot and bothered, though, and she made a note to look up the benefits of HRT when she got back home. It had been on her mind for a while, and it might not be too late to start taking it…

Charles was almost fully submerged, and she guessed he must have reached the bottom step as the waves were washing up his body to his chin, before they retreated to his hips. He turned his head to look at her and she giggled at his shocked expression.

'It's nice when you get used to it,' he added unconvincingly.

'I'll take your word for it.'

'I can see the bottom, the water is so clear,' he noticed, bending over as far as he dared without getting a face full of water. A couple of other swimmers were a little further out, and he called to them, 'Is it deep enough to dive?' In a quieter voice, he said to her, 'I can't tell. It looks it, but I'd hate to be proved wrong.'

So would she. She didn't want him to take a needless risk.

'Ten metres. More, maybe,' a heavily accented voice called back and Charles thanked the man. 'I haven't done this since I was a kid,' he said to her, climbing back up the steps and retreating a few paces. He aimed for the side of the jetty where there weren't any steps, took a run, and just as he became airborne, he tucked his knees into his chest, his arms around his knees and entered the water with an almighty splash.

With her heart in her mouth, Elspeth scrambled to her feet, only to sink back down when his head broke the surface, a massive grin on his face.

Dear God, she could do without shocks like that at her age. But he was evidently having the time of his life and his excitement was catching, so she found herself grinning back at him while shaking her head at his foolhardiness, and in the process she also realised that she was having one of the best days she'd had in a very long time.

Chapter 12

Elspeth loved speedboats. The only occasions she'd been on one was when she and Ray had returned from Masca Gorge via water taxi before, but as far as she was concerned this was the best bit of the whole trip.

Eager to get on and sit near the front of the boat, she positioned herself at the end of the jetty to be in prime position to clamber aboard.

'You're eager to get back,' Charles said, and she gave him a sharp look. He'd sounded almost… disappointed?

'Not really. What I'm eager for is a front spot on the boat.'

She got her wish, and Charles sat next to her, his arm draped over the side as he leant against the craft's side and turned his face up to the sun.

'That was fun,' he said. 'Thank you.'

'I'm glad you've had a nice time. We'll be in Los Gigantes in about fifteen minutes and we can catch the bus from there to Santiago del Teide. The next one isn't due for another hour and a half though, so how about we find a bar and have a drink?'

'That sounds good. I could murder a cold beer right now.'

Elspeth smiled. So could she, and it would be a good end to the trip.

'Here we go,' she cried, as the boat reversed away from the jetty, turned slowly, then ramped up the speed as it shot out of the small bay and into the open ocean. 'Woohoo!'

Charles gripped the side of the boat as the acceleration caused Elspeth to be pushed back into him, and she allowed her weight to fall against him, even though she knew it was a ridiculous thing to do, but Ray used to do the exact same thing and—

'Dolphins! Look!'

The pilot's shout had her scanning the waves, desperate for a glimpse of the beautiful creatures.

'Over there,' Charles said, and she followed his pointing finger, zeroing in on two sleek dark shapes powering through the water, their speed easily matching that of the boat.

Mesmerised, she watched as the dolphins leapt out of the water and dived back in again, until eventually they sank below the surface and were gone.

'That was wonderful,' she said, twisting around to see Charles's reaction, hoping he'd found it as breathtaking as she had done.

What she read in his face really did steal her breath.

He was gazing at her with a rapt expression, his head tilted a little to one side as he stared back at her. 'Yes,' he said, 'it was.'

And for some strange reason, she didn't think he was talking about the dolphins.

Then the mood was broken as she realised how close she was to him, that her lips were only inches away from his and that they were staring into each other's eyes like a couple of lovers. She shuffled back uncertainly, putting a good couple of feet between them.

'I adore dolphins,' she said, hoping she didn't sound as inane as she thought she might.

She was saved from further embarrassment by the boat slowing dramatically as it approached the harbour, and Elspeth made a point of concentrating on the scenery as the skipper steered between the harbour walls and into the calm water beyond.

As soon as the boat docked and she was on dry land again, Elspeth headed towards the row of shops, bars and restaurants lining the landward side of the harbour, Charles at her side.

She picked the first bar and they sat at an outside table, angling their seats so they both had a view of the boats.

'It's busier than I thought,' Charles observed, gazing around at the myriad of boats, jet skis, small yachts and a couple of larger boats at the furthest end of the moorings.

The harbourside was busy, too, with people embarking and disembarking, vendors selling water excursions and tourists taking a stroll around the shops and restaurants. It was a far cry and a hundred miles away from the peace of Masca Gorge and its almost empty beach. The contrast was disconcerting and a little jarring, if she was honest.

After they had ordered and their beers had arrived – in nicely chilled glasses, as Charles was delighted to discover – they reminisced about the day so far.

'That bit with the ledge was far too hairy for my liking,' Charles said, taking a sip of his beer.

Elspeth was tempted to swallow half of her beer in one go, but she held back. 'Mine, too. I think I forget about that drop on purpose,' she said, 'because it always comes as a shock when I'm confronted with it. I think if I had a clear memory of it in my head, I might never hike down the gorge again.'

'It was worth it though; the gorge is so unspoilt and wild.'

Elspeth was about to reply when her phone trilled at her. She so rarely received texts that she jumped, then delved into her rucksack to find it.

It was from Amanda, asking what time Toni should pick Charles and his luggage up this evening.

Ah. Once again, in the excitement of the day, she'd forgotten that Charles was due to leave the villa later today. He'd spent his last night under her roof and suddenly she didn't feel ready for him to go. She'd become used to having him there, even though it had only been a few days.

'You've gone very quiet. What's wrong?' His face was full of concern.

'Nothing, I was just working out what time we'd have to be back at the villa for Toni to collect you to take you to your hotel.' She gave what she hoped was a bright, reassuring smile.

It couldn't have come across how she meant it to, because Charles didn't reply. Instead, he focused on the nearest shiny boat whose tall mast was moving slightly in the breeze, the flag on top fluttering and snapping.

It was rather a nice boat, she had to admit, but Elspeth didn't think it warranted the amount of attention Charles was giving it.

'I bet you're looking forward to transferring to the hotel,' she continued, to break what had become an uncomfortable silence. 'Sorry again for the mix-up. It must be a real pain having to unpack, then repack, then unpack once more.'

Charles shrugged slightly and still didn't say anything. Elspeth hoped she hadn't misjudged the situation entirely, and that far from being OK with having to stay at her place for three nights, he was far more cheesed off about it all than he'd let on.

'I'm sorry about you having to move again,' she repeated, feeling partly responsible, even though it was nothing to do with her and not her fault in the slightest.

'So am I,' he said finally, his gaze now on a pair of jet skis pulling into the harbour.

She gave the water skiers a fleeting glance. 'If I can do anything to make the transition easier for you...?' Though moving him from one lodging to another was hardly up there in the Top Ten list of life's traumatic events. And it wasn't as though she hadn't looked after him; as far as she was concerned, she'd gone above and beyond in order to make his stay as pleasant as possible.

'At least you get a choice of meal tonight,' she pointed out. 'You don't have to eat what's put in front of you and lump it.'

He turned his attention back to her. 'I liked lumping it.'

'Excuse me?'

'Too much choice can confuse a person.'

'Oh, I don't think Hotel Aventuras' menu is too extensive. You'll have a choice of about six or seven starters and—'

'That's not what I meant.'

'It's not?'

He shook his head.

Elspeth waited for him to continue, but the people climbing off the jet skis seemed to fascinate him.

'The food there is very good,' she added, in case he was concerned about it. 'I've eaten there myself many times.'

'It's not about the food.'

'What is it, then?' She was genuinely confused.

'I... um... never mind. I'm sure the hotel is great.'

'It is! And Amanda and Toni are such good hosts. It's the perfect base for hikers and cyclists.'

'Hmm.'

She took another sip of her drink and hunted around for something to say. 'Tell me more about your day yesterday. Where did you go?' They'd touched on his bike ride during dinner last night, but he'd not gone into a great deal of detail.

'I cycled up to the base of Teide, then down through Vilaflor to Güímar and then onto the TF-24, through the caldera, and back to Santiago,' he said.

'That's quite a distance.' Elspeth had never cycled the route, but she had driven it, or rather Ray had back in the days when they'd owned a car, and she'd enjoyed the view from the passenger seat. 'I love Vilaflor – there's a little cafe on the side of the road on the edge of the town with the most fantastic views over the whole of the southern part of the island. What did you think of the caldera?'

'It is like a moonscape, just as everyone says it is. I thought it was incredibly beautiful and rather scary at the same time.'

'I know what you mean.' The caldera was the remains of an ancient volcano that had exploded thousands of years ago, leaving a circle of jagged mountains surrounding a rugged plain of newer, solidified lava where the immense peak of Mount Teide rose in conical glowering splendour. Elspeth loved the place, yet was awed by it too, and was very conscious of its dangerous allure. Tenerife's slumbering heart wasn't to be taken lightly.

'I can't wait to hike up the volcano next Sunday,' Charles declared, his eyes shining.

'Which route are you taking?'

'Um…I haven't decided yet.'

'The most common is the one from Monta Blanca,' she reminded him.

'Then I'll take that one.'

'You're planning to go on your own, aren't you?' It should have occurred to her before now.

'I am.'

'You'd be better off if you went with someone.' The thought of someone unfamiliar with the area hiking to the crater rim, sent waves of alarm through her.

'Who do you suggest?'

'Have you thought about taking the cable car and then just hiking up the last stretch?' It was quicker and not nearly as taxing. It was safer, too.

'And miss the best bits?' he laughed.

'The climb is incredibly steep and an awful lot further than you think. It'll take anything from five to seven hours to hike to the top, depending on your fitness level. And what about the altitude? It can make you very ill.'

'I've been at altitude before.'

'I'm serious.' Elspeth knew she was fussing, but couldn't help herself. 'Altitude sickness is a thing. And it doesn't matter how fit or athletic you are, it can affect anyone. You shouldn't go on your own; it's not safe or sensible.'

'I've got my pass,' he reminded her. 'If I don't go then, I won't be able to go at all.'

She had to concede that he had a point. Anyone could hike most of the way up the volcano or go in the cable car, but in order to venture beyond the cable car station and climb the last few hundred feet or so of the mountain, a pass was required. 'Why didn't you book to go on an organised tour?' she asked.

'I couldn't find any that didn't involve going up in the cable car first. I want to walk up all of it.'

'I am sure there are tours that do that,' she insisted. 'Groups. Guides for hire.'

'I couldn't find any,' he repeated, and she remembered him asking her that very same question on his first night in Tenerife, which was why she'd ended up going with him on the walk on Saturday, and why she had also scrambled down Masca Gorge with him today.

'You can't go on your own,' she reiterated firmly.

'What do you suggest?'

'I'll come with you,' Elspeth said, surprising herself as she spoke. She knew the route, she was familiar with the dangers and, more importantly, she could look out for any signs of altitude sickness in him. The condition wasn't easy to recognise in oneself and there was the very real possibility he'd pass off a headache as being caused by glare from the sun, or nausea as being a result of exertion.

'But you won't be able to get a pass at such short notice. They're booked weeks in advance.'

'I know.' Passes to the summit were tightly regulated to prevent too many pairs of boots tramping to the top of the crater at once. 'There's another way. There's a bunkhouse called the Altaviste Refuge about two-thirds up the side of the volcano. If you hike up in the evening, you can spend the night there, and as long as you get to the summit by 9 a.m., you don't need a permit.' If he was determined to make it to the top and she was determined to go with him, then the Refuge was the only viable alternative.

'I read about it, but discounted the idea. I didn't fancy doing it on my own,' Charles said.

'There'll be other hikers there – there always are.'

'It's not the same.'

'No,' she agreed. 'It's not.' The thought of sleeping in a bunkhouse and sharing it with fifty or so strangers didn't fill her with much enthusiasm either.

'Have you ever stayed at the Refuge?' he asked.

'No.'

'So how would you feel about staying overnight there with me?'

Elspeth hesitated. Ray had once suggested doing this route and using the walkers' shelter, but she hadn't been too keen. He'd even bought sleeping bags for the occasion, but she still hadn't been swayed, not when she'd already had the experience of hiking to the crater's edge once before. She preferred to sleep in her own bed, and not even the promise of watching the sun come up whilst sitting on one of the highest peaks for hundreds of miles changed her mind. And yes, she probably would feel awkward, even though Charles had spent the last three nights under her roof, barely metres away from her in the next room.

'Probably a bit strange,' she admitted.

He nodded to himself. 'We'll knock that idea on the head, then.'

'No, we won't. I'm coming with you. And… and… I want you to stay on at Villa Cruz, too,' she blurted out. If she was going to see more of him during his stay, then he might as well not have the inconvenience of having to move out of hers. It would be strange to think of him staying a stone's throw away. And, damn it, she'd become used to having him there.

'If you want to, that is,' she added, as a thought occurred to her. 'Please don't feel obliged. Oh, silly me, forget I said anything! Of course you'll want to move into the hotel. It's got all the facilities you need, and you must be fed up with my company by now.' She didn't know what had possessed her to make such an offer.

'Are you done?' His eyes were soft as they stared into hers.

She gazed back at him without speaking.

'I'd love to spend the rest of my holiday in your home,' he said.

'You would?'

'Yes.'

'Oh, my.' Elspeth put a hand to her chest, her heart was thumping so hard she thought it might leap out of her ribcage. Then she began to get flustered. What about Amanda and Toni? Would they think she was deliberately poaching their customer? She'd better call Amanda right away. Although, maybe it might be better to leave it until later, when she was somewhere more private. Oh, dear... what had she done?

She didn't know whether Charles sensed her dismay and confusion, or whether he was simply being practical and organised, but while she dithered (it was so unlike her – but there she was, dithering again) he'd pulled out his phone and now had it clamped to his ear.

'Hi, my name is Charles Brown. I don't know if you remember me, but I should have booked into your hotel last— You do?' He paused as someone on the other end of the line spoke. 'Great, that saves me explaining further. I just wanted to let you know that Mrs Evans and I have agreed that I will stay at Villa Cruz for the remainder of my holiday. I know I've paid to stay at the hotel, and I don't expect any—' Another pause. 'That's very generous of you. I will, of course, make sure Mrs Evans—' He listened for a second. 'Elspeth, yes. As I was saying, I'll settle up with her.'

Elspeth shook her head and waved her arms at him. 'No need,' she mouthed, but he ignored her.

'Thank you for being so understanding. Yes, yes she is.' His eyes found hers and flickered away again. 'Yes, I agree. Of course, wait a sec.' He handed her his phone. 'The hotel wants to speak to you.'

Elspeth took it, inhaled deeply, and gingerly put it to her ear. 'Amanda?' She was treated to a loud squeal which made her wince, followed by, 'Are you serious? You're happy to let him stay? He's not got some weird hold over you, has he?'

'Yes, that's correct.'

'Which one? Happy or coerced?'

'The former.'

'God, you've gone all formal and stilted on me. Is that because he's listening?'

'Uh huh.'

'Seriously, Elspeth, you don't have to do this. There's no obligation.'

'No that's fine, and extremely generous of you to refund him, considering the time of year and the short notice. I don't want you to have an empty room.'

'Pish, I can sell his room twice over. Easter is a busy time for us.'

'I know, but still...'

'Don't worry about it. It's lovely to see you coming alive again.'

'What?' Elspeth squeaked. 'I'm not! Please don't think there's anything—' She stopped and shot Charles a worried look, but he seemed to be scanning the boats in the harbour again.

'I don't,' Amanda chuckled. 'You can fill me in on the details later. For now though, just enjoy yourself. You deserve it.'

Elspeth handed Charles his phone back, her mind whirling. Did Amanda honestly believe she was being anything other than friendly towards Charles? What did her best friend think – that she was sharing *more* than a few meals and the occasional walk with him? Her cheeks flamed and another flush spread from her stomach, up her chest, to burst up her neck and face. Dear God, to add insult to injury, she was now having a hot flush.

'Is everything OK?' he asked.

'Yes, fine,' she replied airily, not wanting him to have even an inkling that Amanda had got the wrong impression about their relationship. Not that they *had* a relationship, apart from a business one. Or, if pushed, maybe friendship. Not a relationship as such. Not in the way Amanda (damn her) had hinted at. *Enjoy herself?* Huh. As if.

Although… she had enjoyed herself today, hadn't she? She'd enjoyed herself very much indeed. In fact, she couldn't remember the last time she'd laughed so hard or had so much fun. But that had been attributable to the speed-boat ride, and the amazing sense of flying across the surface of the water followed by the rhythmic thud of slamming down on the waves, with the wind in her hair and on her face, and the dolphins cavorting in the wake was life-affirming stuff. It had nothing to do with Charles.

Nothing at all.

Chapter 13

'It's my turn to take you out to dinner,' Charles announced an hour or so later, when they were on the bus from Los Gigantes back to Santiago del Teide.

'No, it's not. There's no need to take me anywhere.'

'Hotel Aventuras is refunding me the amount I've paid for my room. For one, you should have the money for putting me up, and for another, I really would like to take you to dinner.'

'I don't want your money.' It was true – helping Amanda and Toni out was one thing, but offering Charles to stay with her for the duration of his holiday was something altogether different, and she didn't want anyone thinking she was doing it for the money.

So why are you doing it, a voice in her head asked. She batted it away. Obviously, it was because she didn't want Charles to wander over the island without a guide, that's why. She was looking out for him and making sure he enjoyed his break. The fact that he could quite have easily used the hotel as a base and she could have collected him from there wasn't something she was prepared to think about in too much detail. It was handier having him under her roof, that was all.

'I insist,' he said.

'No!' Her tone was sharper than she'd intended, and she immediately felt contrite. 'I mean, I didn't ask you to stay because I wanted paying for it.'

'I know.'

She sent him a curious look. What did he know, exactly?

'I still want to take you to dinner,' he urged. 'It's the least I can do. Think of it as a thank you for such a wonderful day.'

'It was wonderful, wasn't it? I can't believe you dive-bombed off the jetty.'

'Neither can I.' He rubbed a hip. 'I think I got a bit carried away. I'm too old for such shenanigans.'

'Nonsense! You're not old. Oh, we get off here.' Elspeth pressed the alert button, and the bus came to a halt.

'Where do you recommend eating?' Charles asked as they got off the bus and strolled across the square to the villa. 'I'm happy to go back to the place we went to the other night, but I was thinking somewhere a little more...'

'Upmarket? Fancy?'

He laughed. 'I can't help it if I like tablecloths and candles.'

'It's not a date,' she stated shortly, stopping when they reached her front door, and slotting the key in the lock and twisting it.

'I didn't for one second imagine it was,' he replied.

Oh. That told her. Not a date. Good. Everyone was clear, then.

'I'm going to have a cup of tea before I have a shower,' she offered. 'Want one?'

'Yes, please. I'll sort out the rucksacks while you make it, shall I?'

They worked in silence, side by side in the kitchen. It was both familiar and disconcerting. She'd done the same thing countless times with Ray; him emptying their rucksacks or shopping bags, her filling the kettle and getting the cups and saucers out of the cupboard. It was almost as though he was still with her. Yet she was acutely conscious that the man sharing her kitchen was a different man entirely. Although, she had to admit that he did remind her of her husband in certain respects – he was polite and gentlemanly, funny, knowledgeable, calm…

There, that was the problem right there – *he reminded her of Ray*. Too much. It was almost as though Ray was back with her, but not quite. Charles was a younger, more vibrant version. And so he *should* be more vibrant – he was considerably younger than Ray had been when he'd died. Those extra years made a difference. She hadn't noticed at the time just how much Ray had slowed down in the last few years of his life, because she'd slowed down too to keep pace with him. She'd never wanted to forge ahead, had always been content to match him step for step. And if he grew to prefer to sit in the garden with the papers on a Sunday morning instead of hiking for miles as they had once done, then she was happy to sit with him too.

Now, though…?

Having Charles in her life, even if it had only been for three days, had opened her eyes. Had she been burying her head in the sand and pretending everything was fine, when it wasn't? Was she perfectly happy to carry on the way she had been since Ray's health had started to decline? Was she holding herself back?

Elspeth placed the tea things on a tray and carried them out into the garden, waving aside Charles's offer to take the tray from her. She could do this herself. She wasn't helpless or incapable, and she resented that he thought she might be.

He's only trying to help, her conscience said. He was being kind and considerate, and she was throwing it back in his face as her emotions were all over the place. And, let's face it, she'd coped for such a long time on her own, it was nice to have someone care for her.

She poured the tea and sat back, her gaze drifting to the orchid tree.

'I envy you,' Charles said.

She swallowed and glanced across the table at him. 'You do? In what way?'

'I've never experienced the sort of love you had with your husband.'

Her eyes suddenly filled with tears and she blinked them away, hoping Charles hadn't noticed. 'It was very special,' she agreed.

'Here I am, sixty-one, and I've never known true love,' he continued.

'You were married, though, didn't you say?'

'Too young, too stupid, too self-centred. Confused lust for love.'

Sympathy crept in around the edges of her mind, colouring her response. 'There's still time.'

He looked at her and smiled. 'You think?'

'I do.' She nodded earnestly.

'For you, too?'

'Ah, well, no, not for me.' Elspeth felt a bit funny as she spoke.

'Because you've had it once and you can't have it again?' he guessed.

His insight stole her breath. 'Yes, that's it exactly,' she agreed.

'Maybe I don't envy you as much as I thought I did,' he said, slowly. 'Your pain is so very obvious and I'm not sure I could handle it.'

'You can. You have to. If I can pick myself up and carry on, then you could, too.'

'But have you? Picked yourself up and carried on, I mean?'

'Of course I have,' she said, feeling a bit affronted. She had, hadn't she? Although, she must admit, she'd been having the exact same thoughts a few minutes ago, when she remembered how she'd slowed down to match Ray's declining energy levels. 'I have this villa, my job, my friends, and I live on an island I love,' she replied stoutly.

Charles inclined his head, but didn't say anything further, and Elspeth was left wondering whom she was trying to convince. A memory of the laughter and joy of the day they had just spent together swept through her mind, a reminder of earlier happiness, of forgotten delights. And once again, she was unnerved and confused. She'd been perfectly content with her life pre-Charles. *Hadn't she?*

'Dinner,' he reminded her, changing the subject.

Thankful, Elspeth said, 'There's a place on the square. It's off the main road, it's quiet, the food isn't too bad and the service is second to none.'

'We'll go there, then,' he said. 'Do we need to book a table? Although, I can't say I'd noticed a restaurant in the square.' He squinted as he visualised the layout of the square. 'There's the government building...'

'It's also a museum. You should take a look.'

'I will. And there's the church. A couple of other houses, and isn't there a tourist information place?'

She nodded.

'I don't recall a restaurant—' He stopped, and his squint turned into a narrow-eyed stare. 'You mean here, don't you?'

She laughed. 'I do.' The thought of going out was nice, but the thought of cooking for him was even nicer. Besides, they'd had a hectic day and she didn't think she could be bothered to dress up.

'In that case, I'll do the cooking,' he said.

'You will not.'

'I will.' His jaw hardened and he stuck out his chin, reminding her very much of a recalcitrant schoolboy.

'My house, my rules,' she argued.

'That's not fair.'

'I don't care.'

There was a stand-off for a few seconds, then his face began to crack into a smile and Elspeth let out a giggle. 'Shall we cook together?' she suggested.

'It depends on what we're having,' he countered.

'Steak, pepper sauce, potatoes, salad?'

'Shall I fire up the barbeque?' He jerked his head towards the barbeque area. It hadn't been used in years, but she'd continued to keep it clean and tidy.

'We've not got any coals or wood.'

'Does the shop next to yours sell any?'

She nodded.

'I'll go and get some then.' He grinned and rubbed his hands together. 'I love a good barbequed steak. Do you think they'll sell corn on the cob?'

'I know they do.'

'Right, then.' He rose. 'Is there anything else we need? Wine? Beer?'

'There's plenty of both in the fridge,' she said. 'Take a look and see if you like what we've got.'

Her eyes followed him as he went into the kitchen, then her ears took over as she heard him rooting around in the fridge.

'I won't be long,' he called a few moments later, and she heard the front door close softly behind him.

For the first time since Charles had arrived on her doorstep, Elspeth was alone, and she wasn't sure what to do with her solitude.

'What do you think, Ray? Are you OK with this? It's only for eleven more nights, then he'll be gone and it'll just be me and you again.' The thought didn't comfort her. In fact, she wasn't much looking forward to life after Charles's departure. He'd awakened something in her that she hadn't realised had been sleeping – and that was the desire to be needed. There was another need too – the urge to be looked after now and again. To be able to leave something for someone else to do, rather than to have to think about and execute everything herself. The humble task of having her rucksack emptied for her was a prime example.

It was pleasant to have someone do it for her. And she wasn't just referring to sorting her bag out, either. It was bigger than that; it went deeper. Caring for, and being cared for in turn, was what it was all about. She hadn't realised this had been missing from her life, until now.

For goodness' sake – she was reading far too much into the whole thing. Elspeth sighed. Maudlin, that's what she was getting, and daft. Not to mention becoming far too introspective for her own sanity. It wasn't healthy, and it wasn't good for her.

With a snort at her silliness, she cleared away the teacups and then checked that the barbeque was fit to use. She was still wiping it over when Charles returned.

The sound of someone else entering the villa and pottering in the kitchen made her heart falter. It *was* just like having Ray back.

Except that it wasn't, because this man was humming to himself. Ray had never hummed. He'd been a tuneless whistler, and it used to drive her to distraction on occasion. Charles smelt different too. Musky and citrusy. Nothing like the Ralph Lauren aftershave Ray had always worn. Charles's scent had subtly changed the ambience in the villa over the last few days. It no longer smelt of the floral perfume Elspeth liked. And if she was honest, it probably no longer smelt of loneliness and grief.

She soon heard other noises, apart from the humming, coming from the villa. Although the everyday sound of water running in the basin was the same, it was somehow new to her ears, because Charles was the one who was doing it. Familiar actions sounded different in some way. Even as she thought it, she realised how bonkers she was being. But she knew what she meant.

She could just imagine Gideon saying, 'so, he's actually nothing like dad, then' in that tongue-in-cheek way he had when she tried to explain something to him. Gideon was nothing like his father either. He wasn't a scholar; he was an architect. His designs were all glass walls and concrete with steel thrown in for good measure. Ray had never seen the attraction of his son's designs, but she had: they possessed a simplistic, modernist beauty of clean lines and no nonsense. Ray had gravitated more towards the ancient stone buildings which graced Oxford and Bath.

'What do you do?' she blurted when Charles stepped into the garden clutching a couple of bags of fuel.

'For a living?'

'Yes.'

'Nothing now. I'm retired. But I used to be a surgeon.'

Elspeth was intrigued. 'What field?'

'Ophthalmology.'

She paused for a moment. 'Are the eyes truly the window to the soul?'

'Maybe,' Charles chuckled. 'Although I can't say I've ever seen a soul staring back. By the time I used to get involved with a patient, the only thing staring back at me was someone who was scared.'

'It must have been interesting.'

'It was. I worked hard and played hard. The play usually involved hiking or cycling, or golf. You might think golf is the softer option, but if you do, you haven't met many golfers. They're a seriously competitive bunch.'

'It's the wiggle that gets me,' she replied, deadpan.

'You mean this wiggle?' Charles assumed the position, pretending there was a club in his hands and a ball at his feet. He wiggled and shifted from foot to foot, and Elspeth hoped he was exaggerating because he looked so ridiculous that she burst out laughing.

'Yes, that wiggle,' she cried. 'I've never seen the point in it.'

'I'll let you into a secret – neither have I.'

'Do you still play? Tenerife has some fantastic golf courses, so I'm told.'

'Not anymore. I prefer more solitary pursuits these days.' He lit the barbeque, blew on it and it began to smoke.

Elspeth sniffed the air: she used to love that smell. She still did. Charles had surprised her when he said he preferred his own company. He came across as so friendly and outgoing that she had no idea he was such a solitary person.

Not at all like Ray, then. For all that he spent most of his working life with his head buried in old manuscripts, Ray had relished company, and had been forever inviting people around for dinner. Friends were important to him, and he used to have a fair amount of them, whereas Elspeth preferred a tight circle of close friends. Or being on their own, just the two of them.

When had that circle shrunk to just Amanda, she mused. Plus Toni, of course, because they came together as a job lot. And Stefan, even though he was technically her boss. One by one, over the course of the last four years, it seemed that most of her and Ray's friends had fallen by the wayside. Elspeth had been so wrapped up in her misery that she'd retreated into herself. And there, it seemed, she had stayed.

Yet did she want to remain there in her loneliness, or was it time she moved on?

As the hot coals began to smoulder and turn grey, she watched Charles through the patio doors as he busied himself with putting the steaks on the grill, while she chopped the salad and prepared the potatoes in the kitchen. She thought about how Charles was still in his solitary bubble, and how he seemed quite happy there. He gave the illusion of being sociable, but the fact that he was holidaying on his own, and had hired a bicycle and had gone off by himself quite happily for the day, should have given her a hint that he wasn't the man she'd originally assumed him to be. He was more like her than she'd first thought.

But if he was as content to be in his own company as he claimed to be, why had he accepted her offer of accompanying him on his hikes? And he'd accepted with alacrity, too. She hadn't picked up on any reluctance on his part or a sense of her overstepping the mark.

And, more to the point, he had readily agreed to spend the rest of his holiday in her little villa, instead of in a less personal hotel where he could have easily lost himself amongst the crowd.

But what Elspeth was asking herself was why.

Was it because he liked her as much as she feared she liked him?

She rather hoped it was.

Chapter 14

The following morning, Charles had taken himself and his hired bicycle off for another ride, leaving Elspeth to go to work. She was glad of the distraction if she was honest, because yesterday had been a strange day – a day in which she'd opened up her home to a man she hardly knew. That he had been previously staying with her was neither here nor there, because he'd been a paying guest. Now, though, she wasn't sure what he was.

'Is everything OK?' Stefan asked, when she dropped her bag in the office and flicked the switch on the kettle for her tea.

'Fine, thanks.'

'I bet you're happy to have your house back.'

'Erm, not really.'

'By this evening you will have forgotten your visitor was ever there.'

'He's staying.'

'Pardon?'

'I said, he's staying on with me.'

Stefan studied her carefully, his eyes scanning her face. 'Are you sure about this?'

'Very sure. I asked him, not the other way around.'

His eyebrows rose and his mouth dropped open. 'It wasn't Amanda who asked?'

'No, there was a room at the hotel if he wanted it.'

Her boss blinked and scratched his beard. The rasping noise of his fingers was loud in the ensuing silence, and it was only broken by the kettle coming to the boil, then knocking itself off.

'This is not like you,' Stefan said eventually.

Elspeth was forced to agree.

'Are you…? Did he…?' Her boss's cheeks grew pink. She might tease him about his love life, but he wasn't used to asking her about hers.

'He's good company,' she said. 'I like having him around.'

'Yes, but—'

'There is no "but". Charles is a friend, nothing more.' She looked Stefan in the eye. 'He goes back to England in ten days.'

'I just don't want you to get hurt,' he muttered, turning away to make the drinks.

That was a first, she thought – Stefan always left the tea and coffee making to her. Which went to show how unsettling he found the conversation to be.

He wasn't the only one.

'Stefan…' Elspeth put a hand on his arm. 'I appreciate your concern, but there's nothing to be concerned about.'

'I worry about you,' he admitted.

'I know you do.' She'd felt his care for her right from the very first day she'd started working at his shop. It was unspoken, but there, nevertheless. And she was grateful for it. Until now though, he'd never mentioned it. Neither of them had.

'How is your dad?' she asked, realising the lines around his eyes and the hard set of his jaw was unlikely to be caused by the news that Charles would be staying with her for a while.

Stefan shrugged. 'He's going to the hospital tomorrow for the results of his tests. Maybe we will know more after that.'

'What about your mother? Is she OK?'

'Not really. I spoke to her last night and she was crying.'

'Oh, dear. It must be very worrying for her.' In some ways, Elspeth was glad that Ray had died so suddenly. She wouldn't have been able to bear the thought of him suffering and going downhill gradually, beyond the natural slowing down that accompanied advanced age. It had been a horrible, horrendous shock when it had happened, but at least she had been spared what Stefan's mum might be facing if the news tomorrow wasn't good.

Still, she was sure it was probably nothing to worry about, and that's what she told Stefan again. Her boss didn't seem to be convinced though, because the smile he gave her was faint and didn't reach his eyes.

Elspeth patted him on the shoulder as she headed for the stockroom. She felt the tension in his body under her hand and resisted the urge to gather him into her arms and give him a hug. This was neither the time nor the place, especially since she heard a customer enter the shop. Besides, he would guess that she was also worried if she did something like that as it would be so out of character.

The morning passed in a blur of hiking socks, walking poles and Lycra, and it was nearly lunchtime before Elspeth checked her phone. Her face creased into a smile when she saw there was a message from Gideon. It widened even further when she read it and discovered that he was planning on visiting her in the next couple of weeks, although he didn't mention a date as yet. No doubt he'd tell her more during their weekly Skype call. He was bringing Sakura and Rai, too, and a surge of excitement built up inside her, but she stamped down hard on it, not wanting her good news to intrude on Stefan's worry. It wouldn't be fair of her to be elated when her boss was so anxious about his family.

Her mind immediately turned to preparing for her son's proposed visit, and Elspeth started to make a mental list of what she needed to do, and what she would need to buy. She'd plan their meals – although she couldn't remember if Sakura liked Spanish and English cooking. She'd better check with Gideon; she didn't want to buy food his wife wouldn't like, but on the other hand there wasn't a great deal of choice when it came to Japanese food in any of the local shops she frequented.

She'd give Charles's room a thorough clean for them—

Ah, Charles! Now she had something else to worry about – *Gideon hadn't given her a firm date.* A couple of weeks, he'd said. What if Charles was still in residence when Gideon arrived? She could hardly kick him out, and neither would she want to, but they couldn't all fit into her little villa.

He would be with her for ten more nights, including tonight. Gideon had said a couple of weeks, which surely meant fourteen days at least, probably longer. Charles most likely would have flown back to the UK by then, so there shouldn't be any overlap.

The thought of Charles leaving, and her possibly never seeing him again, made Elspeth feel sad. He was great company and she thoroughly enjoyed having him stay at the villa. But another unwelcome thought crept into her mind unbidden. How could she be sure that she enjoyed having Charles in her home, or did she like just having *someone*? Would anyone do? Now that she'd broken the seal on having another person around, was she just anxious about being alone again? But then again, what if she invited another guest into her home and it simply wasn't the same as having Charles with her?

Well, once he'd gone and her son's visit was over, she'd soon have the answer, wouldn't she?

But she was secretly worried that particular discovery might not be to her liking, and that she'd miss Charles more than she had any right to.

Chapter 15

Lasagne was Elspeth's speciality. Ray had loved it, even the vegetarian version she foisted on him now and again, much to his feigned disgust. Her husband had grown up in a time when meat and two veg were the staple diet, and although he'd done his level best to move with the times, lasagne had been as exotic as he liked to get. He had, though, fallen in love with Chinese food, and she could never eat Yeung Chow fried rice without thinking of him.

This evening, though, she was making the Italian dish with roasted red peppers and aubergines, and serving it with a colourful salad and slices of thickly cut fresh bread to mop up the sauce.

At least, that's what she'd planned on doing when she got home from work later that evening.

Charles, it seemed, had other ideas.

He'd prepared spicy enchiladas. From scratch, no less.

To say that she was impressed was an understatement. She was also extremely hungry, because the aroma coming from the kitchen assaulted her nose as soon as she opened the front door made her mouth water.

'I was going to make a lasagne,' she said, walking into the kitchen, her eyes wide. The room was spotless. He'd cleaned up behind him and put every single thing away, apart from a couple of plates which he was in the process of popping into the oven to warm through. 'I don't expect you to cook.'

'Why ever not?'

'You're a guest.'

'A non-paying one. And you've been at work all day.'

'You're on holiday.'

'I enjoy cooking.'

The pair of them stared at each other for a moment, until Elspeth chortled, 'Is this a Mexican stand-off?' leaving Charles to frown at her in confusion, before he, too, got the joke and smiled.

'Go and sit in the courtyard,' he said, 'and I'll bring you out a glass of wine. Will red do you? I thought it would go better with the enchiladas than white, although you can have whichever you prefer, of course.'

'Red will be great,' she called over her shoulder as she dashed upstairs to change.

He was being incredibly sweet. Fancy going out of his way to cook for her.

'Here you go.' Charles handed her a glass of fruity red as soon as she came back downstairs, and she took an appreciative sip.

After the day she'd had, the alcohol was welcome indeed.

'Where did you go today?' she asked.

'Nearly as far as Los Cristianos. I fancied some flat terrain, although it was a drag coming back up from sea level to the villa at the end of my ride.'

Elspeth grinned. 'It would be. I'm surprised you had any legs left at the end of it.'

'I almost didn't. No wonder the famous cycling teams train here. These gradients are killers.'

'Tenerife is popular with cyclists of all abilities,' she said. 'Though the less experienced tend to keep to the coastal roads in the south where it's considerably flatter.'

'I don't blame them.' He reached down to massage one of his calves with a rueful expression. 'Still, it's a fantastic way to see the island. You miss such a lot when you whizz by in a car.'

'Walking is even better,' she countered. 'You get to see even more.'

'True. I'm seriously looking forward to going up Teide next weekend.'

Elspeth was looking forward to it, too. It had been a while, although she was still a little uncertain about spending the night on the mountainside with a strange man.

Then she nearly laughed out loud. She'd spent the last four nights alone in her villa with him, and here she was baulking at the idea of sleeping in a hostel with him along with several others. She couldn't be less alone with him if she tried!

She made a mental note to find the sleeping bags to make sure they were still serviceable and to give them a good airing, else she and Charles would be spending a decidedly chilly night because she didn't fancy using the quilts the Refuge supplied – too many other bodies had slept under them for her liking. If one or both of them weren't useable, then the shop sold sleeping bags, so she could always purchase a couple from Stefan.

Which reminded her...

'Stefan's father gets his test results tomorrow,' she said. 'Poor Stefan is really worried and it doesn't help that they live so far away; it's more than a four-hour flight to Germany. I'm sure it's nothing to worry about, but Dieter has been having a few issues with his balance and slurring his words. Stefan's mum had to practically force him to go to the doctors, and he was sent for tests straight away.'

Charles's face became grave. 'I see.'

'Do you think it's anything to worry about?' He wasn't that kind of doctor, she knew, but he might have more of an idea than she did.

'I honestly couldn't say.'

'No, of course you can't.'

'You're probably right, though, and it's something simple or easily treatable.'

'Hmm.'

'You're not convinced, are you?' he asked.

'It's not that, I'm more concerned that this might be a tipping point for Stefan. Don't get me wrong, he loves living on Tenerife, but it can't be easy living so far away from home when things such as his dad's poor health crops up.'

'Are you worried he'll pack it in and go back to Germany?'

She nodded, nibbling at her lip with her teeth. That was exactly what was bugging her. 'He might, and even if he doesn't move back, if the news about his father isn't too good, he may have to be away for an extended period.'

'Who will run the shop?'

'Me, I expect. There is no one else, and I've done it before, but only for a week or so when he's taken a holiday. It wasn't easy on my own.'

'I'm sure you'll cope, and maybe if he does need to fly back home for a bit, he'll rope in some extra help.'

'Maybe. But what if—?'

'Don't worry too much, not until you know for certain one way or the other. You don't want to be fretting over what might never happen.'

Charles was right. She'd never been much of a worrier when Ray was alive, but now that she only had herself to rely on, she found she was more cautious and tended to pick over things a little more, which was exactly what she was doing now – panicking before there was any real reason to do so.

'On a brighter note though, it sounds as though Gideon is coming to visit in a couple of weeks' time, and he's planning to bring Sakura and Rai with him. Ooh, I can't wait! It's ages since I last saw them, and I bet Rai's grown loads.' Elspeth clapped her hands, and gave a deep, excited sigh.

'That's wonderful news. I expect you're over the moon,' Charles said, reaching for her hand to give it a pat. The pat turned into a clasp, as his hand remained on hers for a few seconds before he let her go to haul himself to his feet and disappear into the kitchen.

Elspeth was left with a warm tingle on the back of her hand where his fingers had rested, and an even warmer feeling in her heart. But she quickly put the little lurch she'd experienced when he'd touched her down to her overwhelming joy at the thought of seeing her son – because let's face it, what else could it possibly be caused by? She certainly didn't like Charles in that sense – she was past all that, and she hadn't looked at another man since she'd met Ray.

Yet a tiny part of her argued that she did like Charles, and because she didn't know how to deal with it, she decided to ignore the tingle.

Tingles were not on her agenda.

Chapter 16

Elspeth would dearly have loved to go for a walk the following morning, but she was too hyped up with the knowledge that Gideon would be here soon, and that there was so much to do in preparation. She understood that her son wouldn't care if the walls up the stairs were a little grubby, or if the grouting in the tiles in the downstairs loo could do with a freshen up, but Sakura might, and Elspeth herself certainly did. She wanted everything to be pristine for her family's arrival, which was why, when she had waved Charles off on his hike, she switched on the radio, and, with the sound of ABBA's 'Waterloo' flooding the villa, she proceeded to dance around singing loudly along to the music and got to work.

Elspeth felt that she should give Charles's room a clean as well, and put freshly ironed sheets on the beds – plus both en suites had to be scrubbed. The fridge would also benefit from being emptied and wiped down, and she didn't want to think what state the inside of her oven was in. After about a few hours of relentless cleaning and tidying, she rewarded her efforts with a cup of tea, which she took outside to drink.

The day was yet another glorious one, with only a little ring of cloud hovering around Teide's summit. It was already warm, and she worried whether Charles had taken enough water with him, before she berated herself. He was a grown man who had looked after himself perfectly well for the previous forty or so years – he was perfectly capable of looking after himself now, and he didn't need, nor want, any mothering from her. Anyway, even if he hadn't, the town of Tamaimo wasn't too far away, and he could always drop into it and buy a bottle of water if he so wished.

There was another reason why she'd declined Charles's offer of going hiking with him today – she felt she needed to spend some time with Ray. She'd been neglecting him lately (ever since Charles had come to stay if she was honest) and feelings of guilt were starting to make their presence felt.

The fact that Elspeth couldn't recall the last time she'd said good morning to her husband – or anything else to him, for that matter – wasn't sitting very well with her.

'I'm sorry, my darling,' she began. 'What must you think of me? I know I've been busy lately, but that's no excuse, is it? Can you forgive me?'

She didn't expect an answer (obviously) but she expected *something*. An acknowledgement, maybe? A feeling that he was listening to her?

There was nothing. Just an aching emptiness, whereas in the past she had always had a sense of him.

Bringing trembling fingers to her lips, Elspeth bit back an unexpected sob.

Ray was gone. The previous closeness she'd felt to him while sitting in the courtyard had deserted her. He was no longer there. Had her connection with him all been in her mind? She had an appalling suspicion that Ray never had been there. Instead it was all just her desperate need to cling onto him, which had made her believe he was still with her, in spirit at least.

Had she been deceiving herself all these years?

'Come back,' she whispered. 'Don't go, don't leave me.'

But he already had, hadn't he? Four long, empty, lonely years ago. And in response, she'd created a shrine that she'd been devoted to every day, keeping him alive and real, and very much with her. Her worship had been the only thing that had kept his spirit alive – but recently she'd forgotten her daily reverence, had let it slide, and now Ray had faded away, lost to her all over again – and this time it was forever.

On unsteady legs, she tottered into the living room in search of her phone.

'Amanda?' Her voice was hoarse and shaky.

'Elspeth? Is that you? What's wrong?'

'It's Ray...'

'Okaaay...?'

'He's gone.'

'I know, my sweetie, I know.'

Elspeth heard muffled whispering and guessed Amanda had her hand over the phone.

'Are you at home?' her friend asked.

'Yes.' Her voice was barely a whisper on the breeze.

'Stay there, I'm coming over.'

Elspeth did as she was told, sinking into the nearest armchair, the one that Ray had always favoured, and waited. Amanda, the woman who had been her rock and her saviour in the dark times after Ray's death, was coming to rescue her again, as she had done so many times before.

Poor Amanda; she'd probably assumed they were past all this by now. Elspeth had assumed the same. Even though her grief sometimes rose up to swamp her, she normally managed to control it, to deal with it. Over time she had learnt to keep it to herself.

But this? This was something new.

She felt as though she was losing Ray all over again.

Amanda still had her own key to the villa, which Elspeth had given to her when she was recently widowed, and Elspeth soon heard it scrape in the lock followed by her friend's firm tread on the tiles in the hall. Ray had chosen those tiles.

Or had he?

She seemed to recall that he'd picked out a darker colour, but she'd vetoed—

'Elspeth, what's wrong?'

Amanda was there in front of her, kneeling at her feet, her eyes filled with sympathy. Her hands reached for Elspeth's, and on finding them gripped them tightly.

Elspeth breathed deeply, her friend's presence anchoring her, pulling her back from the blackness that threatened to consume her.

'What's happened?' Amanda asked.

'I can't feel Ray. He's not here.'

'Oh, sweetie.'

Amanda gathered her up and enfolded her with her love, pouring strength into Elspeth, and the pair of them stayed like that for a long, long time. Eventually, the darkness began to recede, and Elspeth was able to breathe once more without shards of glass stabbing her chest.

Amanda gradually pulled away and searched Elspeth's face. 'It's been a while. What brought it on?'

'I forgot him.'

'You'll never forget him,' Amanda was adamant.

'I did. I haven't spoken to him in days. Only once since Charles...' She trailed off.

'Do you honestly think Ray would have held that against you? You've been busy.'

'Busy enjoying myself,' Elspeth replied, bitterness oozing through her.

'Aren't you allowed?'

She shrugged.

Amanda got up from her knees and slid her bottom onto the arm of the chair. Wrapping her arm around Elspeth's shoulders, she hugged her close. 'Was Ray really such an awful man?' she asked softly.

'Excuse me?' Elspeth was appalled.

'That he would begrudge you having fun?'

'Of course not! How could you say such a thing?'

'It's not me who is saying it.'

Elspeth twisted round in her seat, to look at her friend. 'Were you baking?' she asked, distracted for a moment by Amanda's appearance. 'Sorry, I didn't mean to interrupt you.'

Amanda had a white apron on, flour smeared across one cheek, and a hairnet covering her brown curling hair. 'It doesn't matter.' Amanda smiled sympathetically.

Elspeth frowned. Her friend was right – that's exactly what she'd been implying – and she knew that if Ray had been granted the time to say goodbye that he'd have made her promise not to grieve for long, not to dwell on her loss, but to embrace the rest of her life and not let it go to waste.

But it was easier said than done.

She thought that's exactly what she had been doing, but she hadn't been, had she? She'd been drowning in her sorrow, barely keeping her chin above the chilly waters of grief, meanwhile trying to convince herself that she was happy and that she would be content if she lived out the rest of her days in this way.

'I tried to speak to him today in the garden, but he's not there.' Despite her best efforts, her voice broke, and she drew in a ragged breath.

'He never was there,' Amanda said, looking in the direction of the orchid tree. 'He's here.' She placed a finger over Elspeth's heart. 'He hasn't gone anywhere – you just don't need him quite as much as you once did.'

'But I do.'

'Is it Charles? Has he upset you, or…?'

It was the 'or' which bothered Elspeth. 'No, nothing like that.'

Amanda cocked her head and raised her eyebrows. 'Do you know that your left eye twitches when you tell a lie?'

Elspeth's hand flew to her face. 'Really?'

Amanda smiled. 'You're entitled to like him, you know.'

Was she? She wasn't so sure. She was still married, for goodness' sake. Spending time with another man felt too much like being unfaithful. And liking that other man was *definitely* being unfaithful. As for fancying that other man… she was at a loss.

Technically, she knew it wasn't the same as cheating on a partner, but she couldn't help how she felt. 'What about Ray?' she asked in a small voice.

'He'd want you to be happy.'

'I know…'

'But don't jump into anything,' Amanda warned, her kind face creased with worry.

Elspeth barked out a wry laugh. 'How have we gone from me not feeling connected to Ray any more to you warning me not to jump into bed with Charles?'

Amanda's mouth dropped open. 'You haven't, have you? Is that what this is all about?'

'No, I haven't, and I don't intend to either! He's a guest, he's on holiday, and he's going home at the end of next week. I'll probably never see him again.' Elspeth hesitated. 'I do think he's been a kind of catalyst, though.'

Her friend looked thoughtful. 'I think you're probably right.'

'I'm sorry I had a meltdown. It's just…'

'No need to explain. I understand.'

And Elspeth knew she did. Amanda, and Toni to a lesser extent, had been with her since the beginning, since the very first time she and Ray had visited Tenerife and fallen in love with the island. They had stayed at Hotel Aventuras and had returned to it several times, getting to know the hoteliers well in the process, before they had finally made the decision to retire to Santiago del Teide. Amanda and Toni had been with them every step of the way, offering their hospitality, their experience and ultimately their friendship. Given what Amanda had been through with her over the last few years, Elspeth felt that her friend knew her almost as well as Elspeth knew herself.

'Get yourself cleaned up and come and have lunch at the hotel,' Amanda suggested.

'What about your baking?'

'Meh.' She waved a hand in the air. 'I left Chef to sort it out. He's better at it than I am, anyway. I swear he'd ban me from his kitchen if he could. He only lets me play in there because I nag him.'

'What were you making?' Elspeth asked as she struggled out of the armchair and made her way to the stairs to get ready for lunch. Amanda was hot on her heels.

'An orange and almond cake.'

'Sounds divine.'

'You can have a piece after lunch. In fact, have the whole thing. Toni and I are trying to watch our waistlines.'

'Great, you foist it onto me so my waistline can expand instead of yours? Charles can have some, and I'll take a slice into work for Stefan. Speaking of Stefan…' Elspeth filled Amanda in on her boss's problems. 'And to top it off, Gideon texted me to say he was coming for a visit in a couple of weeks and is bringing Sakura and the baby with him.'

'You must be over the moon.'

'I am. It's been ages since I saw him last, and Rai will have grown loads. Skyping is great, but it isn't the same.'

'No, it's not.' Amanda's own family were back in the UK, so she knew all about long-distance calls. 'No wonder you got a bit upset – you've got such a lot going on. You're not used to it.'

'That's true,' Elspeth agreed.

But as she washed her face and slipped into something more appropriate for lunch at the hotel, she couldn't help feeling that the most momentous part of this morning's emotional outburst was the sense of clarity she had about her growing feelings towards Charles.

There was no going back now; she felt like a genie had been released from a bottle, and she didn't think she'd be the same ever again.

Chapter 17

Despite eating a decent lunch (just two courses though – she refused a starter), Elspeth had a meal prepared for Charles when he arrived home later that evening. She had planned to eat with him, even if it was only a couple of mouthfuls, because she didn't like to think of him eating on his own.

'Where did you go?' she asked as she carefully put an oven-hot plate down in front of her place setting. Charles was waiting for her to sit down before he tucked into his own meal.

'Along the main road and out the other side of Santiago for about half a mile, then I cut left and hiked into the mountains. I had a feeling I would come out somewhere above Masca village, and I was right.'

'I don't suppose you hiked down the gorge again?'

'Damned right I didn't. Not only did I not do that, I also didn't walk back from Masca. I took a taxi back to Santiago.'

'Sounds nice. Did you have a coffee and a sandwich in Masca village?'

'Guilty, as charged.' Charles held up his hands as he talked. 'It was very pleasant sitting outside and watching the world go by. I don't do enough of that.' He smiled to himself. 'I can't believe how much I've fallen in love with this place. I can see the attraction of coming to live out here. I don't know…' He shook his head slightly. 'It feels like home. I honestly don't want to leave.'

'Tenerife can do that to you,' Elspeth said, thinking back to her and Ray's first visit. Ray always said he wanted to retire to Tenerife, even then. 'But living here isn't the same as being on holiday,' she warned.

'A lot of people do it, though – retire to the Canary Islands, I mean.' Charles looked thoughtful, as if he were giving the idea some significant consideration.

'You're not seriously thinking about it, are you?' Her heart gave a jolt, making her a little cross. She could do without feeling as though she was being electrocuted at the mere idea of him moving to the island. Especially when it was only a pipe dream – she couldn't believe how many tourists said the exact same thing when they were in the middle of their annual fortnight in the sun. 'You've got a life back in the UK – your daughters and your grandchildren, for a start,' she pointed out.

'I know, but I can dream, can't I? Besides, I didn't see that much of them before I retired; they had busy lives and so did I, and we lived in different parts of the country. The difference between then and now is that they still have busy lives but now I don't, and I still don't get to see much of them.'

'Living here isn't the same as being on holiday,' Elspeth repeated, wishing her tippy-tappy pulse would slow down. The last thing she needed was another hot flush.

'I accept that, but I'm tempted, nevertheless. I've spoken to a few ex-pats on my walks since I arrived, and none of them seem to regret making the move.' He narrowed his eyes at her. 'And neither do you.'

'Ray and I had visited the island many, many times before we considered relocating here. And we thought about it for a long time. Mind you, I was still working at the time, so it was more of an upheaval for me than it was for Ray, when we did eventually decide to move.'

Even though Charles didn't have a job to resign from, Elspeth still wasn't convinced it was the right thing for him. It was all well and good falling in love with the place when you were on holiday – when everything was rosy and on its best behaviour – but whatever troubles and issues you had in your real life tended to follow you wherever you went. Although, to be fair, Charles didn't appear to have much in the way of problems, or none that he'd shared with her. The only thing he appeared to have was too much time on his hands and not enough to fill it with now that he'd given up work. Having no one to share retirement with probably didn't help either. Which meant if he did decide to relocate to Tenerife, his situation would still be the same: he'd still have as much time on his hands, and would still be as alone, except with better weather.

Ah, but what about you? a little voice asked, a voice she was trying to ignore because it seemed intent on sabotaging her hard-fought-for peace of mind. Charles would certainly have her for a friend, so maybe he wouldn't be quite as alone on the island as she anticipated.

And that was the word she needed to focus on – *friend*. That's what they were becoming. Correction: *had* become. Despite the way her heart beat faster sometimes, despite Amanda telling her that she deserved to be happy and that Ray would want this for her, Elspeth had decided friendship was the only thing on the cards. There was no way she would ever leave herself open to experiencing the kind of pain she'd been in when Ray died. Once in a lifetime was enough for anyone. Letting someone else into her heart (she ignored the fear that she'd already done just that) was not going to happen.

She was aware that if Charles left, she'd lose his friendship. Yet liking his company wasn't enough of a reason to encourage him in giving up everything in England to move to Tenerife, no matter how many days of sunlight the island enjoyed per year, or how spectacular the scenery. If it hadn't been for Ray wanting to retire here, Elspeth would never have entertained the idea of leaving the UK. Also, her circumstances were not the same as Charles's. He had a family to go back to. Her nearest family was close to eight thousand miles away in Japan. So here was where she'd stayed when Ray died.

She decided that Charles would undoubtedly do what thousands of other holidaymakers had done before him – he would go back full of idealistic plans, but once back home, real life would make its presence felt, and the ambitions would fade into nothing more than wonderful memories of a nice holiday.

After dinner, the pair of them were lost in their own thoughts as they cleared the table and washed the dishes together. Elspeth couldn't be bothered to reject Charles's unspoken offer of help (not after the day she'd had) and he wiped the table down and put things away while she dabbled her hands in hot soapy water.

She was scrabbling about for an elusive teaspoon at the bottom of the sink, when her phone rang.

Hastily, she wiped her hands on a towel and reached over for it on the counter, worried about who it might be. No one ever called her in the evenings, except Gideon, and today was Wednesday, not the scheduled day for their weekly Skype call. 'Hello?'

'It's me, Stefan.'

'Oh, hello, chicken, is everything all right?'

'No, it's not. I am sorry, but I have to go home tomorrow to Germany.'

'Oh…' Elspeth's mouth went dry as she guessed the reason. 'What did the hospital say?'

'It's motor neurone disease.' Stefan sounded numb, his voice flat.

'I see.' She didn't really, because she didn't know much about it, but she knew it wasn't good.

'My father didn't want me to know—' He stopped abruptly and she heard him fighting back tears. 'Mutter called, she thought I had a right to know. But he… my father… he knew I'd come back to Germany, and he didn't want to worry me – the shop…'

His anguish was palpable, and Elspeth's heart went out to him.

'I have to go,' he repeated.

'Of course you do, Stefan. Don't worry about the shop. You can tell your father it's in safe hands, and I'll take care of it for you until you get back. I'm sure things are not as bad as you think they are.'

'I hope you're right. Are you sure you will manage? I may be gone a while.'

'Take as long as you need. I've covered for you before, haven't I, without burning the place down or driving all your customers away.' She tried to joke, to lighten the conversation.

Stefan's responding chuckle was weak and forced, but she'd got her point across. He'd got his across too, and it made her forehead crease with worry; a break for a few days, a week at the most, was one thing – but Stefan was telling her that he might be gone for much longer than that.

'What's up?' Charles was at her side and offering her a glass of brandy from the stash of bottles Toni and Amanda had given her, when he saw her face as she hung up the phone.

Elspeth accepted the glass gratefully. 'It's Stefan, he is flying to Germany tomorrow because his father has just been diagnosed with motor neurone disease.'

'Oh dear, that's awful!'

'He sounded so upset, the poor lad. I hope it's not as bad as he thinks it is,' she said, echoing her earlier words. She caught sight of Charles's expression, and her heart sank even further. 'Tell me,' she demanded. 'Warts and all. I'm not totally sure what the condition is…'

Clutching his own glass, Charles went to sit on the sofa, and she joined him, sipping the smooth fiery liquid. She soon felt the alcohol track a warm path down her throat to her stomach.

'It's a disease that affects the nerves in the brain and spinal cord which control the muscles,' Charles said. 'It usually starts gradually, and the symptoms can often be the same as many other diseases.'

'Like a brain tumour?'

'Yes, it can present like that, and it's difficult to diagnose in the early stages. But once the neurologist knows what he or she is dealing with, there are treatments in place to help manage it.'

'But no cure?'

'No. Physiotherapy and speech therapy, plus a combination of drugs can reduce the impact of the disease and may even slow its progress somewhat.'

'But not get rid of it?'

'Unfortunately, it can't be reversed or stopped…' Charles paused.

'Tell me the rest. It's going to get a lot worse for Stefan's father, isn't it?'

'I'm afraid it is.' He took her hand and she let him hold it, grateful for its warm strength. A glass of brandy was nowhere near sufficient fortitude for what she suspected she was about to be told.

'Patients with MND will deteriorate over time,' Charles said. 'The progress of the disease varies from person to person in the severity of individual symptoms, but Stefan's dad can expect to have greater difficulty with his movement, and this will affect the whole body, including speaking, swallowing and breathing. There may also be emotional and behavioural changes.'

Elspeth was stunned. 'That's dreadful.'

'It's not pleasant, either for the sufferers or their families, and it must be a terrible shock to Stefan, especially with him living so far away.'

'That's also what I'm worried about,' Elspeth admitted quietly. 'I know it's awful to be thinking of myself at such a time, but what if he's gone for weeks? Months? What if he doesn't come back at all?'

'Is it just you and him in the shop, is that right? He doesn't employ anyone else?'

She shook her head. 'We've always managed in the past just the two of us; there didn't seem any need to have another staff member, although I sometimes find it tough when he has a holiday; it's a lot for one person to manage and Stefan's much younger than me.'

'If you do have to run it single-handedly for a while, what will you do about taking days off? Lunch breaks?'

Elspeth smiled gently. 'Ever heard of a siesta? Many shops and businesses close some time in the afternoon for an extended lunch break. Stefan's shop is no exception, although if there are two of us in on that day at peak season, he stays open and we take it in turns to have lunch. I usually man the place if he wants a day off, but what generally happens is that Stefan will come in late or leave early that day. He tends to work seven days a week.'

'Ah, I see.'

'Exactly. Do you know, there are times when I think he didn't need to employ me at all, but he just gave me the job out of the goodness of his heart,' she confided. 'It's not as though I don't pull my weight – I do – but honestly, I think he could manage without me if he had to.'

Elspeth was sure that Stefan had felt sorry for her when she was widowed. Ray used to frequent the shop regularly, and Amanda and Toni often pointed their guests in its direction, but when she thought about it, Elspeth wasn't convinced that she had even applied for a job there. She couldn't remember seeing an advert – the details of those first months after she'd lost Ray had grown fuzzy around the edges due to grief – and neither could she remember having had an interview.

Amanda had mentioned that there was a job going – she could remember that much – and her next memory was of speaking to Stefan and him telling her the job was hers if she wanted it. And to think, that at the time she hadn't been sure whether she wanted a job or not – what a lifesaver it had turned out to be!

'He can't manage without you, especially now,' Charles pointed out.

'True. But I'm not sure how I can possibly manage without *him*. A week is fairly exhausting when you have to man the place on your own at my age; it's OK for a young man like Stefan, but for me to run the place for longer...' Elspeth grimaced. It was hard work and although she might not be over the hill yet, she was heading rapidly for sixty and she didn't have the stamina or energy that she once had.

'I can help. If you'll let me,' Charles said.

Elspeth blinked owlishly at him, not sure she'd heard correctly. Why on earth would he want to do that? He was on holiday, for goodness' sake. Besides, this might turn out to be a long-term problem; as thoughtful as his offer was, she had to think beyond Charles's departure. Although, any help she could get would be welcome...

'You want to help?' she echoed, in case she'd misheard him.

He nodded.

What a thoughtful and considerate man he was. How many other people would offer such support to someone they hadn't long met, especially when they were supposed to be on holiday, enjoying themselves? Despite her worry over Stefan and her anxiety over how she'd cope over the ensuing days (weeks?), Charles's kindness and support made her feel warm inside. His help would be greatly appreciated, but there were other things to consider, such as the fact that this was his holiday, and having him spend some of it working in a shop was hardly fair on him. Then there was the question of, what would Stefan think? She trusted Charles – he had a key to her villa, didn't he? – but she didn't feel right letting him loose in Libertad without Stefan's knowledge, and she didn't want to ask her boss right now and give him yet another thing to be worried about.

Something else occurred to her. 'Please don't worry that you will be neglected; I won't shirk my hostess duties and I'll still hike up Teide with you, too,' she promised.

Charles put a hand out, and placed it on top of hers. 'Please don't feel you have to cook for me or change the sheets on my bed. I'm perfectly capable of doing those things. And I don't expect you to trudge up a bloomin' great big mountain either, not when you're working flat out. I can go on my own.'

'You are not going on your own,' she stated firmly. 'We've discussed this already. It's safer with two, and the shop will be closed on Sunday because it's Easter – not many places will be open – so I'm still game, if you are. If we go up on Saturday evening, we can sleep in the Refuge and we'll come back down on the following morning. It'll give me all day Sunday to recover.'

It was an arduous hike; she'd probably need more than the Sunday, but she didn't share that with Charles. She didn't want to trouble him, not when he was being so kind.

And he was right – she would need help in the shop if Stefan was away for any length of time. Not Charles's assistance, either, as kind as the offer was. It wasn't fair on him and besides, this was her problem to deal with not his. She'd manage, somehow. She'd have to, because even if she did accept his help, it could only be for a short time. After he'd gone, she'd be on her own again.

The thought wasn't a happy one, and she wasn't just referring to the shop. She enjoyed spending time with him far too much, and there was a very real danger that she was beginning to feel more for him than was wise, and that would never do.

Did she have to continually keep reminding herself of her utter devastation when she'd lost Ray in order not to get involved with anyone else? But if she didn't, she might fall for this man and she'd vowed to never, ever let herself get in that position again. Love was too risky, especially at her age when there was no way of predicting how long she might have a new love for. Look at her and Ray… yes, he was older than her, but he hadn't been *old* old. And if he could be snatched so cruelly from her, so could anyone else she gave her heart to.

She simply wasn't prepared to let that happen.

And, as she'd thought so many times previously and especially now since Charles had arrived on the scene, Ray was still very much a part of her life and she couldn't imagine loving another man as deeply and as thoroughly as she loved him. Therefore there was no point in even trying, so she might as well get the idea out of her head.

Not only that, he'd be leaving soon. So there wasn't any point in giving in to her feelings.

Charles was a friend. And that's all he ever could be.

Chapter 18

Elspeth loved working at Libertad: she always had done, right from the start. She enjoyed chatting to the customers, despite not being much of a people person normally and usually preferring her own company if given a choice. There was a certain satisfaction in helping people purchase the best item for their requirements and she took pride in her product knowledge. She also took pride in ensuring the shop looked the best it could possibly look.

The following morning, though, she had a bit of a run-in with a gentleman who was cross that she didn't have the time to swap a bike saddle over for him, even though the bike he'd brought in wasn't one of theirs and neither was the saddle. The cheek of it! She'd been on the go since before nine that morning, hadn't had a break for a cup of tea at all, and now it was one in the afternoon, and her bladder was shouting at her that she needed the bathroom urgently, but with three people still in the shop there was no way she could leave them unattended.

It was typical that she hadn't seen the place this busy in quite a while. What a time to be running it single-handedly!

There was something else that was bothering her – being left in charge felt different to the other times. In the past, there'd been a finite end to her role as manager. She'd known when Stefan was due back, and it had given her a goal to aim for. But now, there was the possibility that he might be away indefinitely, and she wondered how he was getting on. She hoped that his father wasn't as poorly as Stefan feared, as she rang up a large purchase, before popping the items in a bag and following the remaining customers to the door. She then locked the door behind them and switched the 'open' sign to 'closed', with a sigh of relief.

Time for lunch and a well-deserved break. She didn't intend to shut for the whole siesta, which was advertised on the notice stating the shop's hours of business, but neither did she intend to rush her lunch.

As she ate, the fragrant aroma of chamomile filled the air from the cup of herbal tea next to her plate. Elspeth usually preferred English breakfast tea, but after this morning she felt the need for something to soothe her ragged nerves. As soon as she'd finished her lunch and had washed and dried her plate, she picked up her phone and sent Gideon a text, smiling as she ended it with her usual 'love you'. Selfishly, and to her disgust, she prayed that Stefan would be back before her son and his family arrived for their visit. She saw them so rarely that she wanted to spend every minute she possibly could with them, because God knows when she'd get to see them again.

Her heart gave a pang whenever she thought of how fast little Rai was growing up. Before long he'd be out of the baby stage and would be a toddler. He was almost toddling already, now that he'd started pulling himself up on the furniture and was using it to cruise around the room. She'd clapped enthusiastically during her last Skype call with her family when Rai had let go and balanced for a second before falling on his bottom.

And that was another thing – the time difference. Japan was eight hours ahead, which made scheduling a call when none of them were in work or in bed a challenge. Gideon was good at sending her cute little videos of Rai, though, so she didn't feel as though she was completely missing out.

Skype tonight instead? Ten p.m. your time? Gideon had texted back, after she'd messaged him with the news that she was in work today and would miss their scheduled call. Elspeth broke out into a big grin.

> That's early for you.

> I'll be awake. Got a big meeting.

> Can't wait. Speak later xxx

The rest of the day sped by, Elspeth buoyed up by the thought of seeing Gideon on the video call – and maybe even Rai, if he was awake. Ooh, she couldn't wait to give him a cuddle and a kiss in person. Several in fact, and there was a strong possibility that she wouldn't be able to put him down for the duration of his visit. Poor Gideon wouldn't get a look in, not with a chubby, smiley baby in the house to play with.

Elspeth was looking forward to seeing Sakura, too. She felt she hadn't got to know her daughter-in-law that well and was glad she would be able to spend some time with her. Not only was there the physical distance between them to contend with, but there was the cultural one as well. Thankfully, Sakura spoke excellent English, so that was one less thing to worry about.

Elspeth had even less to worry about when she got home at the end of a very long day, and discovered that Charles had cooked dinner. Between mouthfuls of delicious beef casserole (who knew the man could cook so well?!) she told him all about her day.

'I'm exhausted,' she declared. 'Easter weekend is coming up; it's super busy and I'm not getting any younger.'

'You're as young as you feel,' Charles told her.

'Yes, well, today I feel about ninety.'

'Any news from Stefan?'

She shook her head. 'Nothing at all. I'm tempted to phone him, but I don't want to intrude. He's always called at the end of the day when he's been away previously, but I haven't heard a peep out of him, which makes me think things can't be good.'

Elspeth and Charles stared at each other for a moment, with sombre expressions.

'On a lighter note,' Elspeth broke the silence, 'Gideon is Skyping me at ten this evening. Poor love, he'll have to get up at the crack of dawn, but he says he's got a big meeting, so I expect he'd be up early anyway. I just hope Rai is awake – I'd love to see him.'

Charles got to his feet and collected up the dishes.

'Let me do that,' Elspeth said hastily, feeling incredibly guilty that not only had her guest cooked a meal for her, but that he was intending to do the washing up as well.

'You sit down; you've had a hard day,' he told her.

'And you haven't? I bet you've either been out cycling or hiking. You're not exactly having a relaxing holiday, are you?'

'Nope, and I wouldn't want to. I don't like lazing around by a pool.'

'So, what have you been doing?' She followed him out to the kitchen, hoping Charles would be distracted by something for long enough for her to swoop in and take control of the sink.

'I caught a bus to Erjos and visited the pools.'

'It's so pretty there! I haven't been to the pools in ages. Did you see much wildlife? I should have thought to mention Erjos to you before.'

'It was so quiet, I can't believe more people don't know about them. I saw rabbits and ducks – and more dragonflies than you can shake a stick at. I'm surprised that the pools are there, though.'

Elspeth told him that the area was once a quarry and that water had then collected in the hollows of the non-porous rock over the course of tens of years. They continued to discuss the local area over coffee and a brandy, as they sat in the courtyard and let the soft night wash over them.

Charles breathed deeply, the scent of night-blooming flowers hanging heavy in the air, and tilted his head back. He looked so relaxed with his eyes closed, that Elspeth considered the possibility that he might have fallen asleep.

It was almost time for her Skype call with Gideon, so she decided to leave Charles where he was for the time being, and quietly got to her feet and made her way into the living room, to sit in front of the dated computer in the corner.

It was high time she invested in a new one, because this old thing was a bit of a chugger, and took ages to load. Maybe she'd treat herself to a younger, slimmer model. The computer was like her, getting old and slowing down.

'Gideon!' she cried when the video call connected at last, and she quickly scanned his face for signs that he was eating properly and taking care of himself. He did look a little tired, but then he was usually up at the crack of dawn. 'How are you?'

'Good, Mum, really good.'

'And how's my grandson?'

'As wicked as ever. He's learnt to say poo-poo,' Gideon said, proudly.

'Nice,' she laughed.

'Oh, he doesn't mean poop – he's trying to say papa.'

Elspeth laughed even more. 'He must have grown so much; I can't wait for you to get here. Have you got a date in mind?'

'We have! Two weeks on Saturday. I've got some business in London first, and Sakura and Rai are coming with me, then once that's finished and Sakura has spent a fortune in Regent Street and seen the sights, we'll fly to Tenerife and spend a few days with you, if that's OK? Then it's onto Berlin for a couple of days and back to Japan.'

'You can stay as long as you like,' she told him. 'I'm just delighted to see you. And it's nice that you're taking a proper break for once. That company works you too hard.'

Gideon narrowed his eyes, and Elspeth thought he was about to say something, when she sensed movement behind her and Charles hoved into view on her screen.

She looked over her shoulder and gave him a little wave as he made his way through the living room and into the hall. He waved back, and she couldn't help smiling at how sleepy he looked.

When she turned back to the screen, however, her smile faded rapidly as she spied Gideon's expression.

'Who was that?' he asked, frowning.

'Oh, that's Charles. He's staying with me.'

Her son's frown deepened.

'Not like that,' she added, hastily. 'Amanda and Toni were over-booked, so they asked if I could put him up as a guest.'

'I'm not sure I like the idea of that, Mum. Couldn't he have stayed somewhere else?'

'It's Easter coming up, and everywhere in Santiago is fully booked. Besides, I don't mind, and the extra money will come in handy.' She tried to look innocent; it wasn't as if she was lying. Not really. Everywhere *had* been full. Initially. Gideon had no need to know that she'd invited Charles to stay on afterwards, or that she wasn't charging Charles for the additional stay. Anyway, it was none of her son's business who she had in her home.

Nevertheless, from the disgruntled look on Gideon's face, she was glad she hadn't shared the whole story with him. He was trying to protect her, that was all, and it wasn't an easy thing to do long distance. After Ray had died, she knew Gideon had been wracked with guilt that he couldn't be with her, and he'd begged her to move to Japan.

She'd refused, of course. He had his own life to lead and it wasn't as though she'd needed taking care of. Or so she'd thought at the time. With hindsight, she knew that she'd needed more help than she'd realised. Thank God for Amanda and Toni.

It also occurred to her that Gideon had worshipped his father so much that he might have some difficulty accepting any relationship she had with another man. Luckily he didn't need to concern himself on that score.

'You should have told me if you've got money worries,' Gideon said. 'I could have helped out.'

'I don't need your help. I can manage perfectly well on your father's pension and my wages from the shop.'

'So why did you agree to let this man stay with you?'

Elspeth stifled a sigh. She didn't want to get into this right now, especially not with Charles in the house. 'Because Amanda and Toni were in a pickle. I've got the room, and Charles isn't any trouble.'

She was about to say more, when she spotted the man in question walking back into the living room again, this time with two glasses of wine in his hands.

Trying not to wince, she watched him draw closer and place one of the glasses gently down on the table, far enough away from the computer to make sure there wouldn't be any danger from accidental spillage, but near enough for her to be able to reach it.

She smiled her thanks at him and waited for him to wander off outside before she faced her son again.

He didn't look at all happy and she realised how it must appear.

'He's being awfully familiar for a paying guest,' Gideon observed.

Elspeth decided to ignore his comment, reasoning that Charles would be long gone by the time Gideon arrived and Gideon would probably have forgotten all about Charles when he got here, therefore the subject would never have to be discussed again. She also ignored the little stab of pain that accompanied the thought of Charles leaving.

All of a sudden, a wave of annoyance surged through her and she began to get cross – it had been four years since Gideon's father passed away. Four long and very lonely years. Her son didn't know half of what she'd been through during that time, and neither had she wanted him to know the extent of her devastation. But she wasn't even sixty. Did Gideon think she was supposed to rot away in Tenerife and never have anyone else in her life? Not that she wanted another relationship, but that was beside the point.

'Look, I have to go, otherwise I'll be late for my meeting,' Gideon said, and blew her a kiss. 'Love you, Mum. Be careful, yeah?' he added, meaningfully.

'I will, and I love you too. Give Sakura and Rai a kiss for me.'

'I will. Bye, Mum.'

'Bye, Gideon.'

The screen went blank as she stared at it for a moment, then she picked up her wine, took a large mouthful and went into the courtyard to join her non-paying guest.

'I take it that was Gideon? He's a good-looking lad,' Charles said.

'It was – and he is.' Her tone was rather clipped, so to soften it she added, 'Thank you once again for cooking – you shouldn't have. You're on holiday.'

'Yes, but you're refusing to take any payment, so it's the least I can do. Anyway, I enjoy cooking. And I enjoy cooking for you. It makes me feel as though I'm living here and am not just on holiday.'

'Perhaps you should try a self-catering option next time,' she joked.

'I might just do that.'

The cross feeling began to leach away, and Elspeth started to mellow. Gideon's reaction wasn't Charles's fault, and she had no right to take out her disgruntlement on him.

'What are your plans for tomorrow?' she asked.

'I'm going to go for another bike ride, I think.'

'You might want to delay setting off for a bit. Tomorrow is Good Friday and there'll be an Easter procession through the town in the morning. It's well worth watching if you're not in a hurry to get off.'

'In that case, I'll go for a ride afterwards.' Charles sipped his drink, gazing into the darkness beyond the courtyard. 'I can't believe I've been here nearly a week. On the one hand it's gone so fast, but on the other I've packed so much into it I feel as though I've been here for ages. The more I see of the island, the more I'm growing to love it. I can understand why you stayed after Ray died.'

'As I said, I had nothing to go back to – unlike you.' This wasn't the first time he'd expressed the very same thought, and she wondered if he was trying to convince himself that staying on Tenerife was a good idea. Was he serious or was it wishful thinking?

'So, you wouldn't consider going back to the UK?' he asked.

She shook her head, wondering why he kept asking her this. She'd already told him she wouldn't. There was no point; she had no reason to. 'No, I wouldn't.'

'Is it because Ray is still here?' Charles glanced at the orchid tree.

'I suppose.' She shrugged. 'There are memories of him everywhere. This is where he – *we* – were the happiest.'

'Pity,' he said. 'I don't want to lose our,' he hesitated, 'friendship, but, as you rightly pointed out, my life is in England, yours is here, and never the twain shall meet.'

Was he sounding her out – trying to gauge if there could possibly be anything between them? She couldn't work it out. After all, he didn't have to rush back to the UK because of work, he was retired. He could extend his stay, or even come back later in the year.

The thought was exhilarating and dismaying at the same time. She might have been forced to acknowledge she had feelings for him, but so far they were compartmentalised because she knew there was a finite end. No doubt she'd keep in touch with Charles for a while after he left, then contact would gradually grow less and less as those things tended to do.

When she failed to say anything further, Charles reached for the bottle of wine and she hastily put a hand over her glass; she'd had enough for tonight. As he topped up his own glass, she drained the last few drops in hers, mulling things over in her mind.

No, she didn't want another man in her life. No one could replace Ray, and things were best left as they were. These silly feelings she had for Charles would fade soon enough and she'd go back to being as she was.

Gideon had nothing at all to be concerned about. She wasn't ready for romance and she never would be.

Oh my God! Charles hadn't thought she was coming on to him, had he, when she'd suggested spending the night with him in the Refuge on Teide, and then she'd gone and offered for him to spend the rest of his holiday in her villa! Elspeth groaned inwardly.

But even as she debated about how she could put this right without making a fool of herself, a part of her couldn't help wondering how it would feel if she didn't...

Chapter 19

Despite not being particularly religious, Elspeth loved the Passion of Christ procession along the main street in Santiago del Teide on Good Friday, and she and Ray used to make a point of watching it every year. Naturally, she'd carried on the tradition after he'd passed away, so that morning she closed the shop, in line with every other business in the town, and waited for Charles to arrive.

Before she turned the key in the lock, she poked her head out of the door and glanced up and down the street. Spectators were already gathering, and there was an expectant buzz in the air.

Just then, she spotted Charles hurrying towards her, and she held the door open for him to slip inside.

'Fancy a quick brew before it starts?' she asked. 'We've got time.'

'Yes, please. I can't believe how many people are dressed up in Biblical-style costumes. If it wasn't for the mobile phones many of them are carrying, I'd feel as though I was in Ancient Jerusalem.'

'Good! That's what the organisers want you to feel.' She led him to the back of the shop and flicked the switch on the kettle.

Charles glanced around curiously and she saw him take in the little office to one side and the stock room. Neither space was very big. The largest room in the building was the room out the back where Stefan stored the bikes.

'Where does most of the revenue come from?' Charles asked. 'The shop itself or the bike hire and repair side of things?'

'It's about equal, I think. As you know, Tenerife is a magnet for cyclists, but if you're not part of one of the professional teams then it's easier to hire a bike over here than to bring your own.'

Charles chuckled. 'Every time a guy passes me on a bike, I check their kit to see if they are a professional. I feel honoured to be riding on the same roads – although I believe my speed is considerably slower than theirs, especially going uphill,' he joked. 'Thanks.'

She handed him a mug of steaming tea and he took a sip.

'It's great that this shop exists,' Charles said after a while. 'I know there are other places you can hire bikes from, but to be honest, those bikes look like they're better suited to a gentle trundle along the promenade at Los Cristianos, than the hard ride up into the caldera.'

'Which is exactly the reason Stefan began hiring bikes out. He saw a gap in the market and jumped right in. Of course, there are other bike hire companies, and some decent ones, too, with quality bikes, but nothing over here on the west of the island.'

'How long has Stefan owned the business?' he asked.

'Just over five years, but the shop has been here a lot longer than that. It was his idea, though, to open up the bike hire part. Finish your tea,' she told him, 'I think they're about to start.'

Charles downed the last of his drink and took their mugs over to the counter, then hurried to the door.

'Crikey, there are a lot of people here,' he said as they shut and locked up the shop behind them and joined the spectators thronging the pavements.

'It's very popular.' A hush descended as the procession started, and Charles craned his neck to see down the road. Elspeth lowered her voice to a whisper. 'Christ's betrayal by Judas Iscariot is being enacted at the far end of the street, and in a few minutes we'll see him carrying his cross.'

Realistic cries of pain floated down the street as the procession drew closer, and the actor playing Christ came into view. He had a crown of thorns on his head, fake blood daubed on his temple and down his neck and face. As the man staggered past, struggling under the weight of the cross, red marks where he'd been whipped could be seen striping his back. They looked incredibly realistic, and Elspeth winced.

Behind the Christ figure were men dressed in Roman centurion costumes, and various other townsfolk looking like inhabitants of long-ago Jerusalem. There was even a donkey. Bringing up the rear were men in clerical office, wearing their cassocks.

Charles was transfixed and Elspeth found she was having as much pleasure witnessing his reaction to the event, as she was from watching it herself.

Charles really was a handsome man, she noted, not for the first time. There was a certain calm, quiet dignity about him, and she guessed he had probably been an excellent doctor. But she got the feeling that he was a bit lost now that he'd retired, and that he was searching for something to fill the void. She hoped he'd find it soon, because whatever it was, she knew he'd be passionate and dedicated about it.

Without warning, heat swept up from her chest and into her face, as Elspeth imagined just how passionate Charles could be with his well-sculpted lips and his caring eyes.

Stop this nonsense right now, she told herself, appalled that she'd somehow managed to transform a simple thing such as his anticipated dedication to a new project or hobby into something far earthier and, let's face it, far ruder.

What was the matter with her?

Maybe she should go to the doctors and get a supply of HRT – her hormones were all over the place and not behaving themselves at all.

By the time the procession reached the square and Christ had been placed on his cross, Elspeth had regained her senses, and was her normal steady self once more, but it had been a bit of a battle to stop her mind running away with her.

'That was fantastic,' Charles said, turning to her, his eyes shining, and she loved his enthusiasm.

She had to agree that the whole event was very well done and the atmosphere was quite emotional, but surely a man as worldly-wise as Charles had witnessed far more impressive things than this? But for him to be so excited about one of her favourite things, warmed her heart.

In fact, it was becoming so warm, that she hurriedly turned toward the shop, her mouth dry and her pulse quickening. Tea, that's what she needed – a nice cup of tea. And of course, she couldn't not offer Charles one, could she?

'Another cup of tea before you set off on your bike ride?' she suggested, and Charles nodded.

'Good idea.'

She'd only just got the door open when she had a customer, and Charles stepped to the side to let him enter. The man was quickly followed by several others, and Charles took one look at her face and then disappeared into the back room, to emerge several minutes later with a cup of tea for her.

'Drink your tea,' he said. 'I can keep an eye on the customers.'

He did more than keep an eye she noticed, as she drank her tea and answered a question from an elderly lady about the benefit of one brand of walking pole over another, and very soon Charles was accompanying a browser to the till and laying several items down on the counter.

'Shall you ring this through, while I help someone else?' he suggested, and Elspeth started packing up the gentleman's purchases.

When trade didn't slacken, Charles offered to stay until it did, then somehow he ended up staying, and she was mighty pleased he did. And not solely because of the help either, though that was welcome too.

Throughout the remainder of the day, she kept half an ear and half an eye on him – mostly to make sure he wasn't getting into difficulties, but also to ensure he was giving the right advice. Once or twice he referred to her expert knowledge, especially when a couple of lads wanted to know about the less-well-known routes up Teide.

She noticed that he was good with customers, friendly, but not overly so, that he didn't become flustered, and was happy to ask for help.

At one point, he even accompanied three middle-aged men into the bike room and advised them on the best machines to hire. Once he'd secured a sale, he handed the admin over to her.

To say she was impressed was an understatement.

To say she wasn't grateful for his help wouldn't be right, but neither did her appreciation for it alleviate her guilt that he hadn't gone out on the bike ride he'd planned.

To say she didn't enjoy working alongside him would be an outright lie.

Every so often she found herself looking at him – although she tried telling herself it was only because she needed to ensure he was OK. And now and again, their eyes would meet and he'd smile at her. It made her feel warm and safe to have him there.

She told herself it was because the shop was too busy for her to have kept an eye on all the customers if she had been on her own.

She told herself a great deal of things, and she wasn't sure she believed any of them.

He even stayed to help her cash up at the end of the day and double-check that the safe was securely locked. She'd have to wait until the bank was open to take the day's takings in, so she was glad to have Charles by her side when she punched in the code to set the alarm on the premises and locked up for the final time that day.

Boy, was she tired, and yet again she had to ask herself whether she was getting too old for all this. On the other hand, though, she felt exhilarated that the business had done so well today. And she'd thoroughly enjoyed working side-by-side with Charles. How many more unexplored facets were there to this man? Not only was he good-looking, he was fun to be with, considerate, polite, quietly confident, well spoken and intelligent, and now she could also throw being a good salesperson into the mix. Oh, and he could cook and was house trained. He'd make some lucky woman a wonderful husband.

She stopped so suddenly that Charles continued to take a few more steps across the square on the way back to the villa before he realised she was no longer by his side.

'What's wrong?' he asked, a little frown dissecting his brow. 'Have you forgotten something?'

'No… it's… never mind. It's nothing.' How could she tell him that the thought of him having a wife had just sent a sharp dagger into her chest?

Biting her lip, Elspeth walked on. This was becoming ridiculous and rather worrying. She hated to admit it, but in all honesty, she had stronger feelings for this man than was wise.

Elspeth gave herself a good talking to. Her life was fine as it was. She didn't need the complication of becoming emotionally attached to a man who would be gone from her life by this time next week, especially one she had only known for such a short period of time.

And emotionally attached was precisely what was happening. There was no point in denying it. No matter how much she didn't want it to happen, no matter how guilty it made her feel, she was growing to like Charles far more than was sensible. She had a horrid suspicion that 'like' wasn't a strong enough word to describe what she was feeling.

To her relief Charles didn't press her about what was wrong, although it must have been obvious that something was on her mind. Instead, he said, 'Shall we go out to dinner this evening?'

Elspeth was tired, her feet hurt, and her back ached, and the thought of not having to cook was wonderful. 'That sounds good,' she replied. 'I've been told there's a lovely little place at the far end of town. My treat,' she added, not wanting him to feel he had to pay.

'Oh no. I suggested it, so I pay.'

Elspeth came to a halt outside her front door and folded her arms. 'I'm not going then.'

'Fine. I'll cook us something tasty, instead.'

She should have guessed he'd say that. 'Dutch?' she offered.

'Will it make you feel better?'

She nodded.

'You look cute when you're being stubborn,' he said, then his eyes widened and a patch of colour appeared on his cheeks. 'I'm sorry, I didn't mean to say that.' When she didn't reply, and just raised her eyebrows, he added, 'It's true, all the same. You do look cute. Your bottom lip sticks out. I bet Rai's does too, when he doesn't get his own way.'

She jabbed the key in the lock, mentally shaking her head. How did he know just the right thing to say to diffuse the situation?

Her stomach did a strange little flip; she'd never been called cute in her life. It made her feel fuzzy inside and a little bit lightheaded, as if she'd drunk too much wine. It wasn't unpleasant, just a little odd and unexpected.

Elspeth continued to feel strange during dinner, which was eaten at a little diner-cum-restaurant on the edge of the town frequented by locals and tourists alike. They'd had to wait a while for a table to become free, but despite her tiredness she didn't mind. It was lively and noisy, filled with families mostly, and was somewhere Elspeth would never have dreamt of eating at when she was with Ray (too noisy) or alone (no other solitary diners). But with Charles it was a perfect antidote to a busy day and it saved her having to be alone with him.

'You do realise you've been working today?' she asked him. 'You weren't relaxing by a pool.'

'I never relax by a pool. I told you, that's not my thing.'

'You were planning on going for a ride, not slaving away hiring bikes out to strangers.'

'I did do OK, didn't I?' he said, concern in his hazel eyes.

'You did brilliantly. I don't know how I'd have managed without you.'

'I can help again tomorrow, if you like?'

'I wouldn't dream of it! You're on holiday – go play on your bike.'

'I wasn't planning on doing anything too strenuous tomorrow, not with a hike up Teide to look forward to later.'

Oh, yes! Elspeth hadn't forgotten exactly, but with the worry of the last few days, she'd pushed their proposed hike to the back of her mind. She wasn't going to find it easy doing a full day's work, then walking uphill for several hours. But she'd offered and he'd accepted, and she didn't like to go back on her word.

Charles must have been thinking the same thing, because he said, 'Let me help in the shop. Two pairs of hands are better than one. I'm going to pick the hire car up in the morning – I've got it until Wednesday, so if there's anywhere you want to go, let me know – but I'll be free for the rest of the day.'

'Definitely not. Besides, if Stefan doesn't return for a while, I'm going to have to get used to running the place on my own.' She gave him a level stare. 'You're leaving in a week, remember?'

His voice was quiet as he said, 'I remember.'

They ate in silence for a while, the laughter and chatter of the other customers swirling around them, and Elspeth felt the beginning of a headache developing.

All at once, there was too much going on. Her life had gone from predictable, ordered, and serene, to unpredictable, chaotic and, well, turbulent. Some of it wasn't of her own doing (the situation with Stefan and his dad, for instance), but most of the blame for the upheaval she was experiencing, which, if she was honest, was more emotional than physical, was all down to her.

While they waited for their coffees and liqueurs, they chatted idly about nothing in particular, and Elspeth let her imagination roam: what if she had let Charles move into the hotel like he was supposed to? She'd still have the shop to run, and she might still be walking up Teide with him tomorrow evening, but would she be feeling calmer and more in control?

Or would she be feeling lost and lonely?

Either way, she was fairly certain her spiritual connection with Ray would be just as severed regardless.

She missed her husband — of course she did; she always would — but if Charles had moved out of the villa when he was supposed to, she realised she would have missed him a great deal, too.

A very great deal, indeed.

And she didn't know how she was supposed to deal with that knowledge, or how she was going to deal with his fast-approaching departure from her life.

Chapter 20

'Have you packed—?' Elspeth began, but Charles held up a hand.

'Yes.'

'You don't know what I was about to say.'

'Water, bananas, cereal bars, hat and scarf – thanks for the lend, by the way.'

Elspeth giggled. Winter gear wasn't something she dragged out of her cupboard very often, but it would get cold at night on the volcano, and she wanted to ensure neither of them became chilled. Charles had looked very fetching in her pink hat and matching scarf. He'd even done a twirl before he'd shoved the offending items into the bottom of his rucksack.

'What about—?' she continued.

'We don't need sleeping bags, I checked. They provide quilts, and the rooms are heated.'

'I'd still prefer to take them,' she said.

Charles gave her a wry grin. 'It'll be more to carry.'

'Don't care. I'd hate to get up there and find they had run out. Anyway, I bet they don't wash the quilts all that often.' She shuddered and he laughed.

'Probably not. But if yours gets too heavy for you though, just say.'

'I'll be fine.' She crossed her fingers, hoping it was true. 'I've got some of those dehydrated meals from the shop,' she said, moving on to the important subject of provisions. 'Two beef stroganoffs and two breakfasts.'

'Grand. That should keep us going.'

Elspeth took another look inside the rucksacks. She usually kept a first aid kit in hers, plus sunscreen, and she doubled checked both items were there.

'Are you ready?' Charles asked, when she tied the bag back up and clipped in the straps.

'As ready as I'll ever be.'

'You don't have to do this, you know.'

'I know, I want to.'

'I'll put these in the car while you lock up.'

Elspeth ran through her mental checklist one more time, conscious of the need to leave shortly. It grew dark around 8 p.m. and it would take them approximately four hours to walk from the tiny car park area up to the Refuge. Elspeth had shut the shop and had not reopened it after lunch. She told herself that the excellent takings yesterday would more than make up for a couple of lost sales this afternoon. It was already two o'clock though, and the drive to the start of the hike would take them a good half an hour.

'Walking poles!' she exclaimed out loud, hurrying to fetch them from the cupboard in the hall where everything she didn't know where else to put, tended to live. There was still an old pair of Ray's in there somewhere that Charles could borrow. She tended not to use poles when out hiking, but the trek to the refuge was incredibly steep, and although they'd be useful on the way up, they'd be invaluable on the way down. It was a well-known fact that most accidents on mountains tended to occur on the descent, and she didn't want to take any risks.

Finally ready, Elspeth locked the door to the villa, and, after shoving the poles in the boot, slid into the passenger seat next to Charles.

Then they were off, Charles driving cautiously at first, as he negotiated the road down to Tamaimo, from where they would branch off left onto the main route which would lead them up into the caldera.

She'd forgotten just how beautiful it was up here, Elspeth thought, as they left the tall trees behind and entered a lunar landscape of bare rocks and jagged, rugged mountains. It was the colours she found particularly captivating – the matt black of the more recent lava flows interspersed with brown, ochre and orange rock. This is what the Earth must have looked like once upon a time, and it was so prehistoric and raw that Elspeth felt rather insignificant.

Neither of them said much as they travelled further into the caldera which, she remembered Ray telling her when they first visited the island (he used to like to read up on the places they went to in advance – that was part of his enjoyment in any holiday), was the blasted remains of an ancient volcano, much larger than the one they were about to attempt to walk up. And she really did mean 'attempt', because getting to the top wasn't guaranteed; no matter how fit and active you were, you never knew how your body would react to altitude, and Teide was seriously high. Elspeth suspected that she should be OK, having been up the volcano before, but she had no idea if Charles could cope with it. At the first sign of a headache, she'd whisk him off the mountain quicker than he could blink.

Distances were deceptive up here, and as they approached the crossroads that dissected the caldera, Teide was on their left. It looked incredibly far away, and although Elspeth knew they would get much closer before they parked the car, the conical peak still rose up at some distance. And she had agreed – not just agreed, but *offered* – to spend the next four or more hours trudging up two-thirds of its height. She must be mad.

She was also quietly excited.

She hadn't had so much fun, or challenged herself in this manner, for at least a decade.

If she weren't careful, she'd start to feel like a teenager again.

With one final check of their equipment after they pulled up into what was little more than a widening of the road, they left the car and began to walk.

Thankfully, Teide broke them in slowly, allowing them to flex their muscles and get their mountain legs. The first part of the ascent was gradual enough for an off-road vehicle to traverse, although it was incredibly rocky and rough underfoot.

After almost slipping on some loose scree, Charles bent down and picked up one of the small rocks about the size of a pebble, and he turned to her in surprise. 'It's so light,' he exclaimed, tossing it in one hand.

'Pumice,' she explained, 'just like your grandma probably had in her bathroom to exfoliate her feet and elbows.'

'Really?' He stared at the rock in amazement before putting it back down on the ground.

She'd half expected him to shove it in his rucksack as a memento, but she was pleased he didn't. 'Leave nothing but your footprints, take nothing but your memories', was a mantra that Ray had drilled into her, and she was glad that Charles appeared to think the same way.

She noticed this consideration for the environment again when they reached the end of the sloping track and stopped for a drink of hot tea and a banana, as she saw Charles carefully wrap his banana peel in a tissue before popping it away in his bag, and she was comforted to realise they held the same values.

As they continued their walk, Elspeth's gaze kept sneaking to Charles's face. She tried to convince herself it was because she wanted to see his reaction to the scenery unfolding all around them, and to check he was bearing up OK, but in reality, she had to admit it was because she couldn't stop looking at him. The more time she spent in his company, the more he fascinated her, and the more she was forced to admit she had feelings for him.

Having finally made her peace with Ray by acknowledging that her husband wouldn't want her to spend the rest of her life pining for him, it was a bitter pill to realise that the only person she would consider letting into her life, was someone who wouldn't be around for long. Less than a week, to be exact. How ironic, and how sad, she thought as she walked.

'What are those?' Charles broke into her thoughts, and she came to a halt, panting slightly. The gradient was increasing (although it wasn't as bad as it would get later on) and she was feeling the pull of gravity.

'They're Teide Eggs,' she replied, then giggled at his expression.

'They're what now?'

She stared at the enormous round balls of black rock littering the landscape, some of them twice as tall as she was, and wracked her brains. Ah yes... 'They're accretion balls. Did you used to build snowmen when you were a child by starting off with a snowball and rolling it across the ground to make it grow bigger?'

She giggled again – Charles was looking at her as if she'd lost her mind, with his mouth open and his head on one side, as he waited for her to explain.

'These huge lumps of rock were formed in the same way, except they're made initially from a small piece of lava, not snow, which, as it rolls, gathers more lava that solidifies around it, and it eventually grows bigger and bigger.'

'Wow.' He walked up to the nearest one and ran his hand across its rough, dusty surface. 'You wouldn't want to get in the way of one of these rolling down the mountain, would you? But there is one thing that's puzzling me.'

'Oh?'

'Who was doing the rolling?'

It took her a second to realise he was pulling her leg, and she nudged him playfully with her elbow. 'Now you're just being silly.'

'I can be serious if you want me to be,' he said, and she was abruptly aware of how close he was; she could smell his aftershave and his eyes were staring into hers with an intensity she'd not seen in them before.

Feeling hot all of a sudden, she turned away to stare over the balls of rock and out at the caldera. 'It's like the Moon,' she said, purely for something to say, even though they'd had the same discussion more than once before now.

Charles nodded, the beginnings of a smile lifting the corners of his mouth, and she wondered what he was thinking. Had she imagined the surge of feeling between them? Had it been solely on her side? Had he not felt anything at all?

She cleared her throat nervously. 'There's an information board a bit further up – it should tell you more about the Eggs.'

They carried on walking, only stopping for Charles to have a quick read about the accretion balls. Soon the relatively wide and well-trodden track petered out.

The pair of them came to a halt and tipped their heads back.

Towering above them was the cone of the huge volcano. From where they were standing, so close to its base, it was impossible to see the top, and the pathway was so steep it was dizzying.

'I take it we are going up there,' Charles said, squinting at the narrow track, rising almost vertically above them in a series of switchbacks. He turned to look at her. 'Good grief.'

'We can turn back now, if you like. We can either go down the way we came or follow that path over there. It's steeper than the one we've just walked up, but it's also a more direct route off the mountain.'

When he didn't respond, she glanced at him.

His eyes were shining, his lips were slightly parted, and he appeared to be enraptured, as he stared at the impossibly high and long climb up the face of Mount Teide.

Lordy, but she wished he'd look at her like that—

What was she thinking! Of course, she didn't want him to look at her with such awe, and respect, and desire – because that was what his expression was saying. And if she didn't think she was being fanciful, she'd say he had fallen head over heels in love with the dirty great lump of rock.

'We'll go up,' he murmured softly, then seemed to shake himself. 'If that's OK with you? I mean, are you feeling all right?'

'I'm fine.' Her reply was brisk. 'Shall we get going?'

There wasn't a great deal of talking from then on, and Elspeth wasn't sure the lack of conversation from her end was entirely due to the fact that the ascent was possibly only slightly short of rock-climbing. It was hard on the thigh and bum muscles, and even harder on the lungs and heart. It didn't help that the air carried far less oxygen at this altitude than at ground level, and the pair of them were soon puffing and panting.

Neither of them stopped for a rest though; for Elspeth the reason was simple – rest meant catching one's breath, which would lead to talking. It might also mean standing side by side and, horror of horrors, seeing Charles's face, and that might lead to inappropriate thoughts again. At the moment she was leading the way on the narrow track, and Charles was bringing up the rear, which suited her fine.

Talking of rears, she was aware that Charles had an eye-level view of hers, but strangely enough Elspeth didn't feel self-conscious about having her backside bobbing about only a couple of feet from his face. Hiking trousers were hardly the most becoming clothes one could wear, and she was convinced that he didn't regard her in that light anyway, despite what was undoubtedly crossed wires on her part. Because, for a moment back there, she'd had a feeling he was—

'It's no good, I'm going to have to stop for a moment,' Charles gasped, and Elspeth was jolted out of her speculations.

'Are you feeling OK? Headache? Nausea? Dizziness?' The symptoms of altitude sickness flashed through her mind, and her stomach knotted with worry.

'No, nothing like that,' Charles panted, and he reached around to work his water bottle free from a side pocket on his rucksack and took a swig.

Relief flooded her tired body, and Elspeth felt her fingers tingle as the sudden rush of adrenalin dissipated.

'Knackered,' he said, taking deep breaths of the thin air. 'It's a bit steep, isn't it?'

As one, they turned around to face the direction they'd come, and only then was it obvious just how high they'd climbed in such a short distance.

'It is a bit,' she agreed, smiling inwardly at his typically British tendency to underplay things. 'But look how far you can see.' In front of them, lay a ridge of mountains – the sun's rays bathed them in shades of orange and russet, and they were punctuated by dark shadows. Over the rim of the ancient caldera landscape, the sea blended into the blue of the sky. 'That smudge on the horizon is Gran Canaria. It has been said that on a really clear day, you can see the coast of West Africa.'

There was silence for a while, as they caught their breath, until, as Elspeth made a move to continue their journey, Charles spoke up.

'Thank you for bringing me up here.'

'Do I have to remind you, that you were all set to do this on your own?' she pointed out.

'But it is definitely more fun with someone to share it with.'

'You could have joined a walking group.'

'I'd much prefer to be here with you than with a bunch of strangers.'

'I know what you mean.'

Charles turned to face her. 'Do you?' he asked, softly.

She swallowed, her mouth suddenly felt dry. She nodded, not entirely certain what she was agreeing with him about.

'Good,' he said.

Then he leant towards her and kissed her, very gently and very swiftly on the cheek.

She froze.

He smiled, his eyes brimming with an emotion she couldn't read, then the moment was gone as his attention was claimed by the extraordinary view once more, and she was left wondering if she'd imagined the whole thing.

If it hadn't been for the lingering feel of his warm lips on her skin, and the way her insides fizzed with the surprise of his touch, she would have done.

Conscious that she was in danger of overreacting and was reading too much into what had only been a friendly peck on the cheek, she said as lightly as she could muster, 'We need to get going. There's still a good hour or more until we reach the Refuge, and we don't want to be caught out here in the dark.'

The sun was now behind Teide, dipping into the west, and the vast coned shadow of the mountain crept along the ground, swallowing the jewelled colours of the volcanic rock as the late afternoon blended into early evening. Elspeth was conscious of the encroaching night and she didn't want to risk having to navigate this almost sheer and ankle-turning track in twilight.

With renewed vigour (which didn't last very long) they stomped on, each step taking them closer to the Refuge. Elspeth wasn't sure how Charles was feeling, but she was beginning to struggle. It wasn't the distance – it was less than 7km from where they'd parked the car to the hut — it was the climb itself. This second half of the hike had been a lift-one's-foot-as-if-one-were-climbing-a-stair-only-to-plonk-it-back-down-again-while-hauling-one's-body-up-a-few-inches-ready-for-the-next-step kind of movement. It was hard work, and after the week she'd had, Elspeth could have done without it.

Although, beneath the exertion and the discomfort, she found she was enjoying herself. It was good to push the boundaries now and again, and if someone had suggested to her a couple of weeks ago that she should hike up the volcano and spend the night on its slopes in a cabin along with fifty or so other people, only one of whom she knew, she'd have scoffed. Yet, here she was, and she was feeling rather pleased with herself. Her fitness level, while not as good as it had once been, was enough to get her up the slope, and the whole event had taken her out of her comfort zone.

In fact, the whole of the past week had been out of her comfort zone, what with having a guest to stay, entertaining that guest, discovering she had feelings for that guest, and that was without taking the issue of Stefan and his dad into consideration as well.

And, if she was honest, she'd felt more alive these past seven days than she'd felt for a good long while. As she climbed, she realised that what she needed to decide was whether it was Charles who was responsible for how she felt now, or whether it was her feelings for him that had woken her up from the inside out.

Her musings took her attention away from her physical discomfort long enough to make good progress to the Refuge, and Elspeth was pleased and surprised when they came around a bend in the path to see the small stone building ahead of them.

Charles let out a sigh. 'Please tell me that's it,' he begged.

'It is.' Elspeth was filled with a burst of energy at the thought of hot tea and the beef stroganoff – not to mention being able to sit down – and she forged ahead, clambering up the track until she reached the small terrace arranged with stone seats and wooden benches which lay in front of the building.

'Yes!' she fist-pumped the air, grinning broadly.

Charles heaved himself on the terrace behind her, headed straight for the nearest bench and dropped wearily down onto it. 'I thought I was fitter than that,' he said with a grimace. 'I've got a way to go before I'm up to your standard. You're hardly out of breath.'

'I'm absolutely exhausted,' she admitted, 'and I most definitely am out of breath! The only thing that kept me going was bloody-mindedness. I'd got this far, and there was no way I was admitting defeat and going back down.'

Charles looked at her, and she saw the respect in his eyes. 'You are one very determined lady,' he said. 'I must confess, if you'd said an hour ago, let's call it a day, I would have raced you down the damned mountain in my haste to get back to the car.'

Elspeth slid her rucksack off her shoulders, and slumped onto the bench next to him, not caring that their knees were touching or that he was so close she could smell the aftershave he wore and the hint of male scent underneath. She leant back and studied the view.

The sky was a deep navy where it met the sea, and it gradually lightened until it was more the colour of cobalt directly overhead. A star was already shining, and she knew the sun would soon be setting to the west, as night crept upon them. In another half hour it would be completely dark, and she was grateful that they had made it to the refuge before night descended.

'I'm starving,' Charles announced, and she realised she was, too.

She would also have loved to have a shower to wash the grime, dust and sweat from her body, but there weren't any showering facilities at the hostel, so she'd have to make do with a good wash instead.

Food first, though.

'Come on, let's see what bunks are left,' she said, getting to her feet and holding out her hand.

Charles looked at it for a second, then took it, his grip comforting and firm in hers as she hauled him upright. 'Bagsy I get the top bunk,' he chortled, dashing past her and heading for the door.

'That's not fair – you could have warned me,' she called after him, following at a more sedate pace. She couldn't manage a dash right now, even if her life depended on it.

'If I had, you might have won,' he called back, earning an amused glance from a young couple who were seated on a bench outside, their arms wrapped around each other, mugs of steaming liquid clasped in their free hands.

Charles had come to a halt just inside the door and Elspeth stood next to him. She'd never been inside the Refuge before, so this was as new to her as it was to him, and she looked around curiously.

A few people were sitting in what she supposed was a reception area, with vending machines that sold hot and cold drinks and chocolate bars, but before she had the chance to check out what was available, a woman approached and asked their names. She spoke to them in English, so Elspeth responded in the same language.

'Elspeth Evans and Charles Brown.'

The woman nodded and said, 'Follow, please.'

They were led into a dorm crammed with bunk beds, and the women pointed out one of them. 'This is for you.

'Light will be off at nine p.m., on at five a.m. Toilets there. Kitchen there. There is internet if you want. OK?'

'Yes, thank you. What time is sunrise?' Elspeth asked in fluent Spanish and the women gave her a bright smile.

'There is a board outside showing the temperature and the time of the sunrise,' she responded in Spanish.

Elspeth smiled her thanks and waited for the woman to leave before she slung her rucksack on the bottom bunk. 'You're welcome to the top one,' she informed Charles. 'I've done enough climbing for one day!'

They unrolled their sleeping bags, and Elspeth was glad she'd brought hers with her; the paper sheets which covered each bunk were a great idea, but God knows how many bodies had lain under the quilt on top.

'Hmm, I'm glad you made me pack this,' Charles said, straightening his sleeping bag out on the bunk above, and she laughed.

'I was just thinking the same thing. I suggest we get everything we need for the morning out now. We'll be up at five, and out of the door by six at the latest.'

'I must have been mad to suggest this trip,' he groaned. 'What was I thinking?'

'That you wanted to experience everything Tenerife has to offer?'

'Except the rowdy nightlife,' he clarified.

'And the theme parks?' she added.

'Oh, I don't know. I'm partial to a water slide or two, and Loro Parque sounds wonderful.' He hesitated, looking up from the inside of his rucksack, the pink hat and scarf in his hand. 'Now that I've picked up the hire car, do you fancy coming with me?'

'Down a water slide?' Elspeth raised her eyebrows.

'I meant the zoo.'

She wished she could – she hadn't been to Loro Parque in years, and she loved seeing the animals – but she had Libertad to run and it was a seven-days-a-week thing, at least until Stefan returned. The only reason she was halfway up Teide this evening was because tomorrow was Easter Sunday and most businesses were closed for the day.

'The shop,' she reminded him with a rueful smile.

'Of course. Look, if you want me to help with that…?'

'It's fine. Thank you, anyway. Please, just enjoy the rest of your holiday. Right,' she rubbed her hands together, 'let's boil the kettle and rehydrate this yummy-looking stroganoff.' She held the silver foil packet up and shook it.

Charles snorted. 'I can't wait.'

To their surprise the meal was fairly tasty, and it was perfect food for when you needed to travel light yet also have a hot meal at the end of the day. They sat in the dining area just off the kitchen to eat it, listening to the conversation of the other hikers ebbing and flowing around them. Elspeth counted seven different languages being spoken, but whenever two groups got chatting, the common language was nearly always English.

Fancying a bit of peace and quiet, she said, 'How about togging up and going outside for a bit? I've heard that the night sky is spectacular up here.'

'Good idea, although, when you say "togging up", what exactly do you mean?' All Charles had taken off so far was his down jacket. He was still wearing his hiking boots, trousers, and fleece.

'Hat and scarf?' She bit her lip to hold in the chortle that was threatening to escape.

'Really?' His expression was so pitiful that the laugh burst out of her.

'Really. At night, the temperature can drop to near freezing at this altitude. Believe me when I say it's chilly out there, and you'll feel it even more now you've stopped walking.'

'Listen to your wife, my friend,' a man sitting opposite them interrupted, in an Eastern European accent. 'It is cold. You will need your coat and a hat.'

Elspeth met Charles's eye, and she debated on correcting the hiker's assumption that they were married, but she decided against it. The explanation wasn't worth the effort, so she shrugged and let it slide, smiling at the speaker instead and saying, 'See, this gentleman agrees with me.'

When she glanced back at Charles, he was gazing at her with an intensity that made her heart constrict, and the desire in his face made the fine hairs on the back of her neck rise.

Without breaking eye contact, he said, 'I'll fetch the hat and scarf. Do you want me to bring yours, too?'

She nodded, not trusting herself to speak in case her voice came out all wrong, and she cleared her throat instead.

After a pause, he got up and she stared after him, uncertain what had just happened.

'Aw, that's so sweet,' said a woman, possibly in her mid-twenties, who was sitting on another table with a young man and another couple. Elspeth recognised her from outside when they had first arrived at the Refuge. 'I hope we're still in love that like when we're their age.' She grimaced, remembering her manners, and then added, speaking directly to Elspeth this time, 'No offence.'

'None taken,' Elspeth murmured absently.

So she hadn't imagined it; Charles *had* looked at her as though he wanted to scoop her up and carry her off.

She swallowed nervously, then bit her lip, her bottom teeth worrying at it as she tried to make sense of what was going on. When she reached for the empty foil packets to pop them into a small rubbish bag, she was shocked to see her hands trembling slightly.

Then he was back, the pink woolly hat on his head and the matching scarf wrapped around his neck. He had his jacket on, fully zipped up, and he held hers out to her, along with her own hat and scarf. Wordlessly, she took them from him and put them on, while he boiled the kettle again and filled their flasks with fresh tea.

'I thought we could have some after-dinner drinks while we enjoy the view,' he said, and she forced a smile to her lips.

Her face felt wooden and her limbs were stiff – she was relatively sure the latter wasn't entirely due to her muscles and joints seizing up from the climb. Almost scared to be alone with him (which was simply ridiculous, considering), Elspeth watched Charles begin to screw the lids on the flasks, then headed outside to wait for him.

She was perched on one of the wooden benches when he appeared carrying the tea, and she shifted across as he approached. He handed her a flask and sat down. She was relieved to see he was more interested in the night than in her, as he gazed skywards.

With a dry mouth, Elspeth gathered her courage. 'Shall we take a short walk?'

He turned to her, brows raised. 'It's dark.'

Finally, she was able to smile. 'I know. But there's too much light coming from the hostel,' she pointed out. It was true – yellow light flooded out through the unshuttered windows. 'Light pollution is a thing.'

'I know,' he echoed. 'Are you sure?'

About what, she almost asked. Was he asking if she was OK about being alone with him? Because if he was, then she guessed he'd felt it too – whatever it was. Or was he asking if it was safe to wander away from the Refuge?

'Yes.' Her reply was firm, but she wasn't honestly sure what she was being firm about.

Carefully, they negotiated the rocks, and picked their way down the path a little, until a bend ensured the hostel was out of sight and no light from it was visible.

Charles made his way to what looked like a flattish rock and perched on its rough surface. Elspeth joined him.

'Goodness me, but it's dark!' he exclaimed. 'Thank God there are so many stars out otherwise we'd not be able to— Oh, my word. The stars! Look at them!'

Elspeth was looking, her mouth open in awe, her eyes wide. She'd never seen anything so beautiful in her life. The inky blackness above shimmered with millions of pinpricks of light, and across the middle was a band of what she originally thought were clouds, until she understood she was looking at the Milky Way in all its majesty.

There were no words to describe what they were seeing, no language to do it justice, and suddenly she was tear-jerkingly grateful to Charles and his ridiculous insistence that he hike up this mountain. Otherwise she'd never have been here to witness such beauty.

'Thank you,' she breathed, her voice little more than a sigh on the breeze.

'For what?' He was just as quiet.

'For bringing me up here,' she replied, aware that she was echoing his words to her earlier that day.

She felt, rather than heard, his chuckle. 'I think you'll find you were the one who suggested sleeping at the Refuge.'

She heard the smile in her voice as she said, 'I did, didn't I?'

'Yes, you did. I never would have thought of that, and look at what I would have missed. It's magical and breathtaking, and it makes me feel very small and insignificant.' He turned to her, his attention on her now and not on the light show overhead.

She was conscious of his gaze caressing her face, warming her cheeks, heating her heart, until she thought it might melt from the intensity.

'I've never felt like this before,' he added, so softly she had to strain to understand him.

'Small and insignificant?' She tried to lift the mood, feeling the need to lighten the almost reverential tone of it, knowing instinctively that what was said next couldn't be unsaid. Elspeth also knew deep down that he wasn't talking about nature, or time, or space. He meant something else entirely, and she didn't know if she was ready to hear it. She didn't know if she would ever be ready, and that was such a shame, but she'd been living a half-life for so long, she wasn't sure she was able to live any other way.

'Giddy, lightheaded…' he said.

And, all at once, she understood she'd misread the situation completely – what Charles was describing were the typical symptoms of altitude sickness. 'Have you got a headache?' she asked sharply, her mind whirling as she tried to think how they were going to get him off the mountainside quickly. 'Do you feel sick?'

'No headache... but heartache, maybe. And that odd feeling in my stomach are butterflies, I think.'

She couldn't see his expression – it was too dark for that – but his eyes glittered softly in the starlight, and she tried to make sense of what he'd just said. Heartache and butterflies...?

'I want to kiss you,' he said. 'May I?'

Her heart swooped and dived, and she wished he hadn't asked her. If he'd had simply done it, then the decision would have been taken out of her hands. But he was a gentleman, and he had asked, and she didn't know what she should say.

In the space of a heartbeat, she made a decision.

She leant towards him, lifted her chin slightly and closed her eyes, her pulse jumping at her throat, as she indicated her consent.

His lips were soft yet firm, and caressed her mouth with the same fluttering touch as she imagined the butterflies in his tummy must feel like. Except they were in hers, too, turning her insides to quivering anticipation and growing excitement.

There was a hunger to his kiss that left her breathless and made it hard to think.

As one, their arms came around each other, his gathering her to him and holding her in a cage of muscle, hers snaking around his neck and pulling him down to her, forcing him to deepen the kiss, until her lips parted fully and his tongue found hers.

Elspeth felt that galaxies could have formed, grown old and died as they kissed, and she lost all track of time and of herself.

She felt she was glowing like the distant stars above them: her breath was ragged, her limbs trembled and bright hot desire coursed through her veins. An emotion, one she'd thought had deserted her long ago, never to return, filled her mind and heart.

Love.

It was a tentative feeling, not fully developed or understood, but it was love all the same, and she sighed, a tiny exhalation of exhilaration, acknowledgement and fear.

Charles ended the kiss, his lips withdrawing from hers like the sun going behind a cloud, and Elspeth shivered, even though his arms were still wrapped so tightly around her waist she thought he'd never let go.

'I'm sorry... it's too much, too soon, I shouldn't have asked it of you. I—' Charles babbled and she heard the dismay in his voice.

'Shut up and kiss me again.'

'But—?'

To stop him from arguing any more, and just in case he hadn't understood what she wanted him to do, she drew his head towards her.

All she wanted right now was his lips on hers.

And that was precisely what she got.

Chapter 21

Who knew metal bunks could make so much noise? Elspeth didn't, but she'd soon found out when faced with trying to sleep beneath the squeakiest upper bunk in the world, and Charles's profuse apologies every time he so much as breathed, due to the racket it made.

Because she was lighter than him, she'd offered to go on top, blushing profusely when he'd sniggered and she'd realised what she'd said. Besides, it made no difference, and she suspected that even the weight of a mouse would have set off the infernal noise. Having little choice, she'd offered to let him sleep with her on the bottom bunk, which made him laugh even harder.

And so they had spent the night together in the same single bed.

It sounded far more romantic than it was.

Neither of them had taken a stitch of clothing off, except for their boots and their fleeces. For one, they hadn't wanted to carry any night things and it was too cold to sleep in just underwear, and for another, there were six other people in the room, two of whom snored and one who listened to music all night via a pair of tinny headphones.

At least Charles didn't snore.

He wasn't a restless sleeper either, as far as Elspeth could tell, because he'd held her all night and had hardly moved.

But she suspected he hadn't slept much at all. She certainly hadn't; instead she'd lain there replaying every delicious second of their kisses, while trying to beat her encroaching guilt back with some common-sense self-talking.

But finally, in those still, dark hours between midnight and dawn, she had let Ray in.

He'd been knocking at her thoughts since she'd made the decision to kiss Charles; it was only fair she heard what he had to say. She might have stopped speaking to him some days ago and she'd also confessed to Amanda that she couldn't feel his presence any longer, but her friend had been right when she'd said that Elspeth would always carry Ray with her in her heart – and that there was nothing wrong in doing that.

But Elspeth still felt as though she needed to seek her husband's approval, and possibly his permission, and she chose the middle of the night while she was snuggled in another man's arms to do just that. The irony wasn't lost on her, and she was sure Ray would appreciate it too – he always did have a dry sense of humour.

Elspeth felt as though she was at a crossroads – she had been kissed by someone who wasn't her husband. But if she was to consider the next step, then she had to make certain she was OK with it, that *Ray* was OK with it.

And as she contemplated the past, the present and the future in that strange and not very relaxing dorm surrounded by strangers, Elspeth realised that she had made peace with her grief quite some time ago, but it had taken Charles coming into her life to allow her to acknowledge and accept it.

She still carried sorrow with her – sorrow that Ray had been taken before she was ready (would she ever have been ready?); sorrow that she was forced to spend the rest of her life without him, and that he wouldn't have the privilege of seeing her grow old the way she had done with him – but she found that the sorrow was bearable now. She realised it was a part of her, and she would never wish herself free of it, because that would mean she'd be wishing herself free of Ray, which was something she'd never do.

However, she now came to understand that there was room in her heart for someone else, and that having Charles there wouldn't mean that Ray was pushed out. There was room enough for two.

But – and here was the big stumbling block – Charles was due to leave in five days' time.

She loved him; she could see that. It would hurt like the devil when he went, and she couldn't believe she'd fallen so hard and so fast for a man she'd only just met and hardly knew. If she'd had a crystal ball and had seen this coming, would she have said no to Amanda when her friend had asked her for that initial favour of hosting the hotel guest?

Possibly.

Then again, maybe not. Because without Charles bursting into her life and rousing her from her grief-filled torpor, then Elspeth might have carried on in the same way for years. Decades, even. Perhaps until her life ended. And what a waste that would have been. She hopefully had many years ahead of her, and she'd do well to remember that.

'You're deep in thought,' Charles suddenly observed in a whisper.

'How can you tell? It's dark.' There was a faint light seeping in from under the door, but it wasn't enough to read a face by.

'I realise it's a presumptuous thing to say given that we've only known each other for a short time, but I know you,' he said and those words were enough for that warm fuzzy feeling to flood through her.

'Are you OK?' he asked. He didn't ask her what she'd been thinking about, and neither did he pry or seem to want to delve into the depths of her innermost secrets. This show of sensitivity meant she fell in love with him a little bit more.

'I am now,' she told him.

She felt his smile in the darkness, then she saw it for real, as the electric lights came on in the room.

Blinking frantically and hoping her eyeballs would eventually recover, Elspeth sat up. The other occupants were stirring too, so she made a mad dash for the bathroom before a queue formed, to splash water on her face and brush her teeth.

She returned to the dorm to find Charles rolling up their sleeping bags. He'd got their dehydrated breakfast pouches out and had laid them on the bed, along with their provisions for the day, which consisted of flapjacks, cereal bars, and a few pieces of fruit.

'We need some more water, so I'll get us a couple of bottles out of the vending machine,' he said.

'While you do that and wash your face, I'll make us some tea, and refill the flasks,' she suggested.

They ate breakfast in relative silence, Elspeth forcing her food down into a stomach that considered it far too early in the day to receive it. Most of the other hikers looked as though they were struggling too, but everyone knew they'd need the calories for the push to the summit, which was roughly a two-hour ascent. Then there was the descent to contend with, which wouldn't be as hard on the heart or the thighs as going up, but would take its toll on the ankles and knees. Thankfully, it wouldn't take as long going down the mountain, but they would still need to take care as they negotiated the steep slope.

'Ready?' Charles asked. It was only 5.35 a.m., but they were the oldest occupants in the Refuge last night, and the odds were that they'd probably be the slowest on the remainder of the hike to the edge of the crater. It was either get a head start, or wait until everyone else had set off, otherwise they'd end up walking with some of the others and Elspeth much preferred being alone on her expeditions. Except for having Charles with her, of course – she'd become very used to having him by her side.

Too used to it, perhaps, considering the circumstances.

Oh well, she reasoned, it was too late now. She'd jumped in with both feet, so there wasn't much she could do about either her feelings or Charles's imminent departure. She'd just have to get through it as best she could, and if there was one thing that Ray's demise had taught her, it was that all things pass. Eventually.

She also decided that she would be better off for knowing and loving Charles than not giving it a chance at all, and she would not permit herself to regret a single second of the fortnight she'd have with him.

With that in mind, she set off on their final assault on the mountain determined to glean every ounce of enjoyment out of today. Never mind that it was darned cold, still dark and she was shattered. And, like Charles, she was wearing a head torch over the top of her woolly hat and its tight band was giving her a headache.

It felt like they'd been trudging uphill for hours, but it was probably no more than forty-five minutes or so, when the path they were following ended as a new path bisected it.

'I think we go left here,' Elspeth said. 'It should take us around the side of the cone to the cable car station.'

'There's a cable car?' Charles exclaimed, slapping a hand to his forehead and nearly hitting himself in the face with one of his poles. 'Why didn't you say so? If I'd had known, I wouldn't have climbed this awful mountain.'

Elspeth stared at him in confusion, the light from her head torch illuminating his face and giving him a rather spooky glow. 'You mean, you didn't know?' How was it possible that he didn't know, and she was sure she'd mentioned it too...

He shook his head, but she could see the corners of his mouth twitching as he tried not to smile.

Of course he knew; he was simply enjoying teasing her.

'You had me going there. For a second, I thought you'd regretted walking up,' she said.

'Never.' His expression turned serious and he moved closer. 'Last night was one of the loveliest nights of my life.'

'Despite the snoring, the squeaky bunk and the complete lack of sleep?'

'Despite all those things – because I was with you.'

Elspeth blushed, feeling the warmth spread across her cheeks, and she was glad the torchlight was poor, because she had a suspicion that she resembled a beetroot.

'I'm not just saying that. I mean it,' he said.

'I thought it was incredibly wonderful, too.'

'Come on, we don't want to miss the sunrise at the top, do we? If you're lucky, I might even kiss you again when we get there.'

'You're rather full of yourself, aren't you?' she said primly. 'I might not want to be kissed.'

'If you don't want me to, then I shan't,' he replied.

Elspeth put her hands on her hips. 'Mr Brown, if you don't kiss me, I'll never speak to you again.' She was flirting, properly flirting, and it felt so right that she let out a laugh.

Charles stopped it with a quick kiss that left her gasping, before propelling her along the path, chuckling to himself.

For a while, the going was easy, as they trudged around the side of the cone rather than going straight up it, but all that changed when they joined the path at the cable car station which led to the crater's rim.

Once again, they found they had to save their breath for the climb, to concentrate on putting one foot in front of the other and to heave themselves up the incline.

Eventually, though, they arrived at the top, and Elspeth paused to draw deep lungfuls of thin air into her chest, her heart thumping, her legs feeling like jelly. After a few minutes, they took the final steps to the crater's rim and picked a spot to sit down, slightly away from the edge and from the other people who'd also made it to the top to watch the sunrise.

The sky was already growing lighter in the east, silver at the horizon and fading to turquoise, then navy towards the west, where night still reigned. One by one the stars faded, and the flat silver light turned to a golden glow which grew brighter as the sun began to show above the arc of the earth.

Elspeth leant into Charles and he pulled her close, slinging an arm around her shoulders and she felt the brush of his lips on her temple. They stayed that way, watching night bloom into day, as the rising sun chased the darkness away, until finally another day was born.

She let out a slow sigh of sheer bliss, her heart filled with the wonder of it all, her soul uplifted and brimming with joy.

'This is what life is all about,' she murmured. 'Moments like these.'

'I prefer moments like these instead,' Charles said, his fingers caressing her chin and lifting her head.

Then he kissed her again, and she knew he was right.

Chapter 22

Tired didn't begin to describe how Elspeth felt when she forced her eyes open the following morning. Not only was she still exhausted, but after the trek back down the mountain yesterday she knew she'd overexerted herself, as her joints and muscles began to seize up on the car journey home.

How Charles had managed to drive back, she had no idea. If it had been left to her, she'd have suggested they curled up on the backseat for the next couple of days at least, and wait for the misery to subside.

He'd been wonderful though, making his way back to Santiago del Teide with minimal input from her (which was good, because she didn't think she was capable of speech at that point), and had unpacked the car while she'd tried to unpack herself from the front passenger seat where she'd become welded into one position, as her limbs had refused to move properly any more.

Charles had then helped her inside (much to her annoyance, considering she was younger than him, and given that she'd also assumed she was the fitter of the two), had run her a hot bath to ease her aches and pains, and had then sorted out lunch for them both.

It was no surprise that the pair of them had enjoyed a nap on the sofa afterwards, each leaning on the other. The evening consisted of a takeaway and a bottle of wine in the courtyard, while reliving the events of yesterday. Conversation soon gave way to kissing, until eventually Elspeth couldn't keep her eyes open, and took herself off to bed, conscious that she had work in the morning.

–

Work! With a groan, Elspeth struggled into an upright position, her muscles protesting, and looked at the clock.

Damn it! She'd slept late. It was already gone ten o'clock, but even without checking the time she could have guessed something wasn't right because the room was far too light and there were more sounds filtering through her bedroom window than was usual for seven in the morning. Cross with herself for sleeping in, she heaved her very reluctant body out of bed (more of a calculated roll off the mattress, if she was honest) and staggered jerkily into the bathroom, where she sat wearily on the loo, trying to summon the energy to have a shower.

However, despite being a bit of a wreck physically, emotionally speaking she felt like singing at the top of her voice. Not literally, of course, because she didn't want to wake Charles. He must have been as shattered as she'd been last night, but he'd been an absolute godsend in making sure she ate, and in clearing up the remains of their curry and rice.

If she could persuade her knees to bear her weight once more, she'd have a quick shower, get dressed and go downstairs to make him a pot of tea before she left. It was the least she could do after he'd taken such good care of her yesterday; and then she must get to the shop and open up. She would have already missed any trade from people waiting for the earlier Masca bus and who wanted to have a quick browse to pass the time.

First though, she needed tea, being unable to function properly without the first cuppa of the day, so she forced herself to have a shower, trying to be as quiet as possible so as not to wake Charles. She then dragged some clean trousers up her stiff legs, pulled on a North Face T-shirt, shoved her feet into her work boots and crept slowly and painfully down the stairs. To her dismay, she found she had to step down each one sideways, because her ankles didn't want to co-operate by bending when they should, and she winced down every stair until she reached the hall and limped into the kitchen.

There was a lingering smell of coffee in the air, along with Charles's by-now-familiar aftershave. The dining table was laid for breakfast with one place setting, and a note was propped against the kettle, where she couldn't fail to miss it.

Frowning slightly, she picked it up and squinted at it, and her frown deepened as she read it.

He'd only gone and opened the shop for her!

What a lovely thing to do. It looked like she hadn't been able to hide her tiredness from him after all, and he'd given her a few precious extra hours in bed.

Charles had laid out fresh bread, jam and hardboiled eggs (when had he found the time to cook those, and what time had he got up?), but how on earth was she supposed to enjoy her breakfast when he was alone in the shop that was her responsibility? He could be in a right pickle and she wouldn't know a thing about it.

Then her attention was drawn to her mobile phone sitting on the countertop where she'd dumped it last night, and she snatched it up to check for missed calls or messages from him. There was a text from Gideon, but nothing from Charles, and she exhaled slowly. No doubt he'd have called if he had an issue. She was panicking over nothing; he was sensible and responsible, and he had decent enough product knowledge to get by.

But what about the alarm system?

Stop it, she told herself. If he'd had trouble with it, he would have phoned or come back to the villa and woken her. He'd been standing right next to her when she'd set it, so he must have seen the number and he must have inputted it correctly this morning.

He was fine.

She'd do as he'd instructed and have a good breakfast and a cup of tea, then she'd go and join him.

So that's what she did. Forcing herself not to dash over there to check everything was all right, she made a cup of tea, sliced some of the incredibly fresh bread (had he gone out to fetch it this morning?) and popped it into the toaster, then peeled the hardboiled eggs he'd cooked for her, while she was waiting.

With breakfast finished and washed up, Elspeth strolled across the square, resisting the urge to hurry. She even made herself stand back for a few minutes while she peered through the shop window. If there was an obvious crisis, she couldn't think of what it could be off the top of her head, but she still wanted to be prepared for it before she walked through the door.

There didn't appear to be a crisis. Charles was chatting to a young couple, one of whom was trying on a pair of Salomon walking sandals, and keeping his eye on the other customers in the shop at the same time.

He seemed to be fine on his own.

If she was honest, he was more than fine, so she put a bright smile on her face as she sauntered through the open door and gave him a wave. Not stopping to ask whether he was OK, she made her way out to the back instead where she stowed her bag and put the kettle on. No doubt he'd like a brew, and the act of making a cuppa gave her time to collect her thoughts.

He'd rung up the sandal sale by the time she emerged with two cups of tea, and was animatedly discussing the benefits of a CamelBak for carrying water on long runs or bike rides with a man who looked as though he did a lot of running.

When he'd finished dealing with that customer, she handed Charles his cup and he smiled at her gratefully.

'Thanks, I need this,' he said.

'It's you who needs to be thanked! What time did you get up?'

'Six-thirty. Old habits die hard. I've always found it difficult to stay in bed.'

'You must be worn out. Why don't you get off home?'

'I'm fine, actually, a little achy, but that's to be expected after yesterday. How did you sleep?'

'Brilliantly. I haven't slept so well in yonks.' As she realised the truth of it, the thought flitted across her mind that the arduous hike and the lack of sleep the night before it might not be the only reason for her deep sleep last night and newfound spark this morning. She might still feel tired and she was definitely sore, but those were only physical symptoms. Mentally and emotionally, she felt invigorated, yet serene at the same time. It was quite an odd feeling, but if she was forced to describe it she would have to say it felt like the clean air that follows in the wake of a powerful storm. Or as though she'd been let out of a cage and was able to stand tall and breathe deeply again.

She knew what, or rather *who*, was responsible, and he was standing in front of her with a soft smile on his lips and an even softer expression in his eyes.

Unable to resist, she stepped closer and kissed him.

'Erm, sorry to... erm... interrupt. Do you speak English? May I try this on?'

Elspeth and Charles sprang apart and Charles cleared his throat. 'Sorry about that,' he said, not sounding sorry in the slightest.

The man in front of them looked quite put out as he held up a waterproof jacket. Elspeth thought crossly that he could have slipped it on and taken a look at himself in the full-length mirror on the opposite wall, without the need to make a song and dance about it. It wasn't as though he needed to use the changing rooms, was it? Then she felt ashamed of herself for putting her own enjoyment (and it had been very enjoyable, indeed) before the needs of the shop's customers.

Charles hurried over to help the man – who didn't need any help at all – and shot her a big grin and a wink.

Elspeth pursed her lips to keep a giggle in, and turned away as the shop began to fill up.

By the time she managed to find a moment to speak to Charles it was lunchtime, and she was flicking the sign on the shop from 'open' to 'closed'.

'Is it always this busy?' Charles wanted to know, stowing several pairs of boots back in their respective boxes after a young lady's marathon trying-on session.

'Not usually quite like this, but not far off. The shop does have its quieter moments, though. Why don't you get off, and have some fun this afternoon?'

'I'm OK. I'm quite enjoying myself.'

'You are?' She squinted at him.

'Surprisingly enough, yes. It's odd isn't it – I like selling people stuff and I don't mind chatting to them, but if I met those same people in a pub and they wanted to have a natter, I'd probably not be too happy.'

'Snap! That's exactly how I feel about this job. I keep telling Amanda that I don't need to go to dinner parties – I get all the social interaction I need in work.'

'Do you know what, I think I might look for a job similar to this when I get back home. I've said before that I've got to keep myself busy, keep the old brain cells ticking over, and something like this would be ideal.'

Elspeth tried not to let her deflation at the mention of his return to the UK show. 'I can't see you selling handbags or cosmetics, though,' she said.

He shuddered. 'Neither can I! It would have to be stuff I know a bit about. Maybe DIY…?'

'Are you good at it?'

'I try, but I'm better with mechanical things like bikes, than with drills.'

'Maybe you could get a job in Halfords? They might take on pensioners.'

'Stop it! I'm still getting used to the idea of being old enough to be one.'

Elspeth didn't think of him as a pensioner either. 'Do you fancy a bite to eat?' she suggested as her tummy rumbled.

'I'm famished. What did you have in mind?'

'Tapas?'

'Splendid! Are we eating out or buying something and cooking it ourselves back at the villa?'

'Let's have lunch out. I think we deserve a treat after this morning, don't you? And once we've eaten, you should go and enjoy the rest of the day. Please,' she begged, 'otherwise I'm going to feel very guilty.'

His gaze met hers. 'What do you suggest?'

'Not a walk,' she said, quickly, 'although a short one might help loosen your joints and muscles. How about a bike ride?'

He shook his head.

'A dip in the pool at Hotel Aventuras? Amanda and Toni won't mind, I'm sure.'

'Will you be joining me?'

'I wish I could, but I have to stay here.'

'Then I'll stay here with you.'

'No, I insist. Go and enjoy yourself.'

'I don't think it will be possible to enjoy myself, if you aren't with me.'

'Oh, gosh,' Elspeth froze, her mind a tumble of conflicting emotions. She was thrilled he wanted to spend time with her, but she was worried he was going to spoil what was left of his holiday. Her heart leapt at the implication that he had feelings for her, but her tummy twisted into knots because this was moving too far and too fast, and she was in grave danger of having her newly healed heart broken again.

She suddenly realised she didn't care, at the exact same time she understood that she wanted him, no matter what. Life was too short and getting shorter with each second that passed. If she didn't take a chance of happiness, no matter how short or fleeting it would turn out to be, she'd forever regret it. And there was no knowing when she'd feel this way about another man again. Maybe never, because she was in deeper than she'd thought was possible in such a short space of time.

'Elspeth, I…' Charles trailed off.

She put a hand on his arm and rubbed gently, his skin warm and smooth. The touch electrified her, sending shocks right through her body, and she inhaled sharply. 'Shall we skip lunch?' she murmured.

'Are you saying what I think you're saying?'

She nodded. 'I am.'

'Are you sure?'

He was such a gentleman; most other blokes would have taken what she was offering without question, and she loved him all the more for his consideration. 'Yes.'

Wonder filled his face, swiftly followed by what she hoped was love, then a hunger in his eyes so hot that it seared everything except him from her mind.

And she knew that whatever happened, whatever the future held, she would treasure this moment for as long as she lived.

Chapter 23

They didn't need words when they returned to the shop a while later; their bodies were speaking for them in the way they caught each other's eye, in the smouldering yet soft glances, in the secret smiles, and in the gentle caress of a hand on a back or on an arm as they worked together tending to customers, tidying up, or sweeping the floor.

To Elspeth, it felt as though she'd known Charles all her life, yet it was so new that it stole her breath when she thought about what they'd done in his bed. Not in hers. Never hers.

Charles hadn't asked, he'd known instinctively that her marital bed was out-of-bounds.

He'd instinctively known a few other things too, but it wouldn't do to linger on those right now, not when she was trying to be professional and keep her mind on the job.

When she popped to the loo later though, the tiny mirror above the sink showed a woman who glowed. Her eyes were bright, her cheeks were pink, and her mouth wore a perpetual smile. Inside she was sparkling, and it showed on the outside. The aches and pains of this morning had gone, and so had her tiredness, although a languorous lassitude filled her, slowing her movements and making her dreamy and distracted.

That glorious feeling lasted until she and Charles closed the shop and picked up some groceries. They made and ate dinner together, working in tandem as though they'd been doing so for years, yet at the same time Elspeth was aware how everything felt uncharted and fresh. She felt like she was sailing into waters she had never explored before. Charles was new, the situation was new – her *emotions* were new.

As they sat later that evening in comfortable silence in the garden, an open bottle of wine between them and with the breeze in the leaves serving as music, playing footsie with each other under the table, she understood that the way she felt about Charles was different to the way she had felt about Ray.

She'd loved Ray with all her heart and then some, and she had been torn apart when he'd died. But never, in all the years they'd spent together, had she experienced the degree of passion she'd felt with Charles. That she was still feeling.

Just the touch of his foot on hers was enough to send her pulse soaring and flip over her tummy. She could almost imagine the electricity sparking between them, like lightning, white-hot and pure.

The thought had crossed her mind that maybe what they were experiencing was nothing more than a holiday romance, burning bright while it lasted but likely to fizzle out when distance failed to provide the fuel needed to feed it. She thought she must be like any other woman who'd gone abroad and had fallen for a handsome waiter – except their roles were reversed as she was the local and Charles was the tourist. It might be clichéd and seedy, eye-rollingly predictable, but that wasn't how it felt. Not to her. And if she was any judge of character, she suspected it didn't feel like that to Charles either.

He seemed just as startled and taken aback by their burgeoning relationship as she was. He also appeared to be equally as delighted and thrilled. And neither of them could stop smiling, or touching each other, or exchanging meaningful looks.

It made her soul soar, and she was skin-tinglingly, stomach-churningly alive, and it felt so, so good.

For a moment, when a phone rang breaking the still of the night air, Elspeth and Charles simply stared at each other, neither of them able to snap back into normal life. Then Elspeth realised it was her phone which was intruding on their increasingly charged evening, and she shot into the living room to pick it up from the coffee table.

'Stefan? Is that you?' she asked as she walked outside and sank back into her seat, the phone glued to her ear. 'How's your father?'

'Not good. It is bad news.'

'Oh, no, I'm so sorry. What's the prognosis?'

'I will tell you about it on Wednesday when I am back on Tenerife,' her boss interrupted.

'You're coming back on Wednesday?' Stefan would be back in two days, thank goodness, and she was filled with relief.

'Yes. Will you be OK in the shop until then?'

'Of course I will. Don't worry about me or Libertad. Everything is good, busier than normal, due to Easter, I think. Takings are up, and you'll need to order more stock, especially the— Sorry, ignore me; you've got more important things on your mind. We'll catch up properly on Wednesday.'

'Good, thank you, Elspeth. I knew you'd keep things going.'

'Take care and try not to worry.' It was futile, but it was so hard to find the right words. He was bound to be worried; she was worried too, but for far more selfish reasons. If the news about his father wasn't good, then Stefan might well decide that going back to Germany was his only option.

'Stefan is back on Wednesday,' she said as she hung up, although Charles had got the gist of the conversation. 'But he sounded dreadful, like he had the weight of the world on his shoulders. The poor boy, I really do feel for him.'

What if he closed the shop and went back to Germany to live? She wouldn't blame him, but it would be such a shame for him to leave everything he'd worked so hard for. He loved living here, he loved his way of life, and for him to have to give it up would be such a blow to him.

'Why is life so unfair?' she cried. 'I feel so sorry for him. Whatever choice he makes, it isn't going to be easy.'

'What do you think he'll do?'

She shrugged. 'The right thing for his conscience and for his parents.'

'Go back to Germany, you mean?'

Elspeth sighed. 'Yes. If things are as bad as I suspect, then he'll feel he has no choice.'

'You'll miss him.'

She most certainly would, and not because she would lose her job either. Trust Charles to appreciate that her distress was also about losing Stefan. It was as though he could see straight into her heart.

'Let me help in the shop tomorrow,' he said. 'But I'll make myself scarce on Wednesday, OK?'

She smiled at him, grateful for his help today and tomorrow, but also thankful that he understood that she didn't want to have to explain his presence to Stefan when he returned.

'You could go to Loro Parque, and make use of the car,' she suggested.

'I'll only go if it's with you. Come here.' He patted his thigh and she got up and went to sit on his lap. 'I want to spend every second of every minute of every hour of—'

She put a finger on his lips. 'I get it. I feel the same way. What are we waiting for?'

He gave her a quizzical look. 'Aren't we spending time together now?'

Her smile was as naughty as she felt. 'I can think of better ways.'

'Oh, yeah?'

'Yeah…'

'Want to show me?'

So that's what she did.

Chapter 24

Elspeth didn't deliberately plan to hide the fact that she was sleeping with her guest from Amanda and Toni when she and Charles were invited to dinner with them on Tuesday evening. Neither did she want to go out of her way to conceal her feelings. However, she didn't intend to broadcast the information, either. No doubt Amanda would work it out for herself. Not much got past that woman, and if Amanda asked her outright, Elspeth decided she would tell her the truth. She just wasn't going to volunteer the news.

'I'd prefer to spend the evening alone with you,' Charles said to her when she came downstairs just before they were due to leave. 'Tell me again, why are we going?'

'Because Amanda asked us.'

'Are you sure she included me in the invitation?'

'Yes.' Elspeth had queried the very same thing, but Amanda said she'd like to meet this mystery guest and Elspeth thought it might be a nice evening out for Charles.

He walked up behind her and wrapped his arms around her waist, kissing the back of her neck, as she put her bag on the hall table and checked her appearance in the mirror.

'If you keep kissing me like that, we won't be going anywhere,' she warned. 'You'll regret it.'

'You mean I'll go hungry?'

'Yes you will, but what I meant is that I want to show you what you've been missing by staying here with me instead of taking a room at the hotel.'

'I've missed nothing,' he retorted, his lips trailing little kisses from her ear, down the side of her neck to her collarbone.

She leant into him, and a delicious shiver almost made her reach for the phone and call Amanda with an excuse. Charles had only two days of his holiday left and, as much as Elspeth loved Amanda and Toni, and as much as she was looking forward to seeing them this evening, she loved Charles more. The thought of waking up, and him not being there, was tormenting her already, and she had yet to experience it for real.

Determined to shake off any sour mood and make the most of the time they had left together, Elspeth squirmed around to face him, gave him a swift kiss, and then wriggled out of his arms.

'Come on, we don't want to be late,' she said.

Charles gaped at her. 'I've been ready for ages,' he said, acting affronted. 'I've been waiting for *you*.' His gaze scanned her from top to toe appreciatively. 'I must say, it was worth the wait – you look gorgeous.' His voice dropped and became a little more serious as he added, 'You always look gorgeous to me.'

'Thank you.' With heightened colour (she was unused to compliments) and a spring in her step, Elspeth marched him out of the door, across the square and along the main road towards the hotel. The building was tucked away at the far end of the little town, almost out of it, yet still within easy walking distance of everything Santiago del Teide had to offer.

The girl on reception recognised Elspeth and gave her a wide smile. 'Amanda is waiting for you on the terrace. Toni is still working.' She spoke Spanish, and Elspeth answered in kind.

'He is always working. Amanda will make him stop when she knows we are here.' She said to Charles in English, 'This way; Amanda is on the terrace and Toni will join us in a minute.'

As soon as Amanda saw them approach, she leapt to her feet. She greeted Charles first, holding both hands out to him, and when he took them in his, she pulled him in for a two-cheeked kiss.

'You must be Charles,' she gushed. 'It's so lovely to meet you at last. I've heard such a lot about you.'

Charles gave Elspeth an amused look before saying to Amanda, 'Nothing bad, I hope?'

'Oh no, quite the opposite.'

'Nice to meet you, too,' he said, letting go of her hands and using one of his free ones to run it through his hair.

Elspeth thought he appeared nervous and she was intrigued. Was he worried what her friend would think of him, especially if Amanda guessed they had become more than host and guest?

'I'll send someone to fetch Toni,' Amanda was saying as she closed in on Elspeth for a hug.

Enveloped in her friend's arms, Elspeth suddenly felt shy. Amanda had been with her when she'd been through the worst experience of her life and had seen her come out of the other side. Would Elspeth be forced to lean on her for emotional support again when Charles flew back to the UK?

'You've got some explaining to do,' Amanda whispered into her hair before she released her. She winked as she stepped back, and Elspeth might have known that her friend would be quick to work it out. Elspeth was right – nothing much did get past her.

'Please, sit down, I've got a jug of sangria on the way. Consuela, can you tell Toni that our guests have arrived?' Amanda ushered them to the table she'd just been sitting at, and they all took a seat.

Elspeth loved the hotel's terrace. It was a quiet area away from the busy outdoor bar and the pool – not that anywhere in the hotel ever got particularly rowdy, but this area was perfect for reading and relaxing during the day, or for having a more sedate drink in the evening. It also had a view of the mountains, and beautiful meadows stretched out on the other side of a low stone wall beyond the hotel's tastefully arranged green shrubs and small trees. It reminded Elspeth strongly of her own little courtyard, as the hotel's foliage gave the appearance of blending in with the natural world on the other side of the wall, and she had a feeling that Ray might well have used it for inspiration when he made an oasis out of the rubble and overgrown mess in the villa's garden.

'How have you enjoyed your holiday so far?' Amanda asked Charles, turning towards him. Her question seemed innocent enough, but Elspeth caught the sneaky sideways glance her friend gave her, and she rolled her eyes.

'It's been fantastic. Really, really enjoyable and great fun, too. Elspeth is a wonderful... um...?'

'Host?' Amanda suggested, her tongue lodged so far in her cheek, Elspeth wondered why it didn't poke out through her face.

'Yes, a wonderful host.' Charles pounced on the word, relief flowing out of him.

Elspeth tried to kick Amanda under the table but missed and caught one of its wooden legs instead. 'Ow.'

'Did you hurt yourself?' Amanda enquired, looking as though butter wouldn't melt, earning herself a narrow-eyed scowl from her best friend. Elspeth hoped her expression hinted at what miseries she was going to inflict on her when she managed to get Amanda alone.

They were saved from further awkwardness by the arrival of a large jug of sangria and four glasses, with Toni following behind.

Greetings were made again, and everyone settled down to their drinks.

'Have you heard from Stefan?' Amanda asked. 'Any news about his father?'

'It's not good, I don't think. He's flying back to Tenerife tomorrow, so we'll catch up then,' Elspeth said.

'What do you think he'll do? Return to Germany permanently?'

Elspeth blew out her cheeks. 'Possibly. I suppose it depends on how much his mum needs him.'

They continued to chat about the shop after their food order was taken, and Elspeth told them that Charles had been helping out, earning herself yet another knowing look from Amanda, who mouthed 'later' at her, when Charles's attention was elsewhere.

However, it took until after dessert and coffee before she and Amanda were alone, and this only happened when Amanda not very subtly suggested that Toni give Charles a tour of the hotel. Elspeth braced herself for an onslaught of questions as soon as the men were out of range.

'Spill,' her friend demanded.

'I've slept with him.'

'*What?!*' The hotel owner screeched, then hastily lowered her voice. 'When? How – I mean, I know *how*, but—'

'But I told you I had no intention of doing anything of the sort?'

'Exactly! You did say that, I distinctly remember it. What changed your mind?'

'It was time I started living again.'

'So you decided to start living with a man who's flying out of your life in a few days' time and whom you'll probably never see again? Way to go, girl!' Amanda clapped her hands.

Elspeth looked down. 'Yes.'

One word was all it took for Amanda to guess the truth, and she immediately sobered. 'Oh, my darling, you've fallen in love with him, haven't you?'

Elspeth nodded, not trusting herself to speak.

'Oh dear…'

'Yes, oh dear.'

'Will you be all right, do you think?' her friend asked, her voice full of concern.

'Do you mean will I fall apart the second his plane takes off? No, I won't. If I can live through the death of my husband and come through that, then I can live with this. It won't be easy – love never is, is it? – but I've gone into it with my eyes wide open. I know our relationship will come to an end on Friday, and I'm prepared for it.'

Amanda was studying her intently, and Elspeth was forced to look away.

'Are you though?' her friend asked.

Thankfully Elspeth was spared having to answer by the return of Toni and Charles.

'You weren't gone long,' Amanda accused her husband, and Toni shrugged.

'Does it matter how long we were?' he asked, confused.

Elspeth chuckled when Amanda shook her head and said, 'Men, they're a pain in the backside.'

'But you love me, this I know,' Toni stated with a broad grin.

'Hmm,' Amanda replied, and Toni laughed. He was secure in knowing exactly how his wife felt about him, and he was right: Amanda adored him, and he, her. It was delightful to see, and a pang caught Elspeth unawares.

She wanted that. After telling herself for so long that she didn't need love or companionship, that she was perfectly happy with her life just the way it was, she now wanted what her friends had.

The idea that she possibly already had it with Charles briefly crossed her mind, but it didn't count because he wouldn't be in Tenerife for much longer. This time on Friday she'd be alone once more, and she wasn't looking forward to it.

Chapter 25

It was only just gone nine o'clock on Wednesday morning. Elspeth had just opened Libertad, and she was shocked to see Stefan shoulder his way through the door shortly afterwards, one of his oversized rucksacks on his back. He shrugged it off and let it fall to the ground with a weary sigh.

She hurried across the shop floor and threw her arms around him, hugging him tightly. She wished she had a magic wand to erase the pallor from his face and the weary hopelessness set deep in his eyes.

'I didn't expect you until this afternoon! You must have been travelling most of the night,' she exclaimed, loosening her grip a little so she could take a proper look at him. Her initial assessment had been correct – he looked defeated and exhausted.

'I had to come back; there is so much to do,' he said with a grimace.

Elspeth's heart sank. It didn't take a genius to work out what he meant. The shop was running perfectly well for now – there was nothing that needed to be done urgently – which meant that Stefan must have plans to make for its future and more important things to resolve than reorganising the stock room or servicing a few of its bikes.

'How is your dad? Your mum?' she asked, letting go of him. She guessed he could do with a strong coffee and a bite to eat, so she grabbed his hand and pulled him into the back room, where she switched the kettle on and thrust a bag of croissants at him.

Stefan slumped into a chair, ignoring the croissants, and her heart went out to him. He seemed to have the weight of the world on his shoulders and had aged a decade since she'd seen him last.

'Awful,' he said. 'My father is in denial. He is refusing to take any medication, saying the doctors are wrong. My mother is…' His stricken expression broke her heart.

He rubbed a hand across his face, his beard making a soft rasping sound. She noticed a slight tremble in his fingers, and she wanted nothing more than to gather him up and tell him everything would be all right.

But it wouldn't be, and he deserved more than inconsequential platitudes.

'What do you need me to do?' she asked.

'Carry on working as normal. I am back, for now, until I…' He heaved a deep sigh. 'God, I am sorry, Elspeth.'

She put a hand on his shoulder and gave it a squeeze. 'You have to do what you have to do. Don't worry about me, and don't be sorry. I guessed you would probably sell up and move back to Germany.'

'You did?'

She nodded. 'Your family needs you.'

She felt so terribly sorry that his dreams of living and playing in the sun were over. Well, for now, at least, because who knew what the future would hold for this young man? Maybe he would come back to the island one day, but if he did, he wouldn't be the same person. His father's illness would have changed him, turned him into someone new, with a different outlook, different values. She just felt very blessed to have known him.

But things change, life takes people in different directions, and this was the start of a new journey for Stefan, one that would undoubtedly be full of difficulties and heartache. However, Elspeth firmly believed that he would cope.

Wishing she could help and knowing that she couldn't do anything of any real impact, was hard – the only thing she could do under the circumstances was to keep Libertad ticking over for as long as necessary.

'Why don't you go home and get your head down?' she suggested. 'I'm fine here, and you look shattered.'

He sent her a grateful smile, but shook his head. 'I can't. I have someone coming to value the business this morning.'

'You've been busy!' She hadn't expected him to start the ball rolling so soon.

'I've had to be. Look, you don't need to be here when they call. Take the rest of the day off, and tomorrow. I'll see you on Friday, as usual?'

'You don't need me to do extra hours?'

'Not this week, although I might need you to step in more next week, or switch your days if you can?'

'Of course, I can. Whatever you need, just ask.'

He stood up and gave her a hug. She could feel the emotion thrumming through him and guessed he was only just holding it together. She desperately wanted to stay, but her intuition told her that he'd prefer to be alone; the company of anonymous customers didn't count, and she knew from personal experience that staying busy would help him get through the next few weeks.

After kissing him on the cheek, she picked up her bag and left quickly, not wanting him to witness her tears.

Blinking furiously, she hurried home, where Charles took one look at her face and wrapped his arms around her.

He waited for her to finish sobbing, then asked, 'Do you want to tell me about it?'

She nodded and let him guide her to the sofa and make her a cup of tea, before he sat next to her and hugged her to him.

'Stefan is back,' Elspeth said, then she paused to gather her thoughts.

'I guessed as much. How is his father?'

She gulped back fresh tears. 'It's not good, but he didn't go into details. He didn't need to – his face said enough. The poor, poor boy. I wish there was something I could do.'

'I take it he's going back to Germany to live?'

'He has to. He said his father is refusing to believe the diagnosis, and although he didn't say it, I got the impression his mum can't cope.'

The pair of them sat in silence for a while, until she said, 'He's selling the business. He's got someone coming around today to value it and put it on the market.'

'That's quick.'

'I know. I was expecting it, but it's still a shock.'

'Do you have to go back to work?'

'No, I've got the rest of the day off, and tomorrow. I think he wants to be alone for a while.'

'With a shop full of customers?'

'It might sound daft, but it'll be easier for him to talk to total strangers about the best pair of socks to wear hiking, than to have to deal with the feelings which must be swirling about in his head.'

Charles nodded, and gave her a squeeze. 'How do you fancy trying to take your mind off things for a while?' he asked. 'I've still got the car. We could go to Loro Parque together after all?'

Elspeth seriously didn't feel like doing anything of the sort, but she was also acutely conscious that she only had the rest of today and tomorrow with Charles, and that this was his holiday after all; she didn't want to ruin what was left of it for him by being all sad and mopey. She'd have plenty of time to do that after he had gone.

She briefly thought about suggesting spending the day in bed, but she realised he was right, and that getting out and about would probably be more beneficial.

'How about Jungle Park instead?' she said. 'They've got meerkats and I love meerkats. It's in the south, not far from Los Cristianos. Maybe we can walk from the far end of Los Cristianos right the way along the promenade to Playa de las Américas afterwards? There's so much of Tenerife you haven't seen yet.'

When he didn't say anything, she twisted around to look at his face, and her stomach did that annoying fluttery thing when she saw the way he was looking at her.

'I've seen everything I need, or want, to see,' he whispered, then bent his head to kiss her.

After far too short a time, he dragged his lips away from hers and said, 'We'd better get going, although for the record I want it noted that I could quite happily take you to bed and ravish you, but I don't want to be responsible for you missing your meerkat fix.'

He stood, pulling her up with him, and gave her a gentle push in the direction of the stairs. 'Go get ready.'

Feeling somewhat calmer and a little less emotional, Elspeth did as Charles asked, splashing water on her face and brushing her hair. She also changed into a skirt and a flowery top, thinking that any memories Charles had of her so far mostly had been of her wearing walking gear. And she also wanted to feel feminine for a change.

She came downstairs to find him on the phone, but he quickly wrapped up his conversation when he saw her.

'You look good enough to eat,' he said and took a step towards her. She held up a hand.

'Meerkats…?' she reminded him.

He gave a resigned sigh. 'Meerkats it is. Although I warn you now, I'd much prefer to look at you than at a cute furry animal.'

'They've got crocodiles.'

'Ah, OK, that does it for me – you've been ousted off the top spot by a dangerous scaly reptile.'

She smiled. He was trying his best to take her mind off things, bless him, and she vowed not to let her worries about the future sour the day.

–

It was good to get out of Santiago and the mountain region, and Elspeth sat back in the car and watched the scenery go by, whilst giving navigational advice to Charles. As he drove, they sang along to the music playing on Radio TEX, which was a station aimed at British ex-pats and UK tourists. They played some mean tunes, and Elspeth found herself belting out the words to Meatloaf's 'Bat out of Hell', with Charles joining in for the chorus.

Charles was right, going out for the day was doing her good, and she was looking forward to spending a couple of hours in the park.

He insisted on paying her entry fee, despite her prot-estations, but once inside Elspeth forgot all about wanting to go Dutch as she normally did with Charles, especially when she saw the sign for the penguin enclosure.

'Ooh, I want to see the penguins,' she cried, earning herself an amused glance from a teenaged girl.

'You can see whatever you want, my love,' Charles said, his arm around her shoulders as they strolled towards the birds in question.

Elspeth oohed and aahed over the antics of the Humboldt penguins, then they headed for a large open-air arena where a display of birds of prey was about to take place.

'Thank you for this,' she said as they sat together on the stone step, shoulders and thighs touching.

'Don't thank me; this was your idea. I suggested Loro Parque.'

'I thought you'd appreciate a splodge of vulture poop on your head instead,' she cried, ducking as one of the birds in question flew perilously close to the tops of their heads as it aimed for its handler who was standing a few rows above them and holding out a piece of meat in his hand.

'Er, not really, but thanks, anyway,' Charles said, laughing at the look of terror on her face when the vulture skimmed the air above them once more, its wings flapping heavily, ruffling their hair.

Elspeth wrinkled her nose. 'I prefer the meerkats. Can we go see them after this?'

'We can do whatever you like,' he said, kissing her forehead.

The little mammals were so cute and she spent ages watching them dig and listening to their engaging calls to one another. 'I want to do a David Attenborough and go and sit in the middle of them. Do you think anyone would object?'

'Probably. Bet you won't feel the same when we see those crocodiles you've promised me.'

He was right. Although the prehistoric-looking creatures were safely ensconced in a steep-sided ravine and were doing nothing more threatening than lazing about, Elspeth got the feeling they were just biding their time and waiting for an unwary human to come too close.

'I can't believe how big they are,' she said, peering over the edge of the wooden bridge which spanned the ravine and praying it wouldn't choose this moment to give way. 'Come on.' She tugged at Charles's arm. 'The butterfly house is this way.'

Although the pair of them had spent an enjoyable couple of hours around the park, and Elspeth was grateful for the distraction from Stefan's news, she couldn't help feeling that something wasn't quite right. She wasn't able to put her finger on it. Charles was as attentive as always, quick to catch hold of her hand or lean in for a sneaky kiss, but she sensed he was preoccupied, and when she saw him checking his phone for what must have been about the fifth time, especially given that he never normally looked at it, she wondered what was up.

Debating whether or not to ask him, she concluded that if he wanted her to know, then he would tell her, so she let it lie and tried to enjoy the rest of the excursion as they drove from the hills towards the coast and the heady sights of Los Cristianos.

'Wow, it certainly is busy,' Charles declared, as he negotiated the car along a one-way road packed with cars, many of them trying to find a parking space just as they were.

'Try down there,' Elspeth said, pointing to a turn-off which didn't look particularly promising as it led to more of an industrial area than to a touristy one.

The road took them closer to the mountain bordering the east side of Los Cristianos Bay, where the beach petered out, but Elspeth's instincts had been correct, and they were able to find a parking space with relative ease.

Once out of the car, they were soon on the wide promenade, with a crescent of sandy beach on the one side which was populated by umbrellas and sun loungers, and a never-ending selection of shops, cafes and restaurants on the other. Everywhere Elspeth looked there were people: walking, on bicycles, on roller skates, on electric scooters, in wheelchairs. The flatness of the terrain compared to the rest of the island, combined with the almost-perfect weather, made the south an ideal place for the elderly and the infirm, as well as being a lively place for families, couples and singleton groups alike. It wasn't her cup of tea as a place to live, but it was fun to visit once in a while. It was vibrant, noisy and full of life, and the promenade was also surprisingly appealing and nicely laid out.

Charles took her hand in his as they strolled, brushing his thumb lightly across her skin. 'Hungry?'

'Famished.' It was way past her usual lunchtime and the enticing smells coming from various restaurants were making her tummy gurgle.

'What do you think of this place?' He stopped in front of a menu board outside the next restaurant they came to and perused it. 'I fancy paella. Would you like to share?'

'Sounds good. I haven't had paella in ages. It's a lot of faffing about to cook it just for one.'

They were shown to a table and sat down under the shade of a wide umbrella. After giving their order, they turned their attention to the view. Or rather, Elspeth did, but she noticed Charles slipping his phone out of his trouser pocket and taking a quick glance at it.

'Everything OK?' she asked, unable to keep a check on her curiosity.

'What?' He looked up, distracted. 'Oh, yes, fine. Just… business.'

She narrowed her eyes slightly. What business could he be referring to? He was retired.

She told herself his business was none of her business, and if he wanted to tell her he'd just had the perfect opportunity. It was nothing to do with her, and as he'd be out of her life in less than two days' time, she put it out of her mind.

'That's the ferry to La Gomera,' she told him instead, pointing to the large white ship anchored at the end of a wide jetty. Cars, vans and lorries were lined up waiting to embark and they watched in fascination as the back end of the enormous boat opened up and the vehicles trundled in one by one.

'My word, this is a fantastic spot,' he observed. 'Not only have you got all the drama of the ferry, there's an endless stream of people up and down the promenade, plus all those on the beach. Then there are all those boats, and the sea itself.'

'Do you wish you'd come to stay here instead of Santiago del Teide?'

'Good Lord, no! For one thing, I think my brain would go into overload after a couple of days, and for another, I'd never have met you. And that doesn't bear thinking about.' He took her hand in his and lifted it to his lips, kissing the back of it, before he turned it over and skimmed his mouth across her palm, sending shivers of delight through her.

'Stop it, you'll put me off my lunch,' she said.

'That was my intention. The less you eat, the more paella there'll be for me.'

She shook her head, a smile playing about her mouth, knowing he didn't mean it, especially when he tried to give her more than her fair share of the shared dish when the waiter placed a sizzling black pan between them.

'Mmm, this is delicious,' she said, tucking in. She never bothered to cook seafood for herself, apart from the occasional prawn, and the rich flavours of the mussels, shrimp, calamari and squid burst across her tongue and she closed her eyes in bliss.

Accompanied by fresh bread for mopping up any spare sauce from the cooking juices, and washed down with a chilled glass of crisp white wine, the meal was perfect.

The day would have been too, if she was able to ignore the upsetting start to it and Charles's distraction. Nevertheless, she knew she would treasure it. This, along with the other memories she'd made with Charles would sustain her in the dark times ahead when he had gone and all she had left were the images in her mind.

After they'd eaten, they carried on with their stroll, pausing now and again to sit on a bench to admire the view and to share a quick kiss.

She had no idea how many miles they'd walked, but by the time they'd both had enough and turned around to make their way back to the car, she was pleasantly tired.

Elspeth almost fell asleep on the drive back, and had to keep shuffling about in her seat to stay awake. She might be tired but she didn't want to waste any of the precious hours she had left with Charles by sleeping. There would be plenty of opportunity for early nights after he'd gone.

In the end though, an early night was exactly what she had, but Charles made sure she didn't spend a great deal of it sleeping.

When she did eventually drop off, Elspeth did so snuggled against Charles, incredibly happy and incredibly sad at the same time, her heart full of love for this amazing man.

Chapter 26

Elspeth woke slowly, languidly, her body feeling fluid and boneless, and she smiled. That's what a fantastic night with a wonderful man could do to you, she thought, stretching out a hand and reaching for Charles, intending to make the most of not having to get up for work this Thursday morning.

His side of the bed was empty and she opened her eyes fully and sat up, patting the sheets.

They were cold, so he obviously hadn't been lying in them for some time. Mind you, she saw it was nearly ten a.m. when she peered at the clock on the bedside table. That was late for her, and she knew he usually woke early, so it shouldn't be any surprise to find him already up.

Hoping he was putting the kettle on, she grabbed her silk dressing gown from the back of her own bedroom door and padded downstairs.

Charles was in the courtyard, wearing nothing more than a pair of boxer shorts and a serious expression, with his mobile phone pressed firmly to his ear. He was speaking quietly, probably in order not to wake her, so she couldn't hear what was being said.

Not that she wanted to, and to make sure he didn't think she was eavesdropping, she called out a cheery 'good morning' and went into the kitchen to make a pot of tea and sort out breakfast.

By the time she inched outside with a tray of breakfast things, Charles had finished his call, the phone lying dark on the table in front of him. Elspeth curtailed her curiosity as best she could and concentrated on off-loading the tray. Charles stood up to help her.

'Sleep well?' he asked.

'I did, thanks. Been up long?'

'A couple of hours. I was about to bring you breakfast in bed, but…' He trailed off, his gaze coming to rest on his mobile.

'That's OK, it was about time I got up. I can't believe I slept so late.'

He shot her a cheeky grin. 'We were busy half the night, so I suppose it's to be expected.'

She blushed, remembering precisely what it was they had been busy doing.

'Do you know how beautiful you are?' he murmured, and she blushed even more.

'Stop it,' she protested. 'You're embarrassing me.'

'It's true, you *are* beautiful.'

'If you don't stop, I'm going to go into work and leave you on your own for the day.' She said, then saw his face. 'What is it?'

'Er, about today… I was thinking of going out for one last ride before I take the bike back to the shop.'

'Oh. OK. Well, of course, enjoy! Where were you thinking of going?' she added, to cover the sudden hurt. This was their last day together. Tomorrow morning she'd have to say goodbye to him and try not to let it show that her heart was breaking. After last night, she thought (hoped) that he'd want to spend every minute with her.

Clearly not.

'I'm going to do a circuit around Teide, then go down through La Orotava and probably come back up via Masca village,' he informed her.

She knew what that meant – he'd be gone for a good few hours.

Her gaze dropped to his phone again. There was something going on back in the UK, something that was taking his mind away from Tenerife and planting it firmly in England.

Blinking sharply to rid herself of the sting of tears at the back of her eyes, she bustled about, getting up to go back into the kitchen for some honey she had no intention of spreading on her toast, then getting up again to fetch a clean knife when she already had a clean one sitting next to her plate.

Charles wore a faint frown and an air of distraction throughout breakfast – a far cry from the man he'd been last night, and she knew she'd lost him already. He might be here in body, but his mind was a couple of thousand miles away, and she understood that he was mentally preparing himself for a return to reality.

It was a pity that his reality and hers were so different.

It would be so easy for him to put the last two weeks behind him, she thought, to compartmentalise his holiday and separate it from his normal everyday life. But how was she supposed to do that? Nearly every room in the villa would have his presence lingering in it. It would be like living with a ghost, just like the way she'd lived with the absence of Ray for so long.

'Oh, my darling Ray, what have I gone and done?' she murmured as she stood at the sink following the meal, her hands in hot soapy water, her mind in turmoil.

She could hear Charles moving about in his room, the opening and closing of the bathroom door, the faint rattle of the cold-water pipe when the tap was turned off, the sound of his mobile as another call came in.

Yes, he was clearly back in the UK in mind, but not in body.

She'd hoped to delay the pull of departure until tomorrow. She'd been there herself, but never usually until it was time to pack – then, as she was shoving things in the case, she used to start planning on how she was going to fit in a grocery shop with loading the washing machine several times before having to return to work.

Elspeth recognised the signs and lamented that Charles was a day ahead of himself. Surely he didn't need to think about real life just yet? Then she recalled the phone calls, the anxious glances at his blank mobile screen, and his preoccupation, and decided that he might not have any choice.

Maybe he needed to spend this last day on his own to clear his head.

Clear it of her.

Of *them*. To make his leaving easier for him.

She only wished the same option was available to her.

So she'd do what she always did when she was stressed or anxious – she'd head into the mountains and let nature soothe her soul. As much as it could be soothed, under the circumstances.

First, though, there were chores to be done.

She waited until Charles had finished getting ready for the day, and then hid in plain sight in the garden, nursing a cup of tea and keeping out of his way, giving him space to clatter around whilst he made sure his bike was roadworthy and his water bottles were full. And with the tires and brakes checked, the water bottles loaded onto the cages, pockets patted for money, key, and phone, Charles was finally ready.

'I'm not sure what time I'll be back,' he told her. 'What are your plans for today?'

She shrugged. 'The bathrooms could do with a clean.' She knew she sounded surly, but she couldn't help it, and when he leant over to kiss her, she dipped her head, so his mouth landed on her forehead and not on her lips.

Continuing to keep her head bowed so he didn't see the hurt in her eyes, she waited for him to stutter out an awkward goodbye and for him to wheel the bike through the gate and onto the rough lane separating her villa from the meadow beyond. She then listened to him snap his shoes into the pedals. The receding hiss of tyres on tarmac told her he was on his way, and with that she could finally breathe and let go.

Except… her chest was tight and her heart felt like a stone. Elspeth had a feeling it would be a long time before the blood flowed freely through her veins once more without carrying the chill of lost love in their depths.

Furious with herself, even though she knew that by letting Charles into her life desolation would be the likely outcome, Elspeth leapt to her feet. The delicate bone china cup and saucer fell to the floor and smashed into pieces. How apt. Her heart was in the same condition, and as she fetched the dustpan and brush from the cupboard under the stairs, she wished she could clean up her wayward emotions as easily.

She decided that cleaning might be just the thing after all, just as she had mentioned to Charles. Tackling the kitchen first, Elspeth set to with a vengeance, scrubbing and wiping until every surface gleamed. Satisfied it was as clean as she was going to get it, she moved on to the living room, the hall, the landing, her bedroom, her en suite, before she finally ground to a shaky halt outside Charles's bedroom door.

Reluctantly, she pushed it open.

The bed was made; the same bed she'd risen from with joy in her heart a few hours ago.

Now, though, she eyed it in the same way that a meerkat might eye a rattlesnake.

A quick check of the bathroom reassured her there was no need to linger. It was clean enough – she'd wait until he'd left before she'd venture into his room again. There would be time enough tomorrow to scrub and mop all trace of him away. Because how else was she going to fill the evening after she came home from Libertad once her working day was over?

There was one other thing to take care of before she could leave the villa and head for the restorative air of the hills, and that was her weekly Skype call with Gideon.

The thought of her son and his family lifted her mood considerably (if fleetingly), so it was with a genuine smile that she sat in front of the old computer and gazed on the handsome (she might be biased, but so was every mother) face of her only child.

'How is my darling grandson?' she asked him. Gideon was at home, sitting in the lounge – she recognised the picture on the wall, and heard the sounds of Sakura making their evening meal. 'Is he in bed yet?'

'No, we kept him up so he could speak to his grandma.' Gideon called to Sakura, who fetched Rai, handed him to his father and gave a quick wave at the screen.

Elspeth waved back, but her attention was on the little boy being bounced on Gideon's lap. She made silly noises and pulled faces at her grandson for a few minutes, but Rai was tired and when he began to grizzle she said, 'Give him a kiss from me,' as Sakura took him.

'I will.'

'Are you excited about your trip?' she asked, when Rai and his mother disappeared off her screen.

His eyes lit up. 'Yeah, it's going to be awesome. Sakura has never been to London and I can't wait to show her the sights. Of course, we can't do everything we'd like to do – I'm there on business, remember? – and we'll have Rai with us, so there's a limit to how much—'

Elspeth sighed; that wasn't what she'd meant at all, and disappointment coursed through her. Her son didn't appear to view his impending visit to Tenerife in the same way she did, and she hoped he wasn't coming to see her out of a sense of duty and no other reason, or that it was merely a few days in the sun for him and his family as a quick diversion from work.

She was yanked back into the conversation when she heard Charles's name mentioned.

'Sorry, could you repeat that, the screen froze for a sec,' she lied to cover her inattention.

'I said, has that Charles guy gone home yet?'

'Uh, not quite. He's leaving tomorrow.' It wasn't an outright lie – she simply failed to mention that he'd spent the whole time at her villa and not the majority of it at the hotel, as was originally intended.

Elspeth hoped her son didn't see the blush spreading across her cheeks.

After the call ended, Elspeth felt bereft, even though she'd soon be able to speak to her son and his family in person, so she picked up her phone and called Amanda, hoping her friend wouldn't be too busy to talk.

'Oh, hi, are you OK?' Amanda asked. She sounded distracted, and Elspeth felt a little guilty for phoning her. Mornings were usually a busy time for her.

'Not brilliant, Stefan came back yesterday. It's not good.'

'Yes, Ch—' There was a bang and a curse, then Amanda was back. 'Sorry, I dropped the phone. What do you mean, it's not good?'

'He is going back to Germany to live. His parents need him.'

'Aw, that's a shame.'

'He's selling the shop.'

'Oh dear.'

'Look, I can tell you're busy. I'll give you a call later on. Is Toni still going to take Charles to the airport, do you know?'

'Er, yes, I think that's still the plan.'

'What time is he picking him up?'

'About seven a.m., I believe. His flight is at ten-thirty.'

Early then. Which suited her just fine, because it meant she could see Charles off and still be able to go to work on time.

'I wonder who'll buy the shop?' she mused out loud to her friend.

'Sorry, Elspeth, I've got to go. There's, um, a towel emergency.'

Elspeth was left holding a silent phone, with a bemused expression on her face. What kind of emergency involved towels?! And did she want to know, or was that mystery better left unexplained?

Still pondering the question (it was better than some of the other thoughts her mind wanted to focus on), she changed into her walking gear, filled her water bottle and headed out of the door.

Chapter 27

It was around four o'clock by the time Elspeth approached the end of the track and walked back along Santiago del Teide's main road. The hike had done her good, although, as she got nearer to the villa, her mood dipped and her troubles returned with a vengeance.

What with Libertad being valued yesterday (how did that go? she wondered) and Stefan planning to sell up as soon as he could find a buyer, Gideon being more enthralled with going to London than coming to see her, and Charles… there was little to say about the latter concern, except that it was already hurting and she feared it would only get worse.

Despite feeling incredibly downcast, Elspeth's stomach growled and she realised she hadn't eaten anything since breakfast, not that she'd eaten much then, either. Her thoughts strayed to Charles and she hoped he had stopped to pick up a sandwich or a slice of pizza on the way, because she didn't think he'd taken any lunch with him.

Knowing that a day on the bike used loads of calories and that he'd be starving come dinner time, she decided to pop into a local Canarian restaurant just off the main road, and book a table for this evening. She intended to put a brave face on it and make Charles's last evening on Tenerife memorable – it was the least she could do.

It wasn't his fault she felt the way she did – both of them had been completely aware of the nature and duration of their relationship before it had started. That it was coming to its natural end was something she had to deal with, and taking it out on him wasn't fair.

With the table booked, she rounded the corner back onto the main road and saw Charles ahead of her, walking into Libertad. He didn't have the bike with him and neither was he in his cycling gear so she guessed he had already dropped it off. Wondering what he was doing now, and assuming he'd probably left something behind in the shop (she never failed to be surprised at the things customers inadvertently left), she dropped onto a nearby bench to wait for him.

Fifteen minutes later, he had yet to come out, so she decided to go and find him.

She got to her feet and crossed the road, and a few steps later she was outside the window and peering in, hoping to see him.

To her surprise, the shop floor was empty. Not even Stefan was there.

Frowning – Stefan never closed before six o'clock – she noticed that the sign on the door had been changed from 'open' to 'closed'.

Concerned that everything was all right, she pushed the door. It swung open.

Now she was getting worried.

Was Charles still here? And if he was, where was Stefan? Something must be wrong.

What if Charles had walked in on a hold-up? It was a bit dramatic, but she heard of this kind of thing happening, although admittedly she'd only ever heard of it on the TV.

Wishing she had some kind of a weapon (just in case – although what use it would be she wasn't entirely sure), she crept towards the back of the shop. She was tempted to call out, but something, some sixth sense that she wasn't alone, held her back.

Knowing what she was doing was foolish, yet unable to resist the urge to see what was going on, she placed one foot in front of the other as silently as possible and inched forward, breathing as quietly as she could and hoping the noise of her heart pounding wouldn't give her away.

A voice from behind the stockroom door made her jump and she stifled a scream with her hand, before sagging against the nearest rail of clothes and almost knocking it over. It was Stefan – and it didn't sound as though he was being held at knife point and forced to hand over the day's takings.

'It is agreed,' she heard him say. 'I will hold off until Wednesday, but after that...'

'I understand,' a second voice said, and this time Elspeth let out a squeal as she recognised the speaker.

Pushing the door open, she found Charles and Stefan shaking hands.

The two men froze.

Charles was the first to recover. He ended the handshake with a pat on Stefan's arm with his other hand, then let go of him and smiled at her.

'What's going on?' she asked, her attention swinging from one man to the other.

Charles looked at Stefan, Stefan looked at Charles, then they both looked at her.

'I was thanking Stefan for loaning me the bike,' Charles said at the same time as Stefan said, 'He was wishing me well, in Germany, with my parents.'

Elspeth wanted to give him a hug; he looked so forlorn.

'How did it go with the valuer?' she asked him.

'Good, good. It's all good.' He scratched his beard and added, 'Very good.'

Elspeth gave a small smile. 'That's good.'

Her boss shook his head. 'Please excuse me, I have work to do. Accounts and stuff.'

She could see how hard he was taking it and she wished she could do something, anything, to make it better.

'Yeah, I'd, er, better, um, get going too,' Charles said. 'Shall we?' He jerked his head towards the door and gestured for Elspeth to go ahead of him.

After saying goodbye to Stefan and stepping onto the pavement, she said to Charles, 'I expect you must be hungry, and because it's your last night on Tenerife I've booked a table at a restaurant around the corner.'

'That's nice. Very thoughtful, thank you.'

'Where did you go today?'

'Just… you know… the same route as I cycled the other day.'

'Did you manage to grab any lunch?'

'Er, yes, I did, thanks.'

Realising that he didn't seem very keen on talking, Elspeth fell silent, and neither of them said another word until they reached the villa.

Two weeks ago, her life was steady and predictable. Now though, she would shortly be saying goodbye to the man she loved, plus Stefan, whom she cared about a great deal, was selling his business and leaving, and she would also soon be out of a job.

It was all a bit too much to bear, and she needed an hour or so to herself.

'I'm going for a shower,' she announced, 'and a lie down in my room. The table is booked for eight.' And with that, she headed for the stairs, desperate to reach her room before she burst into tears.

'I've got a couple of phone calls to make, so I'll see you later,' Charles called after her.

She nodded and walked heavily up the stairs. She wouldn't cry – she *wouldn't*. Not yet. There'd be plenty of time for tears tomorrow after he'd gone. But despite her resolve, she did shed a tear or two as she dropped onto the bed and lay there, her cheeks damp, staring up at the ceiling and wishing he had already left the island, because she didn't know how she was going to be able to sit through a meal with the man she loved when she might never see him again.

Elspeth, determined not to let Charles see that her heart was breaking when it was time to get ready for dinner, dressed with care, wanting to look her best. She'd known what she was doing when she'd slept with him – it wasn't as though they'd declared their undying love for one another and then he'd dumped her. This relationship of theirs was a finite thing, bound and defined by the date he was to return to the UK (*tomorrow* – how could it have come so soon? She wasn't ready for it). The ending was known, the outcome was already written, so she needed to behave like an adult and not like a teenager with an unrequited crush.

Charles cared for her, she was certain of it, and she didn't think he made a habit of hopping into bed with women he didn't have feelings for – he wasn't that kind of man – but that was as far as it went. And she needed to accept that.

So, she went out for dinner with a stone in her heart, but with a bright smile on her face, and her dignity intact. Until, that is, Charles turned her world upside down.

Chapter 28

'It's nice here, isn't it?' Charles observed, his gaze roaming over the haphazardly plastered walls with pieces of bare stone artfully showing through. He looked up at the ceiling. 'I like the beams. Very authentic.'

'The food is good, too,' Elspeth told him.

He turned his attention back to the menu he was holding. 'Mmm, it all sounds wonderful.'

It did, but Elspeth found she didn't have much of an appetite. The wine, however, was slipping down her throat a little too easily.

She took a smaller sip than her previous ones and placed her long-stemmed glass back on the marked and pitted table. The fixtures and furniture were rustic and well used, but the cutlery shone, the simple white plates gleamed and the glassware sparkled in the subdued lighting.

A faint aroma of smoked garlic hung in the air, and even though she didn't feel like eating much, Elspeth thought maybe she could manage a morsel or two if she put her mind to it. She didn't think it polite to sit there pushing food around on her plate. With that in mind, she looked at the menu for the least heavy dish, which definitely meant no chips or Canarian potatoes.

'Can you bring me another glass of wine, please?' she asked, catching the attention of a passing waiter. 'Would you like another?' she said to Charles.

He shook his head. 'Not with a day of travelling ahead of me tomorrow. Besides,' he sent her a slow smile and her traitorous tummy turned over with desire. 'I'd like to keep a clear head for later tonight. On second thoughts...' His eyes suddenly twinkled and he beckoned the waiter back. 'Do you have champagne?'

'Of course, sir.'

'Could you bring a bottle to the table?'

The man inclined his head.

'And I think we might be ready to order?' Charles turned the statement into a question as he looked over the top of his menu at her.

Elspeth shrugged, not caring. 'I'll have whatever you're having,' she said. If he wanted to watch her pick at her food while he slurped champagne in some kind of weird celebration of their last night together then so be it.

The two of them sat in silence until the waiter returned with a bottle and a couple of champagne flutes. He poured the sparkling liquid with a flourish, then retreated.

Charles picked up his glass and held it up in front of him.

Elspeth made a grab for hers and went to take a sip.

'Not so fast,' he said with a chuckle. 'I want to propose a toast.'

Elspeth raised her eyebrows.

'To us,' he said, and reached across the table to clink glasses with her.

Elspeth didn't move. 'What us?'

'Me and you.'

'You're leaving tomorrow or have you forgotten?'

'I haven't forgotten. Yes, I'm leaving, but I'll be back as soon as I can.'

Yeah, right, as her son used to say.

Her scepticism must have shown on her face, because Charles set his glass down and reached for her hand instead.

'Don't you want me to come back to Tenerife? To come back to you?' he asked, and she could see the sudden doubt in his eyes.

'Yes, I do. But you won't. When you get home and settle into your usual routine, Tenerife will become nothing more than a pleasant memory.'

'That's where you're wrong—' he began, but she cut him off.

'It happens all the time. By their very nature, holiday romances don't last. You'll soon forget about me,' she insisted.

'No, I won't. I can't, since we'll be working together.'

Elspeth took a second or two to process what he'd just said. When she realised that she had heard him correctly, all she could say was, 'Excuse me?'

Charles was bubbling with excitement. His eyes were alight and he was grinning so widely she thought he was about to burst.

'I've put an offer in on Libertad,' he blurted out.

'Come again?' Elspeth leant forwards, her head on one side, her brow creased as she struggled to understand. Charles wasn't making a great deal of sense.

'Of course, we've got to go through a heap of rigmarole first, what with the solicitors and the accountants, and all the legal stuff that goes with purchasing a business over here, but I've been assured that as long as the books are sound and there aren't any unforeseen problems, then it should be a relatively straightforward process.'

Elspeth was still struggling. She knew what each word meant, but the way Charles was stringing them together made it sound as though he was— 'You want to buy Libertad?' she exclaimed.

'That's what I've been telling you. Isn't it wonderful?' He wore the same expression as a child in a sweetshop who'd been told he had an unlimited amount of pocket money to spend.

'Um, yes, I suppose it is…'

Some of the light and life drained out of his face, and Charles sat back in his seat. 'You don't think so.' He didn't phrase it as a question.

'It depends,' she replied, cautiously, 'on why you're doing it.'

He nodded slowly, thoughtfully, before he replied. 'There are several reasons: I envy your life here, the slower pace of it. I love the climate, the atmosphere, the food, the hiking. I enjoyed working alongside you in the shop; it was fun, although I'm not naive enough to think it will always be fun – it won't. I need a challenge; I'm getting stale, bored even. I've worked all my adult life and I've been a bit lost since I retired, if I'm honest.'

He paused to gather his thoughts and Elspeth took the opportunity to jump in. She wanted to make sure he'd thought seriously about such a big step, and she also wanted to keep a lid on the hope bubbling inside her – just in case it didn't happen.

'OK, I'm going to play devil's advocate, so hear me out,' she said. 'You talk about my slower pace of life? That's because I only work part-time and Libertad isn't *my* business. As soon as I leave the premises, I can forget about it. If you own it, you won't do that. I say "won't" not "can't", because some people might be able to do so, but I don't think you would be one of those.'

'Stefan doesn't—'

'Oh, he does, believe me. How do you think the business is doing so well? He hardly ever takes a day off. You won't, either,' she predicted. 'Climate? – OK, I'll give you that one. Even if you do spend all day in the shop, you'll be able to sit on your balcony or in your garden in the evening without getting frostbite. However, don't think you'll see much of it during the daytime, because you'll be working. I'll grant you the food argument, too, but as for the hiking, ditto working all day. You won't have much time for it. Or cycling. Unless you take on an employee, which will cut into your profits, like Stefan did with me. But unlike Stefan – and I'm being brutally honest here – you're not in your twenties. Stefan works damned hard but he's young enough to be able to do a full day's work then go surfing until it's dark. At your age, *our* age, we're lucky if we've got enough energy to pop the cork on a bottle of wine when we get home after working all day.'

He was watching her intently, absorbing everything she was saying, and his serious expression spurred her on.

'Then there's the fun part,' she continued. 'Hmm, where do I start with that? Take it from me, it isn't fun all that often, although Stefan and I have our moments. And you won't be working alongside me, either,' she added, thinking that there was no way she was going to have Charles as her boss. How could they remain lovers if he was her employer? It wasn't a good idea at all.

'Have you finished?' He didn't seem sarcastic or dismissive, he seemed curious, as though he genuinely wanted to know if there was anything else she was going to add.

There was.

'No, I haven't. What about your family?' she asked. 'They'll still be in the UK, and you think you might not see a lot of your daughters and grandchildren now, but being two thousand miles away isn't going to help the situation. It's hard being so far away, especially if they need you – or you need them.' She was thinking about when Ray died and she was left all alone.

He held his hand up. 'I know all this. Well, nearly all of it – we can discuss your job later. I have thought through what a move like this entails. Ever since you told me Stefan is selling Libertad, I've done nothing but think about it.'

'For all of two days?' she said. This was a big step. For him. For them. She was terrified that if he did buy Libertad, things mightn't work out the way Charles anticipated and where would that leave them then? She didn't want him to regret it. And she was also selfish enough to hope that he was doing this for her, for their relationship – but there wasn't even a hint of it.

'Longer than that. I've been considering my options for a while now, thinking about what to do with the rest of my life – because it's far from over, you know. I might have another twenty, thirty years in me, and I want as many of them to be as useful and as productive as possible. I might have retired from ophthalmic surgery, but I haven't retired from life.'

'That's an impressive speech.' Elspeth leaned back in her chair and folded her arms across her chest. At some point during their discussion, their starters had appeared and the food in front of them was now growing cold. She eyed her plate with indifference.

'Are we having our first argument?' A smile was playing about Charles's lips, and she found, despite her frustration, that she desperately wanted to kiss him.

'I'm not sure. Are we?' Her gaze remained defiant, challenging him to carry on.

'If we are, I'm not really clear why. I thought you'd be pleased.'

She should be, shouldn't she? Charles would be back in Tenerife before too long – she won't have lost him after all. They could take up where they'd left off, enjoying spending time with one another. She wouldn't be just another fond holiday romance.

But – and this was the part that she couldn't move beyond – not once had he mentioned that he wanted to stay in Tenerife because of *her*. The only time he'd brought her into his deliberations, was because of the 'fun' they could have working together. No indication of how he felt about her, or how she would slot into this new life of his, except as a paid employee.

'At least I know where I stand,' he muttered when she failed to respond, and he pushed his untouched plate away before throwing his napkin on the table and getting to his feet. 'I'd better call Stefan. Excuse me.'

'Wait.'

'Why?'

She took a deep breath. 'Are you doing this for you and you alone?'

'Yes.'

'Oh.' Crestfallen, she felt the familiar prick of imminent tears.

'Because I'm selfish,' he added, sinking back down onto his chair. 'I want to be with you. I had hoped you wanted to be with me, too… Do you?'

She nodded, the tears now perilously close to the surface. 'You don't have to buy Libertad to stay here,' she pointed out softly.

'But I do, for all the reasons I've just mentioned. I can't stagnate, Elspeth, and that's what I was doing before I came here.'

'What if the sale falls through? Have you set your heart on Libertad?'

'I've set my heart on *you*. The shop is an added bonus. If it falls through, then so be it, but I would find something else. It would be a shame, though, because I loved working there.'

She opened her mouth but before she could say anything he reached out and put his finger on her lips.

'I know what you're going to say about fun and hard work. If I do buy the shop, I intend to hire someone who can take over from me if we want to have a holiday, or take a couple of days off, or spend the afternoon in bed...'

His smile made her go weak. 'Ask for the bill,' she said. 'I suddenly feel a bit faint and need to go home and lie down.'

His lips parted, as he stared into her eyes. 'I'll ask if they can wrap this up to go, shall I, because I get the feeling we might be rather hungry later on.'

As it turned out Charles's premonition had been correct – it was considerably later before the pair of them reheated the food together, because, once back at the villa, a different kind of hunger consumed them for quite some time.

Chapter 29

Elspeth opened first one gritty eye and then the other, squinting heavily as she slapped the alarm clock off and flopped back onto the pillows with a groan. Five-thirty. Not particularly early on a normal day, but on most normal days she usually managed to achieve a decent night's sleep.

Charles sat up, rubbing his face. 'What time is it?'

'Time to get up, if you want to have a shower, a decent breakfast and finish packing.'

He looked at the clock. 'Just how long do you think it'll take me to shower, woman?'

'Toni is picking you up at seven,' Elspeth said, wishing she could turn over and go back to sleep. And not solely because she was shattered, either. Being awake and conscious meant she had to face the reality that Charles was leaving today.

He would be coming back shortly, but the knowledge didn't make her feel any better. She felt like she had when she was seventeen and had fallen hard for her first boyfriend, Duncan. When he'd informed her that he was off to university, her world had fallen apart and she'd been inconsolable for weeks.

It had been a mere ghost of the loss she'd felt when Ray had passed on, but even now she was able to recall the terrible insecurity she'd felt that Duncan would forget all about her (she was right, he had), that his life would move in the opposite direction to hers (she'd been right again – he had become a vet and emigrated to New Zealand), and that he'd become far too sophisticated and worldly-wise and that she'd be left behind (the sophisticated part hadn't quite panned out, while he was at university at least, unless drinking snakebites and White Lightning could be considered classy).

That she felt the same way this morning was troubling. She was forty years older, had married, had brought up a child, had experienced losses that her seventeen-year-old self could never have imagined, yet she was as scared of losing Charles – of being left behind, of being moved on from, and forgotten about – as she had been of losing Duncan.

It appeared that older didn't necessarily mean wiser.

Determinedly pushing the what-ifs to one side, Elspeth made to get out of bed. They might have an hour and a half before Charles needed to leave, but she had a feeling it would fly by.

Charles, though, seemed to think he had all the time in the world, and he pulled her back under the covers.

'Again?' she squeaked.

'Again.'

Dear God, the man was insatiable, she thought as his lips met hers once more.

–

'It really is time to get up,' she said a good while later, feeling breathless and a bit wobbly as she sat up and swung her legs to the floor.

'I don't want to. I want to stay here all day,' was his slightly petulant reply.

'I need a cup of tea.'

'I need *you*.'

'You've just had me,' Elspeth replied smartly.

His slow smile made her toes curl. 'I didn't mean in that way, although now you come to mention it...' The smile faded. 'I really *do* need you.'

She paused and studied him. 'I'm not sure I know what you mean?'

'The thought of going back to the UK and not having you by my side fills me with such sadness.'

'It does?' Despite herself and her misgivings, her heart skipped a beat.

He nodded.

'I feel the same,' she said.

His smile lit up his face.

'I wish you didn't have to leave,' she added.

'So do I. But if I'm to go ahead and buy Libertad – which I most certainly am, if everything goes to plan – then I have lots to sort out.'

Elspeth agreed and didn't envy him in the slightest as she remembered how much organising and planning she'd done when she and Ray had relocated to Tenerife, and that was without buying a local business. Ray had left the emigration details to her, focusing his attention on the plans he had for Villa Cruz.

Elspeth wandered into the bathroom and turned the dial on the shower, trying to keep a check on her emotions. It wasn't as though Charles was going for good and she'd never see him again. He'd be back soon enough. She had to hold onto the thought, because thinking positively, along with the phone calls they would inevitably have, would be the only things to sustain her until he did.

Breakfast was a subdued affair, with both of them catching each other's eyes then giving a small smile and looking away. If it hadn't been so heart-wrenching, it would have been awkward. Everything had been said that could be said, and Elspeth worried that his future in Tenerife – their future together – depended on whether the purchase of Libertad would go ahead. Despite Charles's optimism, it wasn't guaranteed.

Which begged the question, for Elspeth at least – if he didn't buy the shop, would he return to Tenerife as he'd claimed he would? Was Elspeth enough to draw him back, or was she merely part of the overall package?

When Toni knocked on the door, she fancied she saw relief in Charles's face, and she was fairly sure there was a hint of it in her expression as well.

Long, drawn-out goodbyes weren't her thing; it was the difference between gently easing a plaster off and prolonging the pain, or simply ripping it off – the pain might be worse in the short term, but it would be over much quicker. Elspeth was definitely a ripper, not an easer.

'Hi, Toni? How are you?' she asked mechanically as she answered the door to her friend.

Charles's luggage was already in the hall, and he hovered behind her waiting for her to move aside.

She did so slowly, reluctantly, torn between wanting to get this over with and not wanting to let him go. Ever.

But of course she had to, and, with a final bone-crushing desperate hug, she released him, and stood in the square watching Charles being driven away, as he peered over his shoulder from the passenger seat at her.

A final wave and he was gone.

And for Elspeth life would never be the same again.

Chapter 30

Elspeth couldn't settle. She kept getting up and peering through the front door to see whether Gideon had arrived. Which was quite ridiculous, because if he had, he would have knocked. She didn't need to keep looking – all it did was make her jumpy. She'd be better off sitting in the courtyard with a nice cup of tea and a paperback. But every time her backside hit a seat, it was as though there was a spring in it, propelling her back up again.

For what must have been the thirtieth time since his flight had landed, Elspeth stared out into the square, hoping to see some sign of her son. He'd told her he was hiring a car at the airport, and she kept expecting to see it pulling up outside the villa any second.

And for what was possibly the hundredth time, she checked her watch.

They should be here by now. Ten minutes to disembark; fifteen minutes to go through Passport Control; half an hour to collect their luggage (and that was being generous); another half an hour to sort out the car-hire paperwork, then find the darned vehicle in the car park; another forty-five minutes, allowing for traffic, to travel from the airport to Santiago del Teide.

So, where were they?

She glanced at the time again, to find it was only thirty seconds later than the last time she'd looked. With a sigh, she went back inside and loitered in the hall.

She knew the flight wasn't delayed because she'd checked online, so the hold-up must be due to another reason. She hoped to goodness that there wasn't an issue at Passport Control, or that their luggage had got lost.

It was probably the traffic, she decided. The TF1, which was the main road along the south west of the island, was always busy.

She poked her head out of the front door yet again, then let out a squeal.

They were here! Really here! She couldn't believe it. With tears spilling down her cheeks, she rushed up to the car and practically hopped up and down as she waited impatiently for her son to get out.

'Gideon!' she cried, hurling herself at him. He managed to stand upright for a brief moment before her weight caused him to fall back slightly against the car.

'Hang on there, Mum, you nearly knocked me over!'

'I don't care.' She hugged him so tightly he made an odd strangled sound.

'Let go, Mum, I can't breathe.'

But Elspeth was busy showering his cheek with snuffly kisses. 'I've missed you so much,' she cried, as Gideon tried to disentangle her.

Abruptly, she released him, and bent down to peer into the car. Her daughter-in-law was still sitting in the passenger side she noticed out of the corner of her eye, but it was the little boy strapped into a child seat in the back who captured her attention.

Elspeth gave Sakura a brief wave, then opened the back door and reached in.

Rai, eyes huge in his chubby face, stared solemnly at her before recoiling as far as he could within the confines of his car seat. His little mouth fell open, his chin began to wobble, and his eyes screwed up as he began to wail.

'Let me, Mum,' Gideon said, gently moving her aside and taking her place. 'He isn't used to you, that's all.' Her son spoke to the boy in fluent Japanese, while unclipping his harness and lifting him out of the car.

Elspeth felt like crying herself.

Rai didn't know her. His own grandmother.

Oh, God, she couldn't bear it.

Plastering a smile on her face and trying not to show that Rai's reaction had upset her, she turned to Sakura, who had climbed out of the passenger seat and was reaching for her bag.

'Hello, had a good journey?' Elspeth asked. 'Here, let me get that. You see to Rai. Come in, come in, I expect you could do with a cup of tea.'

Sakura smiled. 'No tea; coffee, please, and may I use your bathroom, Okaasan?'

'Of course! I'll show you.' It had taken Elspeth a while to get used to the title Okaasan, and she still wasn't entirely sure what it meant, but Gideon had assured her it was a polite term for mother.

'No need, I remember from last visit.' Sakura bowed slightly, her black bob shining glossily.

'Oh, yes, I expect you do. You go on ahead, I'll help Gideon.' Elspeth knew she was babbling, and hoped she wasn't coming across as slightly hysterical. She was feeling rather overwhelmed and tearful, and it was an effort to keep her tears in check.

When Gideon opened the boot and hefted out a suit-case with one hand, she took it from him, sending a reassuring smile to her grandson as she did so.

The little boy had stopped wailing, but he still wore a wary expression.

Maybe he'd come round a bit after he'd settled in, she reasoned. He'd just had a long journey and this was so new and strange. Hopefully he'd soon recognise her as that nice woman on the computer, the one whom he had happily smiled and waved at before.

Dragging a suitcase, she ushered Gideon and Rai inside, before depositing the luggage at the bottom of the stairs.

'I'll hold Rai if you want to take the cases up to your room. I've put you in mine.' The thought of Gideon and Sakura sleeping in the room she had made love to Charles in, didn't seem right, somehow. In fact, she'd spent the last week sleeping there, because it made her feel closer to Charles.

She had attempted to sleep in her own bed on the night Charles had departed, but had been unable to settle, so she'd slipped between the sheets she'd yet to change in the other bedroom, and had lain awake for hours, with the scent of Charles lingering around her.

'I'll wait until Sakura can hold him,' Gideon said. 'He's calm now and I don't want to upset him again.'

Neither did Elspeth – that was the last thing she wanted – but she was so desperate to hold the child it gave her a physical ache in her chest.

'I'll make the coffee then,' she said, moving past her son and going into the kitchen, feeling flat and upset. This wasn't how she imagined their reunion would be, and she wasn't sure how she could make things better.

Look, she told herself as she took some cups out of the cupboard, they've done a lot of travelling over the past few days, which was draining in itself, without adding a young child into the mix. They were probably tired, and could do with a freshen up and a quiet hour to relax, before she bombarded them.

By the time the drinks were made, Gideon had taken the cases upstairs and Sakura had changed Rai's nappy and had given him some juice, Elspeth was feeling a little better about everything. She'd been over-excited, she could see that now, and with them all seated in the courtyard, the atmosphere had lightened considerably.

'You're looking well,' she said to Gideon. He was a hard worker and she often worried that he was taking too much on.

'I feel it.'

Elspeth drank him in, scrutinising his light brown hair so like his father's, the eyes he had inherited from her, the nose which could have come from either set of grandparents. He looked a little older than the last time she'd seen him in the flesh, a little more mature, but that was to be expected. Weekly Skype calls helped, but they didn't lay her worry to rest, and seeing him for herself calmed her ever-present concern regarding her only child.

Sakura hadn't said much, and when Elspeth turned her attention to her, she saw how tired and strained her daughter-in-law appeared to be. Her heart-shaped face was tense, and there were dark circles below her eyes. Always petite, she now was positively gaunt, and Elspeth's heart went out to her – looking after a young child was never easy.

'How did you enjoy London, Sakura?' Elspeth asked.

'It was tiring. So many things to see. The shopping was good, and I am looking forward to—'

'Why don't you have a lie down for a couple of hours?' Gideon interrupted. 'You look worn out, and Rai could definitely do with a nap.' He jiggled the little boy sitting on his knee and spoke to him in Japanese.

Elspeth noticed Sakura's frown, and saw that she began to say something, but Gideon spoke again in Japanese, and Sakura's face cleared and she nodded.

'Sleepy time, Rai?' she said instead, and Gideon handed the child over. The little boy didn't look enthused at the idea, his face scrunching up as he shook his head.

'I used to say that to you,' Elspeth said to Gideon. 'Do you remember?'

'I do; that's why we say it to Rai.'

Elspeth knew that her grandson understood some English because of her interactions with him on Skype, but she was pleased to hear that Sakura was also using English with him.

She watched mother and child go inside, before she said, 'Is Sakura all right? She seems a bit down.' Sakura wasn't what Elspeth would call effervescent, but she was usually far livelier than this.

'She's fine – a bit tired, that's all. We all are. It's been a hectic few days. Do you mind if I have a lie down, too? I know we've only just got here, but we can have a proper catch-up later.'

'Of course I don't mind. You go and have a rest – you've got plenty of time before dinner.'

Gideon slapped a hand to his forehead. 'I was going to buy some champagne in Duty Free but I've had so much on my mind...'

'We don't need champagne,' Elspeth chuckled. 'Having you here is enough of a celebration, and I do have wine, you know.'

Gideon grinned. 'I've got some news,' he said. 'That's what the champagne would have been for.'

'Ooh!' She clapped her hands together. 'What is it?'

But all her son said was, 'I'll tell you at dinner when we can raise a toast.'

Despite further pleadings on her part, Gideon's mouth was firmly closed on the subject, and after he'd gone upstairs for a nap, Elspeth was left on her own to do some serious guessing.

She may as well start dinner, she decided, unable to sit still. She hadn't regained her composure from her son's arrival yet, and she was full of unresolved energy. As she got the various ingredients for this evening's meal out of the fridge and the cupboards, she ran through several possibilities, before narrowing them down to three: either Gideon had been promoted, Sakura was pregnant again, or they'd bought another house.

Out of the three contenders, the only one she had mixed feelings about was another grandchild.

She hardly knew the one she'd got. Rai was unsure about her, and she hated not being around more to see him grow up. It would be doubly hard with another baby on the scene. But Sakura expecting again would explain her washed-out appearance and subdued attitude, Elspeth thought to herself.

Of course, she would be delighted for her son and his wife, if this were the case! It was wonderful news. Her only hope was that she'd see a tiny bit more of this new baby than she had of Rai – she'd only seen him once since he'd been born, and she envied his Japanese grandparents, who lived near the family, with all her heart. Elspeth had never more keenly felt she was missing out on Rai's growing up than she did now, and the fact that he had not recognised her earlier only added to her regret.

There wasn't anything she could do about it, however. Gideon and his family lived in Japan, she lived in Tenerife, and that's the way it was.

She was busy chopping and slicing when her mobile rang, and her heart leapt as she hurried to answer it, wiping her hands on a towel as she did so.

'Charles! How are you?'

'Missing you like crazy.'

She giggled. 'Apart from that…? Hang on.' She scooped the chopped vegetables into a pan.

'Oh, sorry, you're probably busy – I'm assuming Gideon and the family have arrived?'

'They're all taking a nap.'

'Great, you've got a couple of minutes to talk; have you missed me?'

'More than you'll ever know,' she murmured.

'That's good, because I hope to be back on Friday. My UK accountant has examined the books, my solicitor is liaising with Stefan's solicitor, and everything appears to be looking OK. There's the due diligence still to do, plus some other legal stuff which I won't go into right now, so I'm not sure how long it will take for the sale to be finalised, but it seems to be progressing nicely. There's little point in my being in the UK, so I thought I'd rather be with you than here on my own – I can always fly back if I need to, but to be honest they can probably email or post anything that I need to sign.' Elspeth heard him take a deep breath, before he continued. 'Besides, Stefan needs to be with his parents in Germany, so we've agreed that

I am to take over the shop on a managerial basis in the interim.'

'Oh, my God! That's fantastic news! I can't wait to see you.' He'd only been gone just over a week, but it felt considerably longer. She quickly calculated that she had enough time to change all the bedding after Gideon left on Friday morning and give both bedrooms a thorough clean before Charles arrived. It might resemble a revolving door with her family heading off in the early morning, and Charles arriving in the afternoon, but at least she'd not have time to brood. No doubt seeing Charles would soon take her mind off Gideon's departure.

'And I can't wait to take you to bed,' he said.

'Is that all you want me for, for my body?'

'Yes, most definitely.'

'Glad that's clear, then,' she retorted wryly.

'Um, there's just one thing,' Charles said, sounding more serious. 'I'm thinking of taking over Stefan's apartment, at least in the short term.'

Elspeth was taken aback. She'd assumed he would move in with her. Stefan lived above the pharmacy on the main street; the apartment above Libertad was owned by an elderly couple. Charles wouldn't be far away from the villa, but...

'Elspeth?'

'I'm still here. It's probably wise,' she agreed. She might have fallen in love with Charles, but from what he'd just said, she wasn't sure he was as committed just yet, despite taking the huge step of moving to Tenerife and making a new life for himself on the island.

'I don't want to assume anything,' he was saying. 'I know what we had – what I hope we *still* have – wasn't necessarily real life, and I want to take the time to court you properly.'

Elspeth couldn't think of anything to say.

'Are you OK?' he asked.

'I'm fine.'

'No, you're not. Something's wrong. What is it?'

'Nothing.'

'I know that when a woman says nothing is wrong, what she means is that something most definitely *is* wrong. Don't you want me to come back to Tenerife? Is that what you're trying to tell me?'

'No!'

'Okaaay – is it because I'm buying the business?'

'Not at all. I think it's a great idea now I've had a chance to think it over.'

'But you don't want to work for me, is that it? I can understand that. If it's going to be an issue, I can pull out of the sale. I don't have to work at all, if you don't want me to.'

Confused, and not sure what he was getting at, she said, 'It's not about what I want.'

'Yes, it is. What's on your mind? You're going to have to tell me, otherwise I'll spend all day guessing.'

'You don't want to live with me,' she said in a small voice.

'You think I really want to rent an apartment?'

'Don't you?'

'No, I damned well don't! What I want is for you to fall asleep in my arms every night. I want to wake up next to you. I want to spend every day and every night with you. I love you and I want to spend the rest of my life with you. Hell, woman, I want to marry you!' he shouted.

There was silence for a few moments as both of them digested what he'd just said.

Then she heard him take a deep breath. 'I didn't intend to say that.'

'No, I don't believe you did,' Elspeth said quietly. She hadn't been expecting anything like that, and she collapsed into a chair, feeling quite giddy. First he had told her he loved her, then he had told her he didn't mean it.

'Not over the phone and certainly not yet,' he continued, a little bashful. 'I wanted to give you a chance to get used to the idea of having me around permanently first, before I told you how I feel about you. And I was hoping for some romance: candles, wine, dinner, a nice sunset.'

'It doesn't matter.' And somehow it didn't. It was the words that mattered, not the setting. Had he really just told her he loved her? And that he wanted to marry her? Elspeth was glad she was sitting down because she felt weak and shaky, while her heart was doing cartwheels in her chest.

'It does to me. I want to woo you properly.'

Elspeth couldn't help it – a giggle sneaked out. 'Woo?'

'Yeah, I know. Corny, or what?'

'Dinner, candles, wine?'

'Don't forget the sunset,' he added. 'I think I fell in love with you that very first night. You looked so beautiful in the courtyard, with the sun setting behind you and all those glorious colours.'

'Are you certain it wasn't Tenerife you fell in love with?'

'Ah, yes, the island might have my heart, but you have my soul.'

Elspeth thought she was about to cry. A strangled-sounding yes, was all she could manage.

'Yes?' The hope in his voice tugged at her heart.

'I'd love to marry you. But not just yet. I want all this wooing you've been talking about. And I want you to come live with me. Not just stay in the villa as a guest, but move in with me.'

'Are you sure?'

'I've never been so sure about anything in my life.'

'You've only known me three weeks.'

'Three weeks, three months, three years... at our age we can't afford to hang about.'

'Hey, we're not that old!' Charles objected.

'Maybe not, but both of us have far more years behind us than we've got ahead of us, and I don't intend fannying about and wasting any of them.'

'I don't fanny.'

'You're talking about renting a flat. That's fannying.'

'Not any more, I'm not.'

'Good, that's sorted then. Oh, one more thing – I expect to be asked again, properly next time.'

Chapter 31

Elspeth knew she would have to fight hard to keep her happiness and excitement under wraps for the remainder of the afternoon, although she thought that if her son noticed that she seemed over-exuberant, she could always put it down to her joy at seeing her family again.

And she really did have so much to be joyful about.

Not only did she have a handsome, successful son, she had a sweet daughter-in-law, a wonderful little grandson, a gorgeous villa in one of the loveliest places in the world *and* she was also in love with a kind, good-looking, generous, gentle man who loved her in return, and had just asked her to marry him. She fully intended that Charles should do the promised wooing first though, and then ask for her hand again in a more romantic manner. On one knee would be nice.

There was a fly in the ointment of her happiness though, and that centred on Gideon.

Gideon hadn't been too keen on Charles being in her house as a guest, so how on earth was he going to feel about him moving in with her? And for that reason (as well as not wanting to steal Gideon's thunder over his promised announcement), there was no way Elspeth was going to tell him tonight, or at any other time during his visit. The short amount of time that she was able to spend with her son and his family was far too precious to spoil with any negativity of any kind.

Gideon would be gone by the time Charles arrived, so Elspeth decided she would tell her son in a couple of weeks.

Maybe she could gently lead Gideon into the idea of Charles still being in her life by mentioning that Charles had bought Libertad. Then maybe, after popping his name into the conversation a few times (in the same way she talked about Stefan with Gideon – purely as part of her working day), she could say they'd been out for a meal. Or two. Get Gideon used to hearing about Charles gradually – she didn't want to spring the planned changes on him all at once, because she knew what he would say. He'd tell her the same thing that she would have told him if he'd broken the news that he was going to marry a girl after only knowing her a matter of weeks. She'd tell him to slow down, step back, and make sure that was what he wanted to do.

And she couldn't blame her son if he ended up telling her this – he did have her best interests at heart.

She was so excited about her and Charles living together – she'd become very used to having him there at the villa and he was such an incredibly easy man to live with. The other option, of course, was to sell the villa and for Charles and her to buy somewhere else new together; but it wasn't something Elspeth wanted to consider, and as long as Charles could cope with Ray residing in the courtyard, finding another place to live was a moot point.

Elspeth continued to let her thoughts run away with her. She'd have to redecorate the room Charles had slept in though, if she intended for that room to become the master bedroom. Even now, there was no way she could contemplate Charles sleeping in the room she'd shared with Ray. It simply wouldn't be right.

And there was the issue of Charles technically being her boss if the sale of the shop went through. Elspeth wasn't certain how she felt about that. She'd worked at Libertad for a long time and knew almost as much about the business as Stefan did, so how would she feel about the man she shared a bed with coming along with different (and possibly unfeasible) ideas, wanting to shake up a perfectly good way of doing things? Would they argue?

Most definitely.

Therefore, it might be sensible for her to look for another part-time job.

With all this on her mind, and the fact that Gideon had something to tell her, especially since Elspeth was convinced she had already worked out his news, by the time he and the rest of his little family ventured downstairs, she was a little distracted as she scurried between the kitchen and the courtyard, busily laying the table while seeing to the final preparations for their meal.

'It'll be about twenty minutes,' she said. 'Did you have a good rest?'

'Yes, thanks, although Rai will probably be up half the night. Sakura usually makes him have a nap much earlier than this.' Gideon made a face, and Elspeth sympathised – even after all this time, she remembered how hard it could be when a small child was out of routine.

'You're on holiday, so if he stays up a bit later, it doesn't matter. I'm sure between us we can wear him out,' she said. And if Rai continued to cry every time she went near him, that should do it, she thought sadly. 'Red or white?' she asked, holding up a wine glass.

'Red for me, please, but Sakura prefers white.'

'Oh, should she… um? OK.' Perhaps one little glass wouldn't hurt. The advice about what you can and can't eat, drink, or do whilst pregnant changed constantly, so maybe there'd been an about-turn on alcohol consumption.

Elspeth poured the wine and handed Gideon and Sakura a glass each before gesturing that they make themselves comfortable in the living room while she finished preparing their meal. 'Can I get anything for Rai?' she asked her daughter-in-law.

'No, thank you. He has water.' Sakura held out a sippy-cup to the little boy, which he ignored. He was more interested in unloading the books from the bookcase in the corner.

'I've got a box of toys for him,' Elspeth said, fetching the playthings from the cupboard in the hall. She'd made a special trip to Playa de las Américas earlier in the week to buy them from the large toyshop there, and it had taken most of her day off to get there and back.

With Rai happily rooting through the unfamiliar toys, and Sakura sitting on the floor supervising, Elspeth began to relax. She'd been on edge and so looking forward to this visit, that she was scared something would go wrong or they wouldn't enjoy themselves.

'Have you got any plans while you're here?' she asked. 'You might want to consider visiting Jungle Park – they've got meerkats.'

'I wouldn't mind going to Santa Cruz,' Gideon said. 'I haven't been there in years, and there is some interesting architecture I'd like to take a look at.'

'Talk about a busman's holiday,' Elspeth joked.

It was a long time since she'd been to Tenerife's capital city too, but she had no real hankering to visit it again. If she thought the big towns such as Los Cristianos and Playa de Las Américas were busy, they weren't a patch on Santa Cruz. She wasn't used to the size of it, the sprawl of urbanisation, the volume of traffic or the number of people. As far as capital cities went, Santa Cruz was a small one, and the older parts were filled with historic buildings and lots of squares with water features. It also had a huge harbour and a magnificent golden beach created with sand imported from the Sahara, along with the best shopping in the Canary Islands. But, despite all the attractions, Elspeth preferred her quiet little corner of the island. With each passing year, she appreciated the peace and the rugged beauty more and more. Gone were the days when she relished the hustle and bustle of city life – she had never truly liked living in London, and it had been a relief when Ray's job had taken them to the more genteel environs of Oxford later on in their marriage.

'This whole trip has been something of a busman's holiday,' Gideon said, and she remembered that he'd had to go to London for work prior to coming to see her. No wonder he was tired.

She vowed to make their short stay as relaxing as possible. Gideon had the same work ethic as his father, the only difference being that Ray had spent hours poring over old manuscripts, and Gideon spent hours poring over architectural plans, interspersed with visits to building sites.

'I don't think I've ever told you how proud I am of you,' she declared impulsively.

Gideon blinked. 'Thanks, Mum. What brought that on?'

'Don't mind me – I'm just a bit emotional. It's been far too long since I last saw you, and I miss my little boy.'

He snorted and gestured at his six-foot frame. 'I'm hardly little.'

'You'll always be my little boy, no matter how big or important you get. I was telling Ch—' She stopped. Now wasn't the time nor the place to bring Charles's name into the conversation. Instead, she changed tack. 'Stefan is selling the shop; did I tell you? He's going back to Germany because his father is ill.'

'What about your job? Will the new owners keep you on?'

'I expect so.' She smiled to herself; the new owner definitely would, but she still wasn't convinced it was a good idea to work for him. 'I'll probably look for something else, though. It's time I had a change. Hang on a sec, I need to check on dinner.'

It wasn't a lie, but neither did she want her face to give too much away, because she was buzzing with excitement once more as she thought about Charles and what he'd said to her earlier on the phone.

Satisfied nothing was burning and everything was under control, she placed some plates in the oven to warm and went back into the living room. It made her heart ache with pleasure to see Sakura and Rai playing, while her son sprawled on the sofa, his long legs stretched out in front of him. All that was needed was Charles in the room and this moment would be complete.

'I'm glad you're thinking of a change,' Gideon said, 'because I've got some news.'

Elspeth arranged her face into what she hoped was a curious expression. She'd better make sure she showed the appropriate level of surprise, given that she already suspected what was coming.

'Mum,' Gideon said, beaming widely, 'we're moving back to London. And we'd like you to come with us.'

Chapter 32

'That way you'd be able to see as much of Rai as you'd like,' Gideon was saying. 'Sakura would welcome the help. At the moment her parents help out an awful lot with the baby. She'll miss that. Besides, she's thinking of going back to work. As you know, her English is excellent, so she could easily get work as a translator. If you could look after Rai in the week, then that would be a weight off our minds. You'd have to live in London, of course. You wouldn't be able to move back to Oxford. Maybe rent a small flat close by, and—'

Elspeth stopped listening.

Her heart felt as though it had stopped working, along with her ears.

Gideon was moving back to the UK?

Her first reaction had been, thank God! He'd be moving closer.

Her second had been a plummeting of her heart as the consequences of what this meant sank in.

Leave Tenerife? How could she? This was her home. Her life was here, her job, her friends, Ray... And now, so too, was Charles.

'Say something,' Gideon urged. 'You look as though you've seen a ghost. I thought you'd be pleased!'

At one time, she might well have been. In the aftermath of Ray's death, she would have been delighted to move to be near her son. His support would have meant so much.

But Gideon had been thousands of miles away, and she'd got through the crushing grief and loneliness on her own, with help from Amanda and Toni, and then from Stefan.

'It's a big step,' she said, after too long a pause, during which she could tell that Gideon was growing irritated.

Sakura, serene as always, was concentrating on showing Rai a round toy peg that fitted in a round hole, rather than the triangular one he was insisting on. A random thought popped into Elspeth's head – she should have bought a highchair for her grandson – it would have made mealtimes a lot easier, but she dismissed it quickly. What was the point? The next time she saw Rai, he'd probably be able to sit at the table on a proper chair.

Unless she moved back to London.

She'd be able to see as much of the little boy as she wanted then. And Gideon, too. She'd have her family around her, just like she'd so desperately wanted for the last four years. Being such a distance from them hadn't been so bad when Ray was alive because they'd had each other. But after he'd passed on, sometimes she'd had to force herself not to jump on a plane to go and visit her son.

'I suppose it is a big step,' Gideon agreed, 'but not as big as when you and Dad came out here in the first place. And it's not as if you won't know the language or the customs, and you'll have company. Of course, my new job will take up a great deal of my time, which is one of the reasons why Sakura was thinking of going back to work herself – so she won't be on her own all day with the baby.'

But you expect me to be, Elspeth thought glumly. The responsibility of looking after Rai for what could amount to five days a week was certainly something to factor in. Babysitting now and again was one thing – having her grandson all week was quite another.

Yet… she so very much wanted to be part of the little boy's life – she'd even banged on about it to Charles.

Oh, God!

Feeling torn and a little ambushed, Elspeth used the excuse of dishing up the food to put some space between her and her son, and the conversation didn't resume until they were all seated at the table outside in the courtyard.

Elspeth ate what she could of her meal, letting Gideon chatter on about how wonderful living in London would be – all the museums and galleries she could visit; all the sightseeing she'd be able to do; the theatres, the shows, the shopping.

To Elspeth, it didn't sound appealing at all. At least Gideon couldn't try to sway her with the weather, she thought sourly, but he was doing his level best on every other front.

'Anyway,' he said, when she'd cleared the dishes and they were finishing off the wine, 'I've said my piece. Have a think about it, yeah? Personally, I think it's a no-brainer, but you have to be happy with the decision.'

Needing time to think and process the information, Elspeth was happy to talk about other things for the rest of the evening, after Sakura had put Rai to bed. Gideon told her all about his new job and how he'd been headhunted by the firm he was going to work for. Sakura shared some funny stories about Rai, and they chatted for a bit about how different Japan was to England.

Apart from the news about Stefan and his father, Elspeth didn't tell her son and his wife about her other news.

Not yet.

Especially since she was now faced with a huge decision to make.

Elspeth decided that she would stick to her original plan of drip-feeding Charles's name into the conversation. If – and it was a big 'if' now that her personal circumstances might change significantly – their relationship progressed.

There was every chance it wouldn't, not after this news.

And that was another thing she had to take into consideration when making her decision.

–

Elspeth was still turning it all over in her mind when she retired to bed, and she let out a long sigh. She spent the next hour tossing and turning, unable to sleep, while the house and the town settled around her. Feeling frustrated, she got out of bed and got dressed in her hiking gear, trying to be as quiet as possible; she could just imagine Gideon waking up and finding her gone. He'd panic.

She left a note to tell Gideon that she'd gone for a stroll.

He'd probably be unhappy about it, but she was a grown-up and this wouldn't be the first time she'd wedged a head torch on and headed out into the surrounding hills in the dark to try and clear her mind. And just because her son was staying under her roof didn't mean she needed to check in with him. She didn't intend to go far. She planned to stick to a route she was familiar with and had walked at night in the past.

The Camino de la Fuente de la Virgen (or the Road of the Fountain of the Virgin, in English) was a distinct path beginning just off the main road marked by a shrine to the Virgin Mary. Elspeth soon passed under a white stone archway and crossed over a quaint white stone bridge which spanned a shallow ravine that had never seen a drop of water in all the years she'd lived in Santiago del Teide.

The night was a dark one, the path illuminated only by the lights from the town and the stars overhead, so when Elspeth stepped off the bridge, she switched the head torch on. The track was rough underfoot, with loose rocks. It began to climb immediately, and within half an hour she was a couple of hundred feet above the town.

A line of fourteen two-metre-high white wooden crosses marched up the side of the track, put up to mark the route to the shrine high above, and she wished it was light enough to see the intricately-carved round plaques at their bases properly, as each one depicted a different Biblical scene. She counted each one off as she reached it, until she finally passed the last but one cross and knew she was nearing her destination. The final cross was positioned on the top of the white marble grotto, which was a shrine to Our Lady of Lourdes. It was so peaceful here, and the atmosphere was one of religious reverence. Elspeth lowered herself onto one of the small stools placed in front of the shrine, and felt peace seep into her weary mind as she gazed at the statue of the Virgin Mary that stood in front of her.

Perfume from the flowers which had been placed around the shrine filled the air, and she breathed in their scent, listening to the wind sighing through the leaves of the surrounding bushes, with the faint noise of the occasional passing vehicle drifting up from the valley below.

The lights of Santiago del Teide were visible, and Elspeth did what she always did when she came up here – she searched for the sight of Villa Cruz's rooftop below.

Could she bring herself to leave all this?

Up on the mountain, she felt calm, centred. What peace would there be for her in a huge metropolis such as London?

She knew she needed to speak to Charles and inform him of this new (and, if she was truthful, somewhat frightening) development, but she had no idea how to explain it to him. It might be best to leave it until she'd made a decision first, but when would that be?

After Charles told her he wanted to marry her, Elspeth thought she had her life mapped out, that she knew what she wanted, but now Gideon had turned everything on its head and she didn't know which way was up any more.

Thinking logically (and if she discounted all the other reasons that Charles had suggested for wanting to emigrate to Tenerife), a move back to England would mean that Charles wouldn't need to relocate. She could join him in the UK, and they'd both be closer to their families. Him moving so far away from his daughters had been one of her concerns and she was worried that he'd regret it later.

But there was also the possibility he would carry on with the purchase of Libertad regardless; she knew he'd set his heart on it, and she had no way of telling what option he'd choose – a new life in Tenerife, possibly alone, or his old life in the UK with her.

Then there was the continuing issue of whether she actually wanted to leave her adopted island; Elspeth kept coming back to this point, no matter which direction her thoughts took her in. She hadn't considered it when Ray died, as there was nothing left for her back in England, but should she consider it now, when her dear wish of being part of little Rai's life could easily be granted?

She couldn't forget Ray in this either. She might not feel his presence anymore, but his ashes were still buried under the orchid tree. Could she abandon him here, possibly to be dug up if the villa's new owners wanted to put in a pool? And she also needed to consider the villa itself. It had been her home for years, and she had so many memories tied up in the house.

Elspeth perched on her cold stool, alongside the statue of the Virgin Mary, and stared out across the valley. The stars twinkled overhead and there was the faint smear of a cloud in the heavens. She wondered again if she'd be able to leave all this behind.

'Goddamn you, Gideon,' she muttered. Why the hell did he have to live halfway across the world in the first place – if he'd been living in Britain when his father had died, then she wouldn't be having this conversation with herself. She'd have moved back to the UK in a heartbeat after Ray's funeral.

Then again, she would never have met Charles and that thought to her now was inconceivable.

Why, oh why, did life have to leap up and bite her in the backside, just when she was ready to start living fully again?

It was always the way – you thought you had everything sorted, that you knew where you were going, then the Gods decided to throw the dice, and you were forced to see how they fell.

With another heavy sigh, and no nearer to deciding what she should do, Elspeth rose to her feet and made her slow careful way back down the path, knowing that she was going to spend the remainder of the night in a fretful slumber.

Because whatever she decided to do, she had an awful feeling that she would be hurting one or other of the men she loved.

Chapter 33

Elspeth sent Amanda an apologetic look and reached into her bag to draw out her phone, knowing who the caller was before she'd even checked the glowing screen.

It was Charles.

She let it go to answerphone. He'd phoned twice today already, but she simply couldn't bring herself to speak to him – not when her life was so uncertain. She had to make a decision soon – it was already Monday, and Charles would be back in the villa in four days' time.

'What's going on?' Amanda demanded, her hands on her hips. 'You've got a face like a wet weekend in Wales. I thought you'd be as happy as Larry to have Gideon here. And speaking of Gideon, why are you moping around at my place when you should be spending time with him?'

'Gideon and the family have gone to Santa Cruz for the day,' Elspeth replied. Unable to bear her turbulent thoughts any longer, she'd popped in to see Amanda. She'd only just arrived at the hotel when her mobile phone had rung.

'Didn't you want to go with them?' her friend asked.

'Not really. I'm quite tired, to be honest – I didn't sleep much last night.' She hadn't slept at all, nor the night before when she'd returned to bed after her night walk, and she had the bags and dark circles under her eyes to prove it.

Besides, she wanted to talk things through with Amanda. And there was also the fact that if Elspeth did make the decision to go to London, she'd very quickly have her fill of cities – except the English ones would be without the beach and the sun. The very thought of it made her shudder.

'Why? You might as well tell me what's wrong, because I'll only nag,' Amanda said, walking through a door marked 'Private' to the side of the reception desk and gesturing for Elspeth to follow her.

Once seated in the office, with a mug of tea and a coconut biscuit in her hand, Elspeth told her friend everything.

Amanda gasped. 'Oh, my goodness, I'm not surprised you haven't been able to sleep much – I don't think I would have, either. What a difficult decision to have to make. Toni? Toni!' Amanda beckoned to her husband as he entered the room. 'Listen to this.'

Elspeth told her tale again. It didn't sound any better for repeating it. 'I honestly don't know what to do,' she concluded.

Amanda grimaced. 'Only you can make that decision, but it has to be made with your heart and not your head. You can list all the reasons why you should go, or why you should stay, but none of them matter a jot. It's what you feel inside that counts. What does your heart tell you?'

'I don't know,' Elspeth wailed. She desperately wanted to live near her family, but she wanted to stay here, too, and her heart was doing a sterling job of arguing in favour of both.

'What does Charles say about it?' Amanda asked. 'Because your decision will affect him too.'

Elspeth fell silent and studied the floor.

'You haven't told him, have you?'

She shook her head. 'Not yet. I want to try to get it straight in my mind first.'

'You're going to have to, before he signs anything,' her friend pointed out, and Toni nodded vigorously in agreement.

'Do you think he'll change his mind about buying Libertad if he knows I'm going back to England?' Elspeth asked.

'Duh, of course he will.' Amanda gave her an incredulous look.

'Don't put that kind of pressure on me,' Elspeth whimpered.

'I'm just telling you how it is, my dear.'

'Are you sure he'll pull out of the sale?'

Amanda and Toni shared a glance, before Amanda spoke. 'I'm sure. It's obvious that he's head over heels in love with you.'

'How can you possibly know that?'

Another shared glance. 'He told us,' Amanda declared.

'When?'

'The day before he left, when he came to the hotel.'

'On the Thursday? But he was out all day on a bike ride.'

'Didn't he tell you that he paid us a visit? He said that Stefan was selling the business and he wanted to pick Toni's brains.'

'He is a good picker. Asked many, many questions,' Toni interjected.

'You're telling me that while I was thinking he preferred to spend his last day in Tenerife on his blasted bike, he was having a pow-wow with you two?' Elspeth folded her arms and glared at her so-called friends. 'The

294

first I knew about Charles buying the shop was when he told me at dinner later that night,' Elspeth continued slowly, as she thought it through. 'I did overhear him talking to Stefan earlier on, and realised afterwards that they had been discussing business – I'm not totally stupid – but I didn't for one minute think that the two of you were in on it, too. It looks like I was the only one in the dark,' she said, feeling a bit miffed.

'I assumed he wanted to keep quiet about it until he'd made a decision.' Amanda shuffled in her seat.

'Ha!' Elspeth exclaimed. 'Got you! That's exactly what I'm doing right now – keeping it to myself until I've come to my own decision.'

'It isn't the same in the slightest,' Amanda objected. 'Charles has every intention of returning to Tenerife regardless of whether he buys Libertad or not – he even asked about a long-term stay at the hotel – and all because he loves you and wants to have a proper relationship with you. The only thing hanging in the balance is whether or not the business is a viable proposition.'

'He told you he loved me, yet he didn't say a word to me.'

Amanda shrugged. 'I bet he's told you now though, right?'

'Yes, but only recently. The Saturday just gone, and completely by accident, I think... on the phone.'

'He didn't declare his undying love for you before he left?'

'Nope.'

'Aww, bless him.'

'Huh, bless him, indeed! He hadn't intended to tell me at all, but he sort of blurted it out. If you must know, he's asked me to marry him, too!'

Amanda let out a whoop and fist-pumped the air. 'See,' she screeched at Toni, 'I told you they were perfect for each other. I knew it, the second I saw them together.' She turned back to Elspeth. 'That's fantastic news!'

'No, it's not,' Elspeth said crossly. 'I've now got to decide whether to leave my life here for a new one in the UK, but I've not only got myself to consider, I've now got Charles to consider as well.'

'OK, look at it from another angle,' Amanda said in a conciliatory tone. 'If you hadn't met Charles, what would your decision be?'

'I don't know!'

'So you wouldn't hop on the first plane out of here?'

Bloody hell, Amanda was persistent. 'No...'

'Does taking Charles out of the equation make things any clearer?'

'No.' Elspeth was certain of that.

'Which means your decision doesn't hinge on him,' Amanda pointed out logically. 'It hinges on whether you are prepared to leave Tenerife. I'd bet my last euro that whatever you decide, Charles will be by your side, so you can safely take him out of the equation when making your decision.'

'I don't want to leave Tenerife.' There, she'd said it, but it didn't make her feel any better at all. 'But I think I should.'

'Because of Rai?'

'Partly. I'm missing out on so much. Plus, it would help Gideon and Sakura enormously if I was around to babysit when they needed me. Sakura is thinking of going back to work, so...'

'So... they want you for unpaid childcare?' Amanda jumped in.

'I'm sure that's not it at all,' Elspeth objected.

'Maybe not.' Amanda didn't look convinced. 'However, it's still something to think about – how would you feel having to look after Rai two days a week? Three? Five? Because if Sakura does go back to work full-time, that might be what they ask you to do. Plus any other times, such as when Gideon has an event at work or they want to have dinner out.'

'I can always say no.'

'Will you, though?'

Elspeth gave it some thought. 'Possibly not,' she admitted. She'd love to spend more time with her grandson, but looking after him all day, every day wasn't something she'd ever anticipated doing. 'Anyway,' she continued, 'it probably won't come to that.'

'And if you are going back to England to spend more time with your family, there's another thing to think about – Rai will only be little for a short time. When he gets to the teenage years he's not going to want to hang out with his parents, let alone his granny. And how about when he goes to school – will you be expected to take him and pick him up? If so, you're going to find it difficult to get a part-time job that fits in around the school run, so you'll be giving up that bit of independence.'

'OK, enough!' Elspeth held up her hand.

'Of course,' Amanda soldiered on, totally ignoring her, 'nothing can make up for missing those precious early years or being able to pop round to Gideon's house whenever you feel like it.'

Elspeth sighed. 'That's the issue, isn't it?'

Amanda reached out to stroke Elspeth's arm. 'Only you can decide,' she said, 'but I think you should tell Charles about all this before he signs a contract he can't get out of and you find your roles reversed, with you based in the UK and him in Santiago del Teide.'

Yes, she should, shouldn't she? But what she didn't want to do was to cause him any worry when she wasn't sure herself what it was she wanted.

One thing she did know, one thing she was entirely certain about, was that no matter what happened, she wanted to spend the rest of her life with him.

The question was, would that be on Tenerife or in the UK?

Chapter 34

Elspeth might prefer to hide her head in the sand and not have a discussion with Charles just yet, but Amanda was right – she couldn't let him go ahead with the purchase of Libertad without him knowing the difficult choices she now faced. It wasn't fair to him, and the longer she put it off the greater the risk that he would be unable to withdraw from the purchase.

She'd better do it now, before Gideon and the family returned from their day out in Santa Cruz.

Picking up her phone, Elspeth began to call Charles's number, then changed her mind and put the phone down again.

Something held her back – a half-formed elusive thought in the back of her mind that eluded her attempts to pin it down. Something significant, some—

She had it!

Where was she going to live? Gideon had mentioned a flat, but she didn't like the sound of that; she wanted a garden or a terrace to sit out in (although how often she'd be able to do that knowing what the British weather was like, was debatable). And how was she going to afford this flat? Property prices in London were sky-high compared to Tenerife, so she might have to rent. But renting wasn't cheap, either. Then she'd have to sell the villa, and that could take a while.

Gideon had mentioned living close to him, but what if she didn't like the area he chose, or there weren't any suitable properties she could afford and she was forced to live further away? What then? She'd be stuck in a city she didn't want to live in, not as close to her family as she wanted to be, whilst paying an extortionate amount just to keep a roof over her head and miles away from the nearest countryside and solitude she treasured.

And what about Charles? Would he want to move to London? Did she have any right to ask him? Surely if he was going to stay in Britain, he'd want to live near enough to his daughters to be able to pop in and see them, too. Which meant that one of them would have to compromise; or else they would have to live slap-bang in the middle of the country, which meant she'd not see that much of her grandson in any case.

On the other hand, if she remained in Tenerife, London Gatwick was four hours away by plane. Budget airline flights were relatively inexpensive. She might have to live a little more frugally (she deliberately didn't include Charles in her calculations), but she would still be able to afford to fly to the UK three or four times a year, more if she picked the cheapest dates to travel, and if Gideon was happy for her to stay with them. She needn't miss out on Rai growing up at all.

Was this it, then? Had she made her decision?

Elspeth rather thought she had, in spite of feeling guilty at not being able to help Gideon and Sakura with child-care.

It might be selfish of her, but she was getting on a bit, and she'd had her fair share of heartache – surely she deserved to grab whatever happiness she could? And Charles most definitely made her happy.

Elspeth reached for her phone again and Charles picked up almost immediately.

'I'm sorry I didn't answer your calls,' she began, comforted by the sound of his voice. It was then that she decided it would probably be a while before she shared the events of the last two days with him. She thought it best to let things settle first, to wait until he'd moved to Tenerife and the purchase of Libertad had gone through, otherwise, knowing Charles, he might try to change her mind and persuade her to live in the UK, because he was far too kind and considerate for his own good.

'That's OK. I guessed you were busy with the family,' he said, and she instantly felt bad for dodging him. He was such an understanding and thoughtful man.

They went on to chat about their respective days, until Elspeth heard Gideon at the door. 'I've got to go, Gideon is back. Love you.'

'Not more than I love you.'

'I'll argue the toss when I see you on Friday,' she promised.

'I'll look forward to it.'

His sexy chuckle as she hung up the phone sent shivers down her spine, and she hastened to compose herself before she faced her family; but the more she tried, the more she blushed, until she was positively glowing as Sakura entered the living room, Rai balanced on her hip.

'Are you feeling well?' her daughter-in-law asked. 'You are very red.'

'I'm fine, thank you, too much sun, that's all. I went out and forgot to wear my hat,' she fibbed. 'How was Santa Cruz?'

'It was great,' Gideon said, from behind his wife. He held up a large carrier bag. 'Sakura went shopping *again*.

And we had a stroll around the Plaza de España. Rai loved the fountain, but screamed blue murder when Sakura refused to let him paddle in the water.'

'Did you go somewhere nice for lunch?'

'Yeah, we found a quaint little restaurant near the Museum of Nature and Archaeology.'

'Did you go inside the museum?'

'Not today – Rai was getting cranky and he's a little too young to appreciate the fossils. Maybe if we come to Tenerife again… Although, now that you're moving to London, I strongly suspect we won't be back.'

Oh dear, she had been hoping to break the news slowly, but she supposed now was as good a time as any. She just hoped that it didn't ruin the rest of their stay. They only had three more full days after this one and then they'd be gone, and she wanted to enjoy it as much as possible.

'Gideon, about that,' she began, taking a deep breath. 'I don't think I'll be moving back to the UK. Thank you so much for suggesting it, but I'd like to stay here. This is my home, and this is where I feel closest to your father.'

Gideon screwed up his face. 'Mum, are you sure you've thought this through properly? You're not making a snap decision based on fear of the unknown, are you? It's important you have a good think about it. We'd love to see lots more of you, and I'd sleep better knowing you were closer. I worry about you, you know.'

Elspeth knew he did, and she appreciated it. Gideon knew how she felt about missing out on so much of Rai's early years and he felt the same, but with the family moving nearer, she'd now be able to see much more of them than if they'd remained in Japan. She wasn't giving something up – she was gaining something. She was gaining time with her family, without having to compromise on her way of life.

'I've thought it through, and I know what's best for me,' she told him gently. 'Thank you for suggesting it, though, and I can't be happier that you're only a four-hour flight away now, as I'll still get to see a lot of you and to see Rai grow up.'

'Well...' He trailed off.

'I love you, Gideon, and seeing you, Sakura and Rai every day would be fabulous. But living here is also fabulous. And this is my home,' she repeated. 'I'm settled, and it's likely that you might get another opportunity sometime in the future to work somewhere other than London, and if I remain here it means that you can then take it without the worry of having to uproot me again.'

She could tell by his expression that the idea of relocating again hadn't crossed her son's mind. But from the small nod Sakura gave her, Elspeth knew it was a valid point, and she wondered how long it would be before Sakura missed her homeland and suggested returning to Japan to live.

Satisfied she'd made her decision, Elspeth considered the matter well and truly closed.

Now she could go ahead and make the most of Gideon's stay – and after that, she had Charles's arrival to look forward to.

Life was most definitely looking good.

Chapter 35

'What's up?' Elspeth looked at the kitchen clock with bleary eyes. It was still dark outside and quiet, so it must be quite early.

It was – four-thirty to be exact.

Gideon was holding a wailing, fractious Rai in his arms and walking him around the kitchen. 'He's been like this for the past hour or so. Did he wake you?'

'It doesn't matter. What's wrong, my little man?' she crooned to Rai, who promptly cried louder.

'He's usually so good. This isn't like him, at all. Sakura has been trying to get him to sleep ever since we went to bed, so I told her to try to rest – we've got a long day travelling ahead of us, although no doubt the little blighter will sleep on the plane. I was hoping I could get him to fall asleep by doing the walking-up-and-down thing – it used to work when he was tiny. Failing that, I might try taking him for a car ride.'

'Do you want me to have him, while you go back to bed?' Elspeth offered.

'Would you mind? What with the flight to Berlin later...'

'Give him to me,' Elspeth urged, reaching out to take her grandson. 'Oh, my, he's rather warm. I think he's got a temperature. His cheeks are red, too. Do you think he's teething?' She put a hand on the child's forehead.

'He could be,' Gideon said, but he sounded doubtful.

'Hang on a sec, I'll see if his glands are swollen. He might be coming down with a cold.' She gently felt the sides of Rai's neck, and the little boy let out a shriek, and tugged frantically at his ear. Elspeth shifted him to her other hip, and inspected him carefully.

'The glands on the one side of his neck are up and the inside of this ear is really red. I think he may have an ear infection,' she declared.

'Bugger.' Gideon let out a sigh.

'Yes, the poor little mite.'

'Do you think we'll have time to go to the pharmacy before we leave?' her son asked.

'I suspect he'll need antibiotics, so the pharmacy won't be any good. He'll need to see a doctor. I can probably get him in to my local surgery, but they don't open until eight.'

'Okaasan is right, Rai needs to see a doctor,' Sakura said, appearing in the doorway of the kitchen.

Elspeth looked up from her scrutiny of her grandson, to see Sakura holding out her arms. She passed Rai to his mother along with a sympathetic look. She used to hate it when Gideon was ill.

'We'll miss our flight, won't we, if the surgery is not open until eight' Gideon said.

'We can get another,' Sakura pointed out then turned back to Elspeth. 'Ear infection?'

'It looks like it to me. It might not be, of course, and I don't want you to miss your flight in case I'm wrong...' Elspeth wrung her hands.

Her diagnosis was proved correct, however, when Rai was pronounced to have a nasty ear infection by the doctor later that morning, and was prescribed a course of antibiotics.

'When will it be safe for him to fly?' Gideon asked.

The doctor said, 'He can fly today as long as he has something to suck on to help alleviate the pressure in the ear, and if you give him some painkillers beforehand.'

Elspeth watched as Gideon thanked the doctor then darted out of the consulting room, probably to check on the next available flight.

By the time she, Sakura and Rai had emerged from the doctor's surgery, Gideon had sorted out the new travel arrangements.

'There's a flight at seven o'clock this evening that we can transfer on to,' he said. 'I'll just let the car-hire company know. Oh, and I'd better inform the hotel in Berlin and ask them if they can arrange transport for us, their end.'

'Right then, we might as well go back to the villa,' Elspeth suggested. 'I'll sort out some breakfast, and then, Sakura, would you and Gideon like to go back to bed for a couple of hours, while I look after Rai?'

'Thank you, Okaasan. You are very kind.' Sakura gave her a small bow.

'It's the least I can do.' A wave of guilt swept over her – this was the sort of help Sakura would need in London, and she had refused them. Hastily, Elspeth swept the feeling aside; she'd made her mind up – there was no point in fretting over the decision because she wasn't going to change it.

After Elspeth had prepared breakfast and everyone had eaten, Gideon and Sakura took her up on her offer to look after Rai and retired to bed for a couple of hours. Elspeth was left with Rai, who was slightly calmer now that he'd had a spoonful of infant painkiller and his first dose of antibiotics. She played with him on the floor for a while, before moving to the sofa so that he too could have a little doze.

It was incredibly soothing rocking a sleeping baby and feeling the warm weight of a child in her arms. Elspeth smelt the sweet scent of Rai's skin and hair and watched his blue-veined eyelids flutter and twitch, before she felt her head begin to nod.

She must have dropped off too, because she woke with a start a while later with a vague problem swirling around in her mind. There had been something niggling at her ever since she realised Gideon and Sakura would miss their flight, but it had taken the nap to bring it to the fore – Charles was now due to arrive before Gideon left!

She didn't want Gideon to find out this way that she had another man in her life, and neither did she want to run the risk of Charles finding out that Gideon had suggested her moving to London with them.

Oh dear, she should have come clean with the pair of them before this, but now wasn't the time to have such in-depth discussions, especially with Gideon, who was already so protective of her. And she wanted to give him a bit of time to process the news before he met Charles.

If she could delay Charles a little, then Gideon would have left, and she could take her time in telling her son that she had fallen in love.

Oh what a tangled web we weave, she thought, even though she hadn't deliberately set out to deceive anyone.

Annoyed with herself, Elspeth eased Rai out of her arms and laid him on the sofa and crept out of the room and into the kitchen. It sounded quiet upstairs, so she imagined that Gideon and Sakura were still resting. She tried to call Charles, but his phone was switched off. He must already be in the air, she guessed, and she made a mental note to try him again at the time he was due to land. In the meantime, she left a hushed voicemail for Charles to contact her as soon as he got her message.

Satisfied she had covered all bases as best as she could, Elspeth brewed a pot of tea.

Crikey, what a day, and it was only just noon!

She had a feeling that the latter half of it might be just as exciting as the first – but for a totally different reason, and her heart did that funny little lurch as she thought of just how different that reason would be.

Charles would be here soon, and she simply couldn't wait!

Chapter 36

'We'll leave at about three-thirty, four o'clock,' Gideon said, around a mouthful of late lunch.

At least she was sending them off with full tummies, Elspeth thought, so they'd be OK until they had a meal on the plane. And Rai appeared to be feeling better; although the antibiotics wouldn't have had a chance to have any effect yet, the infant painkillers, a decent sleep and some food were going some way to perking him up and making him less grouchy – the poor little chap.

'These things can't be helped,' she said. 'Children pick up germs all the time, and they do say that the more bugs they are exposed to earlier in life, the more robust their immune systems will be when they grow up.'

'Let's hope so,' Gideon said.

He was about to say something else when an unexpected knock at the door made Elspeth frown, and she got to her feet and went to answer it.

But before she reached it, a voice called 'Surprise!' then the front door opened and Charles strode into the hall.

Sweeping her into his arms, her cry of 'Charles, no!' was muffled by his shirt as he hugged her to him.

'God, I've missed you— Oh…' Through the hallway, Charles had noticed Gideon and his family sitting at the table, and released her quickly. Elspeth stepped back out of his reach, feeling flustered. 'I'm sorry, I thought your family would have left by now. I don't want to intrude.'

'Didn't you get my text?'

'No, sorry. My charger is faulty and the blimmin' thing didn't charge my phone before the flight. I'll have to get a new one.' He was speaking to her, but his attention was on Gideon, who was standing in the doorway to the living room.

'Is this the guy who was staying with you?' her son asked. 'The one from the hotel that your friend Amanda owns? I thought he'd left.' He was on his feet and staring at Charles.

'Um, he had. He's come back,' Elspeth said, her heart plummeting to her feet.

Gideon continued to stare. 'What gives him the right to walk straight in?'

Heat spread up Elspeth's chest and neck and into her cheeks, and she was unable to meet her son's eyes.

There was a long silence, broken only by Rai tapping his spoon against the table.

Finally, Gideon broke it. 'Oh, I see. God, Mum, that's... that's... Words fail me.'

'Clearly,' she replied, the initial shock wearing off in the face of her son's dismay. She was an adult, for goodness' sake. He had no right to get on his high horse. It wasn't as though she was still married and Gideon had caught her in the throes of an affair. 'I think you need to consider your next words carefully,' she added, moving closer to Charles and slipping an arm around his waist.

Charles hugged her to him, and she was grateful for his unspoken support.

The expression on Gideon's face made him look more like a bewildered teenager than a grown man, but in those few seconds between Charles's reappearance and her son's reaction, she suddenly understood that time hadn't moved on for Gideon.

He was still hurting from his father's death.

And she also understood that by her showing an interest in another man, to him it felt as though she had forgotten Ray.

As if that could ever happen! But how to convince her son? Especially since he was due to leave in half an hour. There wasn't enough time to have such an emotional conversation, yet she couldn't let him go without at least trying. Explaining how she felt over the phone would be ten times more difficult.

'Gideon, I—' she began, then hesitated when Sakura stood up and walked towards them, covering the short distance in a couple of strides, Rai balanced on her hip, his chubby legs dangling.

Sakura held out a hand to Charles. 'Hello, I am pleased to meet you. I am Gideon's wife, Sakura, and this is our son, Rai.' She jiggled the little boy, who made a grab for his mother's necklace.

'Sakura,' Gideon warned. 'Stay out of this.'

Charles took her hand and shook it. 'Pleased to meet you, too, and you, Rai.'

Sakura looked over her shoulder and said to her husband. 'There is nothing to stay out of.'

'I beg to differ.'

Elspeth said. 'You sound just like your father.' Ray had used to say 'I beg to differ' when he disagreed with someone, and it gave her a pang.

'Glad to hear you haven't forgotten him entirely,' was Gideon's cool response.

'I could never forget him,' Elspeth replied softly.

'Are you sure about that?'

'Gideon, you are behaving like a child. Stop it,' she retorted.

'Better that, than behaving like a—'

Elspeth never knew what Gideon had been about to say.

'That's enough!' Charles roared, making everyone jump. Little Rai's bottom lip began to quiver and his eyes grew large. 'I will not have you speaking to my future wife like that. Mind your manners, lad, and be more respectful to your mother.'

Gideon's jaw went slack. 'Your future *wife*?'

'That's right. Your mother has kindly agreed to be my wife. In good time.'

'Since when? You barely know each other! Oh, hang on, just how long has this been going on?'

'If you're asking how long we've been in love, I can't answer for your mother, but for me I fell for her the moment I saw her.' Charles gave her another squeeze.

With tears in her eyes and threatening to spill down her cheeks, Elspeth hugged him back. She wasn't going to lie and say it had been the same for her, because falling in love with Charles had been a slower and more subtle process, but it didn't mean she loved him any the less now.

'If you're asking how long we've been together,' Charles continued, 'then I'd say that our story properly begins right now, here, today, because this is where the rest of our lives starts.'

Gideon blanched and Elspeth saw he was close to tears too. Her heart went out to him. She thought back to how he'd held it together when his father had died, how he'd been so resolute and strong, and she was struck with sudden insight. Had he been so strong, precisely because she had fallen apart? Had he felt unable to grieve because he'd had to focus on her and not on his own feelings?

She instinctively knew she was right. Unlike Elspeth, who had mourned long and hard for a very long time indeed, Gideon had barely shed any tears at the funeral and had then been her rock for the short amount of time he'd been able to spend with her before he'd had to return to his life in Japan. She also guessed that he'd immersed himself in work and his family, as a way of burying his sorrow.

She should have paid him more attention, she should have helped him come to terms with it – after all, she might have lost her husband, but Gideon had lost his father. And here she was, telling him that she had fallen in love with another man whom she would one day marry, when he'd never, ever get his father back. It must seem as though she'd replaced Ray with Charles; that Gideon was a grown man who should be able to see the truth of the situation was irrelevant when it came to such raw emotion.

'Just here for a holiday, are you?' Gideon snapped at Charles. 'Then once you've had a good time, you'll sod off back home. Is that the way it works?'

'Hardly, not when I'm buying Libertad,' Charles said.

'He's doing *what*? Mum, are you aware of this?' Gideon rounded on her.

'Of course, I am.'

Her son threw up his hands. 'So he's the reason why you don't want to come to London with us, isn't he?'

Elspeth was aware that Charles was staring at her curiously. 'Not at all,' she replied, much more calmly than she felt. 'I don't want to go to London with you because

I don't like cities, and I know I won't be happy there. Tenerife is my home, and this is where I intend to stay.'

'I give up!' Gideon cried.

'Good,' Sakura said. 'Your mother is right: you are being a child. If Okaasan does not want to come to London, that is her choice. She is happy here.'

'She could be happy in London,' Gideon persisted. 'She'd see more of us, more of Rai.'

'She can visit whenever she wants. We can come here. Tenerife is not as far as Japan.'

Gideon narrowed his eyes.

'And Charles-san will be welcome, too,' Sakura added, sending her husband a pointed look. 'All family will be welcome. So, now I can tell you my sister will be staying with us.'

'What's that?' Gideon frowned. 'Your *sister*?'

'Yes. She wants to study in England, so I said she can stay with us.'

'When were you going to tell me?'

'When you were in a better mood,' Sakura replied, disingenuously. 'But now is good, too. She will help with Rai, so I am happy. You do want me to be happy, don't you?'

'I… er…'

'And you want your mother to be happy?' Sakura added, and Elspeth had to hold back a teary smile.

'Of course I do.'

'Then you must let her be. Charles-san makes her happy.'

'What if it doesn't last?'

Sakura cocked her head at Gideon. 'What if *we* don't last? Does that mean we should not try?'

'You are incorrigible.'

314

'Yes, I am.' Sakura turned back to Elspeth and whispered loudly, 'What does "incorrigible" mean?'

Gideon shook his head. He still didn't look convinced, but at least he appeared to have calmed down. 'It's time we made a move; we don't want to miss *this* flight.'

'You have something to say to Okaasan first,' Sakura said, her mouth in a straight line. Then she added something in Japanese.

'You're joking.' Gideon looked aghast.

'No, I am not.'

Elspeth's attention was pinging from one to the other. Please, no more shocks. Not today.

Gideon took a deep breath. 'I'm sorry, Mum. For what I implied.' It was forced out between clenched teeth, but at least it was an apology. He nodded at Charles.

Sakura raised her eyebrows. 'That is not sorry.'

'God, woman, you'll be the death of me. Mum, Charles, I owe you an apology. I overreacted and I'm sorry.' Gideon ran a hand through his hair. 'It's just... I...'

'We understand,' Charles said. 'I'm not your father, and I don't intend to be. It's a lot to take in. No one can take his place, but I do hope we can be friends one day. I know you want your mother to be happy, and I promise I'll do everything in my power to make that happen. She's still a young, vibrant, beautiful woman, and I know you wouldn't want her to be lonely for the rest of her life.' He held up a hand as Gideon opened his mouth. 'You can be surrounded by family who love you and still be lonely,' Charles explained. 'Now she has someone of her own, and so do I.'

Gideon nodded his understanding but didn't say anything further, and although Elspeth knew he needed time to process everything, she couldn't let him leave like this.

'Gideon, I still love your father. I always have done and always will. He's here,' she touched her heart, 'and here.' She pointed towards the courtyard and the orchid tree where Ray's ashes lay. 'And that's another reason why I don't want to move to London; I can't leave him.'

Gideon's brow creased and he turned his attention to Charles. 'Are you OK with that?'

'Yes. Ray is part of your mother, part of who she is. How could I not be OK with it?'

Finally, Elspeth's tears fell, trickling down her face, and she let out a small sob.

'Mum, Mum, please, don't...' Gideon swallowed noisily. 'I'm sorry, I didn't mean to upset you. It's a bit of a shock that's all. And a bit sudden.'

She could tell he was still apprehensive because of the look he sent towards Charles, and if the shoe was on the other foot, then she might well be thinking the same thing Gideon undoubtedly was. But he'd come to terms with it, she knew, when he saw how happy Charles made her, because, after all, that was the main thing. Happiness.

'Come here.' She held out her arms and Gideon stepped into them, burying his face in her hair as he bent to embrace her. 'I love you, son.'

'I know, and I love you too.' He lowered his voice, 'But if Charles doesn't treat you right, you let me know. Promise?'

'I promise.' She hugged him tighter, knowing that was one promise she'd never have to keep. 'Go on, you'd better get going,' she told him, squeezing him hard before releasing him and giving him a gentle push.

As her son and his family retreated upstairs to gather their things Charles gave Elspeth a long hug. 'You can see who wears the trousers with those two,' he said chuckling to himself. 'Who knew that such a slip of a girl could be so forceful.'

Who knew, indeed? Elspeth felt that she'd discovered more about her daughter-in-law's personality in the last ten minutes than she had throughout all the time she'd known her. And she was incredibly grateful to her, too. With Sakura by his side, Gideon would be OK.

'Now the introductions are out of the way, are you ready to become Mrs Brown?' Charles murmured.

'Not so fast, mate. I expect some of that wooing you promised me, and besides, I haven't met *your* family yet,' she replied.

'Ah, yes, about that… how do you fancy a visitor or two over the next week or so?'

'It can't be any worse than this, can it?'

'I don't know – I haven't told my girls about you yet.'

Dear God, Elspeth thought as she snaked her arms around Charles's neck and pulled him down to kiss her – life was certainly going to be more interesting with him in it.

Chapter 37

When Charles joked with her that he wanted to propose to her properly, with candles and wine, dinner and a sunset, Elspeth had imagined an intimate meal for two in an eye-wateringly expensive restaurant. Which was why, when he told her they were going out to dinner and that she might want to treat herself to a new dress and maybe have her nails done, she suspected what was going on.

In the eight months since Charles had returned to Tenerife, he'd made good on his vow to woo her. Elspeth had been taken on picnics, to the cinema (the dubbed Spanish over the top of an American film had proved challenging to Charles, who was desperately trying to get to grips with the language), and for many meals out. Charles had bought her flowers, massaged her feet after a day at work – the decision to continue working in Libertad hadn't been made lightly, but so far Charles had proved to be an easy boss to work for – had drawn her baths laden with scented oil and had cuddled up with her on the sofa while listening to music. He was so good at wooing her that she half hoped it would never end.

He was good at the other stuff, too, like holding her when she cried on the anniversary of Ray's death; he did his fair share of the housework, and he'd nursed her lovingly when she came down with a nasty cold earlier in the year.

She couldn't wish for a kinder, more considerate, or more loving man, and knowing he was about to propose made her believe she was the luckiest woman in the world.

The dress she had chosen was a silver sparkly number, in recognition of the season. Christmas was fast approaching and everywhere she looked there were twinkling lights and decorated trees. Christmas Eve was the day after next, and she wished she could have spent the festive period with Gideon, Sakura and Rai – and no doubt Charles would have loved to see his daughters during the festivities, too, but Christmas, after Easter, was one of the busiest times of the year in the Canaries for tourists, and, as Charles very rightly said, it would be madness not to open the shop when there were so many potential customers around.

One of the first things he'd done after he'd taken over the business, though, was to employ an additional pair of hands as the shop was doing so well, so he had more free time for them to spend together. Luciana was enthusiastic, capable, and also an avid hiker and cyclist. She had managed the shop on her own for five days when Elspeth and Charles had flown to the UK to visit both their families but to leave her to run the place single-handedly over Christmas would be deeply unfair.

Never mind, thought Elspeth, this would be her and Charles's first Christmas together, which was a special enough occasion, and they'd agreed to travel back to Britain in February.

With a last look in the mirror, Elspeth was ready, and she trotted downstairs to find Charles waiting in the hall, wearing a dinner suit, complete with a bow tie.

'My, don't you look handsome,' she said, reaching up to smooth his hair. She loved the steadily encroaching silver at his temples highlighting the already salt and pepper strands; it made him look incredibly distinguished.

'And don't you look beautiful,' he responded, giving her an admiring look. 'But then, you always do to me.'

'Aw, you say the nicest things.'

'I'm going to say something even nicer, later on.' His eyes were twinkling and there was a big grin plastered on his face.

'I know you're going to ask me to marry you again,' she told him. 'It's hardly a surprise.'

'I don't care. I simply want it to be the most romantic proposal I can think of.'

'I hope you've got me a nice ring?'

He shook his head, still beaming. 'That's very mercenary of you. Seriously, though, I thought you might like to choose your own.'

'Oh, OK.' That was hardly romantic, was it? What was he going to use instead? The ring pull off a can of beer?

Slightly disappointed, she followed him out of the house and got into their car. It had originally belonged to Stefan, but he had sold it to Charles along with the business. She had to admit that it came in handy, and she and Charles had enjoyed some great days out that they wouldn't have been able to manage if they'd had to rely on public transport.

'Where are we going?' she asked as he drove out of the square and turned right, heading out of the town.

'Not far.'

It certainly wasn't, she saw.

Almost immediately after turning onto the main road, the car pulled into a long drive.

'Hotel Aventuras?' she queried. Not that she minded – the food at the hotel was excellent, but she was expecting something a little more intimate. If they were dining here, then Amanda and Toni would also be there, even if they didn't join them for the meal itself. Elspeth would prefer for Charles's proposal to be a private affair, and not to have her friends gawping at them.

'The very same,' he said, pulling into a parking space.

That was fine, she could adapt. Perhaps Charles thought the idea of him proposing to her in the hotel that had played such a significant part in the two of them getting together was a sweet touch. And she had to admit that it was – as long as there weren't fifty or so other diners watching. Although, what had she expected? If Charles had chosen somewhere else, then there would be strangers there, too.

Get over yourself, she muttered silently. He's trying his best, and it was the sentiment that mattered and the intention behind it, not the venue, or the food, or even the darned ring.

Surprised not to see Amanda or Toni hovering in reception, she was even more surprised when the familiar-looking receptionist gestured for her and Charles to go through to the terrace and not into the dining room. She could hear people inside – it sounded quite busy – and she was relieved that they wouldn't be joining them. Perhaps Amanda and Toni had set a table on the terrace instead?

Or not...

Charles carried on past the terrace, where several people were sitting enjoying either pre- or post-dinner drinks and a glorious view of the setting sun, and pointed her in the direction of an archway set in the low wall which surrounded it. She couldn't remember seeing that before and wondered why it was there, because beyond the terrace there was nothing but untamed meadow filled with wild flowers, cacti and busily humming bees, much like the one beyond her own garden.

'Where are we going?' she asked.

Charles came to a halt in front of her, obstructing her view. 'Close your eyes.'

'Why?'

'Do you trust me?'

'With my life.'

'Then close your eyes.'

Elspeth closed them, wondering if he'd be down on one knee when she reopened them, but then he took her hand and began to tug at it.

'Just a couple of steps and you'll be able to open them again,' he said.

She had no idea what was going on. As she hesitantly let him lead her, she kept expecting to feel rough ground under her strappy sandals, but all was smooth and paved. Definitely paved, as the gentle tap of her heels testified.

Charles brought her to a halt. 'You can open your eyes now.'

Suddenly feeling shy, it took her a moment.

When she saw the scene in front of her, she clapped her hands to her mouth and squealed.

The meadow beyond the terrace had been transformed into a wonderland of fairy lights and lanterns hanging from the surrounding trees and bushes. A substantial part of it had been paved with pale marble slabs, and flowers had been planted around the edges, blending into the wild meadow grasses beyond, so it was hard to tell where the one ended and the other began.

Fire pits chased away the slight chill of the December evening, and newly planted palm trees provided shelter and slowed the evening breeze until it became little more than a murmur. The whole scene was bathed in an orange glow from the setting sun, and the sky was streaked with purple and pink.

Tables were dotted here and there, dressed with crisp white tablecloths, the cutlery and glasses reflecting the fairy lights, and arrangements of fresh flowers in sunset colours sat in the centre of each table.

Elspeth took all of it in with a single glance.

What she found more difficult to take in were the people sitting at the tables.

'Gideon,' she breathed, her hands still over her mouth, her heart hammering wildly. 'Sakura and Rai.' She began to laugh. 'There's Gina!' Charles's eldest daughter was sitting with her husband and two children on the next table. 'And Hayley, too. Is that her boyfriend?' Hayley raised the glass she was holding and nodded. 'What are they doing here?' Elspeth rounded on Charles. 'You didn't tell me your daughters were coming to visit.'

'I didn't tell you Gideon was, either,' he pointed out.

'There's Stefan!' Elspeth cried, hurrying over to him. 'Oh, my God, I can't believe it. How's your father?'

Stefan grinning from ear to ear, said, 'We are coping. And I am happier now I have Klara.' He pointed to a slim blonde-haired girl sitting next to him.

'She's pretty,' Elspeth said.

'I know. I think I might, as you English say, settle down.'

'That's fantastic news. I'm delighted for you!' Elspeth's heart swelled with emotion and she gave him a quick hug, before letting go and scanning the rest of the people gathered there.

Amanda and Toni were seated nearby, and she wagged her finger at her friends, amazed that they'd managed to keep planning this event a secret.

'I love this new space,' she called to them. 'I hope you didn't do it just for me!'

'Hardly! We love you but not that much. This is our new wedding venue.'

'It's lovely!'

She had a final look around, hoping she hadn't missed anyone, and saw that even Luciana was there, with her girlfriend and their little boy. Charles had brought together the people that meant the most to them all in one place.

But—

'Where is everyone staying? How long are they here for? What about—?' Elspeth began, before Charles stopped her from saying anything more with a kiss.

By the time she'd surfaced again, everyone was on their feet and staring at them with huge smiles on their faces.

Elspeth blushed furiously.

'One, two, three,' Amanda chanted, and everyone shouted in unison, 'Elspeth, will you marry Charles?'

Charles dropped to one knee in front of her. 'Will you?' he asked, holding out a black velvet box. Inside lay a ring with a square-cut single stone in the most vibrant shade of orange.

'Yes, please.' Her voice was barely more than a whisper, but their family and friends heard her plainly enough, and the night was suddenly alive with clapping, cheering and whooping as Charles slipped the ring on her finger.

'I love you,' Elspeth said, her eyes filling with tears and trickling down her cheeks.

'I love you, too, and I can't wait to spend the rest of my life with you.' Charles gave his bride-to-be a deep kiss and for a wonderfully long moment she forgot the rest of the world existed.

—

One by one, everyone gathered around to congratulate them.

'I love your ring,' Charles's younger daughter, Hayley, said. 'What stone is it?'

Elspeth looked to Charles for an answer, because she had no idea what it was, either.

'It's a sunstone, because this enchanting lady has brought light and warmth into my sunset years,' he told his daughter. 'Just like the sun.'

'Gorgeous, just like you lovebirds,' said Amanda, giving her friend a warm squeeze. 'When you get married, can I be Matron of Honour? Please? I've never been a Matron of Honour before.'

'Only if I can give my mother away,' Gideon said, coming up to stand by the happy couple. 'Congratulations, Charles,' he continued, as he held out his hand, 'I know you'll make Mum very happy.'

Elspeth, laughing through her tears, said, 'He already has.'

When she slipped an arm around Charles as he hugged her to him, and she gazed at those people who meant the most to her, she realised she'd come full circle on this enchanting island she called home. Love had turned to grief and now she was in love once more. And not only did she have the rest of her life to look forward to with this remarkable man, she also had her incredible friends and family, no matter how far across the world they were scattered.

The glow in her heart was reflected by the glorious glow in the late evening sky overhead, and she knew that although it might be sunset on Tenerife, it was the dawn of a whole new life for her and Charles.